BROWSING COLLECTION
14-DAY CHECKOUT
No Holds • No Renewals

THE GHOST
ILLUSION

Also by Kat Martin

THE GHOST ILLUSION

KAT MARTIN

KENSINGTON
PUBLISHING CORP.

www.kensingtonbooks.com

KENSINGTON BOOKS are published by

Kensington Publishing Corp.
119 West 40th Street
New York, NY 10018

Copyright © 2023 by Kat Martin

All Kensington titles, imprints, and distributed lines are available at special quantity discounts for bulk purchases for sales promotion, premiums, fundraising, educational, or institutional use. Special book excerpts or customized printings can also be created to fit specific needs. For details, write or phone the office of the Kensington Special Sales Manager: Attn. Special Sales Department. Kensington Publishing Corp., 119 West 40th Street, New York, NY 10018. Phone: 1-800-221-2647.

Library of Congress Card Catalogue Number: 2023938815

The K with book logo Reg. U.S. Pat. & TM Off.

ISBN: 978-1-4967-4402-9

First Kensington Hardcover Edition: October 2023

ISBN: 978-1-4967-4404-3 (ebook)

10 9 8 7 6 5 4 3 2 1

Printed in the United States of America

ABOUT THE BOOK

I wanted to write a ghost story. The two I had previously written were both challenging and interesting to write, so I began my usual search for a place to set the novel. England, I thought. Plenty of ghosts in England. I began searching abandoned historic buildings, and that was the beginning of a journey that led me to a place I did not want to go.

More research pulled me deeper. I am bringing you a tale I felt compelled to write. It is not one I would have chosen. But I believe it is a story I am meant to tell.

Soon you will understand why.

They shall grow not old, as we that are left grow old.
Age shall not weary them, nor the years condemn.
At the going down of the sun and in the morning
We will remember them.
—Laurence Binyon, "For the Fallen"

CHAPTER ONE

May
Sunderland, England

THE OLD HOUSE CREAKED AND GROANED. EVE SHIVERED AND PULLED her robe a little closer around her. She'd told herself that in time she'd get used to the place, grow accustomed to the ominous sounds and eerie, shifting movements in the shadows, but she had lived in the home she had inherited from her uncle for more than two months and the unsettling disturbances had only grown worse.

She tried to tell herself it was just her imagination, the wind playing tricks on her, the movement of the wood inside the walls of the hundred-year-old home. But the ghostly moans, whispers, and cruel laughter, the sound of running footsteps in the hallway, were impossible to ignore.

At those times, the darkness came alive, the air in the room seemed to thicken and pulse, and it took all her will just to make herself breathe.

Eve shivered as the howl of the wind outside increased, rattling the shutters on the paned-glass windows, but no wind she had ever heard sounded like angry words being whispered in the darkness.

Rising from the antique rocker in the living room, she moved the chair closer to the fireplace, hoping to dispel the chill. The smokeless coal she was required to burn wasn't the same as a roaring blaze, but the glowing embers somehow made her feel better.

A noise in the hall caught her attention and she went still. It was the whispering she had heard before, like men speaking in low tones somewhere just out of sight. Time and again, she had gone to see who was there, but the hall was always empty.

Goose bumps crept over her skin. Today she had finally done something about it. Setting aside her closed-mindedness, she had gone on the Internet and googled information on ghosts, haunted houses, anything she could think of that might give her some answers.

It didn't take long to realize she wasn't the only person who had trouble with spirits or ghosts or whatever they turned out to be. Not everyone believed in ghosts, but there were people out there who were convinced they were real.

Eve had sent an email to a group in America called Paranormal Investigations, Inc., a team of experts who traveled the world to research problems like hers. Their website was discreet. No photos of the people who worked there, no names, just a picture of the office in a redbrick building near the waterfront in Seattle. At the bottom, the page simply read, *If you need help, we are here for you.*

Interested, but not satisfied with the limited information provided, Eve continued her research. The man who had started the company was a billionaire in Seattle named Ransom King. King owned dozens of extremely profitable corporations, including several hotel chains, one of them the five-star King's Inns, as well as high-rise buildings, and real-estate developments around the country. He was a good-looking, broad-shouldered man, tall, with blue eyes and wavy black hair.

Paranormal Investigations wasn't a business King ran for profit. According to one of myriad articles she'd read about him, researching paranormal phenomena had become his passion, a hunger for knowledge that seemed to have settled deep in his bones. He had founded the company after losing his wife and

three-year-old daughter in a car accident. King had been driving
the night a violent rainstorm had sent the car careening off the
road into a tree.

Eve could only imagine how grief-stricken he must have been.

Intrigued and desperate for help, Eve had filled out the brief
contact information form on the website, giving her name, phone
number, and address. Her message simply said:

> My name is Eve St. Clair. I'm an American living in England. I
> think there is something in my house, something dark and sinis-
> ter that is not of this world. Can you help me? I live alone. I'm
> not crazy, and I'm not making this up. Please help me if you can.

She glanced over at the burgundy settee where she had been
sleeping for nearly a week. On the surface, it seemed ridiculous,
but she couldn't face going upstairs to her bedroom. Down here,
she would at least be able to run if something bad happened.

She reminded herself to put away the blanket and pillows in
the morning before her weekly housekeeper, Mrs. Pennyworth,
arrived. The older woman was a notorious gossip. Eve certainly
didn't want her knowing she was too frightened to sleep in her
own bed.

A scratching noise sent a chill sliding down her spine. It was
probably just branches outside the window, scraping against the
glass. At least that's what she told herself.

Eve settled back in the chair and started rocking, the movement easing some of the tension between her shoulder blades.
When what sounded like a dozen footsteps thundered down the
hall, she prayed she would hear from the Americans soon.

Ransom King sat behind the computer on his wide, glass-topped
desk in the King Enterprises's high-rise building in downtown
Seattle. The office was modern, with all the latest high-tech equipment, from a top-of-the-line iMac Pro to a seventy-inch flat screen
with a wireless HDMI transmitter and receiver kit.

A gray leather sofa and chairs provided a comfortable conversation area with a chrome and glass coffee table, and a wall of glass overlooked the harbor and the blue waters of Elliott Bay.

On the computer screen in front of him, he reread the most recent email message that had come in from Eve St. Clair. They had corresponded several times. Her case looked interesting. Part of her note read:

> I keep praying this isn't real. If it is, at least I'll know.

Ran understood the words in a way few people could. In the months following the accident that had killed his wife, Sabrina, and their daughter, Chrissy, he had seen Rina and Chrissy's faces in his dreams a hundred times.

In his dreams. That's what he'd told himself. But a person didn't dream in the middle of the afternoon with his eyes open.

Talking to a shrink hadn't helped. Every explanation centered around the overwhelming guilt he felt for the death of his wife and child. Which was true, but not a satisfactory explanation of the visions that had continued to plague him.

Desperate to do something—anything that would give him peace—he had finally gone to a psychic. He had managed to keep his visits secret, but in the end, it hadn't mattered. Lillian Bouchon had turned out to be a fraud.

The woman was a fake and a con artist, like most of the charlatans who supposedly possessed supernatural abilities. He had run through a list of them, but during his pursuit of the truth, he'd met people whose abilities were real.

In a move that had caused him endless ridicule, he had assembled a team of paranormal experts. People with open minds, an interest in the field, and a determination to find answers to age-old questions—or some version of them.

Kathryn Collins and Jesse Stahl had been his first hires. The best in their fields, Katie handled the video equipment, while Jesse handled audio and other miscellaneous instruments. Ran dug up background information on each case and probed the history, looking into past events that might have influenced whatever was happening on the premises they were investigating.

A woman named Caroline Barclay had been the first psychic on the team. On certain occasions, she'd been able to sense and communicate with unseen energy, but she wasn't always successful. Other people followed, mostly women, who seemed to be more intuitive than men.

Aside from the members of the team he kept on payroll, including a team coordinator to handle the logistics, Ran also brought in part-time help on occasion. A psychometrist named Sarah Owens, who could touch an object and know its past, and a former priest named Lucas Devereaux, formerly known as Father Luke.

What Ran had seen in the years since his formation of the team had convinced him that spirits were real, and though he'd never made contact with Sabrina or little Chrissy, the visions and dreams had finally faded, allowing him to find a fragile sort of peace.

Two years ago, he had hired Violet Sutton, a woman he had met in an online chat room for gifted people. Tests supported her claim that she was a sensitive, and occasionally clairvoyant. He had watched her work and hired her.

Ran glanced back at the screen and thought of the case in England. What the team did could be perilous. It could be wildly exciting, a rush like nothing he had ever felt before. But under certain circumstances, it could be deadly.

And there was Eve St. Clair, a woman he found surprisingly intriguing. He liked her intelligence and what seemed like sincerity in her emails. From photos he'd seen on social media, she was attractive, with a slender figure and very dark hair. He liked the open-mindedness she had shown in reaching out for help.

And there was the fear she worked so hard to hide. If what she was reporting was true, Eve might have good reason to be afraid.

Making a sudden decision, Ran called his executive assistant and asked her to clear his schedule for the next three days. If the team found something or encountered some kind of trouble, he would be there.

Ran checked his gold Rolex. Ten a.m. in Seattle. Six p.m. in Sunderland, England. He'd go out, maybe walk down to the Bell

Harbor Marina, where he kept his forty-foot sailboat. He loved that boat, loved being out on the water, loved the solitude, the peace that usually eluded him.

Maybe when he returned, he'd find a message on his computer.

Maybe he'd have another email from Eve.

CHAPTER TWO

THE OFFICES OF PARANORMAL INVESTIGATIONS, INC. SAT ON THE ground floor of a four-story brick building on Alaskan Way, across from the Seattle Aquarium. There were restaurants all along the quay, and through the windows, the blue waters of Elliott Bay sparkled in the morning sun.

The guard in the lobby, an older, gray-haired man named Mitch, sat behind a computer at the front desk. He waved as Ran walked past. Ran waved back and continued down the hall to the conference room.

Like the rest of the offices, the conference room had a homey feel, with exposed redbrick walls, wide-plank, golden oak floors, and comfortable leather seating. Four familiar faces looked up from their cell phone screens and smiled at him from their places around the long oak table.

"Hey, boss." Jesse Stahl, his audio expert, a good-looking African American man, lifted a hand in greeting.

"Morning," Ran said.

Next to Jesse, Kathryn "Katie" Collins, a thirty-year-old blonde who knew her way around a video camera like the pro she was, tucked her cell phone into her pocket. "I'm really hoping you have something for us to do. I'm going crazy sitting around the office." After a dry spell, all of them were edgy, ready to get back to work.

"There's a house in Sunderland, England," Ran said. "Looks promising so far."

Katie grinned. "I've never been to England."

"Neither have I," Jesse said, obviously intrigued.

Next at the table, Violet Sutton, the sensitive on the team, shifted in her leather swivel chair. "Actually, Britain's kind of dreary. But with all the old buildings, there are certainly plenty of ghosts."

Violet was in her early sixties, with silver hair she wore swept back in a twist. She tended to mother team members, including him. Ran adored her.

The fourth person in the room, Constance Dutton, was the team coordinator. A forty-year-old woman with light brown hair cut in a bob, Connie made all the travel arrangements and handled anything else that came up. Though she didn't go with them, she took care of everyone's needs and managed to keep all of them happy and under control.

Ran turned at the sound of the door opening as another person entered the conference room.

Like Ran, Zane Tanner was a tall man, about an inch shorter than Ran's six feet two, with a leaner build. He had brown eyes, a square jaw, and dark brown hair with faint auburn highlights. He wore it cut short, unlike Ran's black hair, which curled over the collar of his blue knit pullover, reminding him he needed it cut. Zane's worn brown bomber jacket seemed to be a permanent fixture.

"Sorry I'm late," Zane said, shedding the jacket. "I had a flat tire on the way over." He smiled. "Not a made-up excuse, I promise."

Ran turned back to the others. "We're adding another member to the team. Katie, Jesse, Violet, and Connie, meet Zane Tanner. Zane's a PI and former Green Beret. He's going to be helping with the research and also provide security when we need it. Which may be the situation with our newest case."

"Nice to meet you, Zane," Violet said.

"Welcome," said Katie, smiling brightly. With her honey-blond hair and big blue eyes, Katie was a guy magnet. She was a notorious flirt, but her interest in men rarely went deeper than the surface. She was extremely smart, and selective in the men she dated, which meant she spent a lot of time alone.

Jesse rose and extended a hand to Zane, who leaned across the table to shake. "Good to meet you," Jesse said. "Welcome to the team."

"Thanks," Zane said.

Connie waved a greeting, while Violet and Katie shook Zane's hand. Zane smiled. "I look forward to getting to know all of you better as time goes on."

They sat back down, Ran taking his usual place at the head of the table. Connie was team coordinator, but Ransom King was the boss.

"I forwarded each of you the email we received from a woman named Eve St. Clair," Ran said. "As usual, I had her thoroughly checked out. Zane has a contact in the UK who was able to fill in the blanks." He turned to the newest member of the team. "Zane?"

"Dr. Eve St. Clair is thirty-one years old, born in England, parents divorced. Mother moved to Boston when Eve was three years old. Father remarried and took himself out of the picture. He and his second, much-younger wife are now living in France. Eve's mother died while Eve was in college."

Zane glanced up, making eye contact with the people around the table. "Recently Eve inherited a house in Sunderland, UK, from an uncle she stayed with every summer as a child, until she was in high school. She was raised in Boston, graduated from University of Massachusetts with a Ph.D. in psychology. Works out of a home office next to her garage."

Zane glanced down at the notes he'd made on his iPad. "Eve was married for two years, divorced a year ago." He looked up. "Apparently, she decided to change her life and moved into the home her uncle left her in his will."

"Any history of mental illness?" Ran asked.

"She's a psychologist. Aside from that, no history of mental disorders." Zane grinned at his joke, and everyone laughed.

Looked like Zane Tanner had a sense of humor, Ran thought with amusement.

"When did the uncle die?" Ran asked, knowing trauma could lead to hallucinations or other psychosis.

"George St. Clair, her grandmother's younger brother, passed away six months ago in his sleep. Death certificate reports it was an aneurysm."

"So she moved in six months ago?" Katie asked.

Zane shook his head. "With probate and transitioning from Boston to England, she's only lived in the house two months."

It took time to adjust to a new home. Clearly Eve St. Clair wasn't used to her surroundings. Which could be important. Or not.

"I looked at the dwelling on Google Earth," Ran said. "Two-story redbrick structure with white trim. Looks like something built in the early twentieth century, nineteen twenties, I'd guess. Nothing particularly unusual about it."

"But you think it's worth a trip to Europe to check it out," Katie said.

"I spoke to Eve on the phone." Not something he usually did. He usually let the team follow up after the initial email contact. This time he'd phoned the prospective client himself, spoken to her via a FaceTime call.

"There was something about her," Ran said. "She's a doctor of psychology. She doesn't want people to think she's crazy, but she's definitely afraid. As far as I can tell, she has no one she feels she can trust with this, and no one else she can turn to. If the problem is real, I'd like to help."

Jesse flashed a wide white smile. "Good enough for me." That was their primary mission—aiding people with paranormal problems, people who couldn't find help anywhere else. "Worst case, she's a fraud. No ghosts but a chance to see England."

"When do we leave?" Katie asked, eager as always.

"Anyone have a reason they can't fly out tonight?" Ran asked.

Nobody's hand went up.

Ran nodded his approval. "The Gulfstream will be ready to leave Boeing Field at eight p.m. You'll arrive at the Newcastle Airport two o'clock tomorrow afternoon. There'll be a car waiting to take you to the Grand Hotel Sunderland. The hotel's only ten minutes away from the destination property. The car and driver will be at your service as long as you're there." He glanced around the table. "Any questions so far?"

"No, sir," Connie said. She flashed a warning glance at the others. "They'll be ready to leave at eight p.m."

Ran nodded. "Great, I'll meet you there."

Violet's silver-haired head came up. "You're going with us?"

"I may not stay, but I'm going over for the initial contact." Ran rose from his chair. "I'll leave the details to Connie." He turned away from the group, long strides carrying him across the room. He wasn't a man who wasted energy.

Pausing at the door, he turned back. "One thing you should know about Zane." A faint smile touched his lips. "Zane doesn't believe in ghosts."

Jesse bellowed a laugh.

Katie grinned. "This should be interesting."

"Zane's objectivity is one of the reasons I brought him aboard. I'll see you tonight." Ran walked out of the room and firmly closed the door.

CHAPTER THREE

THE PASSENGERS BEGAN TO STIR AS THE KING ENTERPRISES GULF-stream G550 began its initial descent into Newcastle International Airport.

Jesse and Katie were still asleep on the long cream leather sofas facing each other in the rear section of the aircraft. Ran had slept for a while, kicked back in one of the wide leather chairs. Now he sat at the burlwood table in the middle section, while Zane stretched out watching a movie in one of the front compartment seats.

The Gulfstream could comfortably accommodate up to four-teen passengers. The King Enterprises's forty-million-dollar jet was configured so that the rear section, with its own separate bathroom, could be closed off and used as a bedroom.

For a moment, Ran's thoughts went to the woman he had met via FaceTime—Eve St. Clair. Her eyes were hazel and seemed to switch mercurially from green to dark brown. Her hair was so dark it looked black, with interesting ruby highlights. Like her eyes, the glints of garnet seemed to shift back and forth as she moved.

Even with an ocean between them, he'd felt a pull toward her. As he'd thought before, Eve St. Clair intrigued him. Ran wasn't a man easily intrigued by a woman.

His thoughts moved from what lay ahead to the luxury provided by the company jet. He smiled. Working for him definitely had its perks.

The job also came with plenty of emotional stress.

They were working in a world few people knew anything about. Along with the physical labor of hauling around and setting up the fragile equipment required to do a paranormal investigation, there were emotions to deal with, those of the client as well as those of the spirits stuck in the earthly realm.

Along with the others, Zane would be joining the team, doing some of the research, as he had done today, and, being former military, providing security when needed.

Violet's job as a sensitive was to feel the presence of energy, to interact with what people referred to as spirits or ghosts. There were any number of names for her skills.

Clairsentience meant heightened awareness or an exaggerated sixth sense, which was different from an empath, who could feel other people's emotions, even psychically communicate with spirits.

A medium was sort of a catch-all phrase for someone who facilitated communication between spirits or ghosts and living human beings, relaying messages from the dead, or at least that was the goal.

Aside from the people he trusted, Ran still wasn't sure how much of it was real.

He thought back to when his experiment had begun five years earlier. Guilt over the death of his wife and child had compelled him to seek answers. Was there life after death? Did heaven and hell actually exist? Was his family now safely in the hands of God? Did God even exist?

He was still searching for answers. Maybe he would find more of them in England.

The jet rolled to a stop and the sound of seat belts popping open combined with tired sighs. The eleven-hour flight and subsequent time change was exhausting. Grabbing their personal items, jackets, and laptops, the team disembarked.

The scientific equipment needed for their research would be unloaded and transported via a separate vehicle to their hotel.

As Ran stepped down on the tarmac, a sullen gray sky hung bleakly overhead. The early May air felt damp and cold. Knowing his expectations, Connie had arranged transportation; a white Bentley Grand limo rolled toward them across the tarmac. The chauffer, in a crisp black suit and white shirt, opened the passenger door, allowing the five of them to settle into red leather seats facing each other while the driver, a slender, gray-haired man who introduced himself as Willard, loaded their luggage into the trunk.

"Wow," Zane said, clearly impressed as he glanced around the interior, illuminated by subtle blue lights.

"Yeah," Jesse said. "The boss has expensive taste."

"Best thing about our job is the perks," Katie said, grinning at Ran.

But the hard part lay ahead, dealing with the unknown, confronting what might be hiding in the darkness beyond their perception. Finding out the truth and giving comfort to the people forced to live with whatever taunted them from the shadows.

Ran settled back in the deep leather seat for the thirty-plus minute ride from the airport to the Grand Hotel Sunderland, an upscale hotel in the area. It wasn't far from the St. Clair house and, best of all, faced the sea.

They discussed the upcoming case on the way to the hotel, arrived as planned, and walked into the high-ceilinged lobby, done mostly in white with blue and gray accents. After an efficient check-in, they received their key cards.

"I'll phone Dr. St. Clair," Ran said. "Let her know we've arrived."

"Connie scheduled Zane and Violet to go over early and do the initial interview," Katie said. "If everything checks out, Jesse and I will go over later and set up the equipment."

Ran nodded, turned to Zane. "We need to be sure there are no security problems." Which included a woman who might have mental issues—or worse. Until they knew for sure, Ran never took chances.

"I've got my permits all lined up," Zane said. "I'll be able to carry a weapon."

Ran nodded, his attention on Zane and Violet. "I'll be joining you."

Violet just smiled. It wasn't part of the original plan, but after working with Ran for so long, she had learned to be flexible.

"In the meantime," Ran said, "unless you have something more you need to do, I suggest you go upstairs and unpack, maybe catch a nap."

"I could use a nap," Katie said, yawning.

Ran's gaze returned to Violet and Zane. "Dr. St. Clair is expecting us at seven. Let's meet for a quick bite in the restaurant . . . say six p.m.?"

"Sounds good," Zane said.

Ran appreciated Zane's strictly business attitude. No flirting with Katie or off-color remarks, nothing out of line. He was a good-looking man, one who seemed to have the confidence that didn't require constant ego reinforcement.

But then, Ran had known all about Zane Tanner before he had hired him. He figured he knew more about his employees than most of them knew about themselves.

Katie yawned again. "That nap is sounding better and better." Even though they'd slept most of the way on the plane, the time change was a killer.

They all headed upstairs to their rooms. Connie usually booked Violet a suite. The team used the living area for conferencing. The suite Connie had booked for him sat on the second floor and had a view of the ocean.

He crossed the living room and opened the door leading out to a narrow balcony, letting a rush of fresh sea air inside. Like the lobby, the suite was done in light colors, mostly white with blue accents. A thick white comforter covered the king-size bed, and the bathroom, he noticed, was modern, with a marble countertop, a shower with a clear glass door, and a tub.

He checked his watch, which he'd reset to local time on the plane. With the time-zone change, the office in Seattle would soon be open. He could check in with his executive assistant before he joined Violet and Zane for supper, then went over to the house.

Interest slipped through him. Until the team was assembled in the house, there was no way to know if Eve St. Clair's story of paranormal phenomena was real or some figment of her imagination.

His pulse kicked up as he thought of their FaceTime discussion. He couldn't deny he was looking forward to meeting her.

CHAPTER FOUR

*T*WILIGHT HAD SETTLED OVER THE FLAT GRAY OCEAN AND THE TOWN along its shores, the last glimmer of sunlight fading. Sunderland had been settled in the year 685. In the fourteenth century it became a shipbuilding port; by 1815, the largest in the world. Today the city was an auto building center.

A long history of changes, Ran thought, over the years.

Standing next to Violet and Zane on the front porch of Eve St. Clair's home, Ran studied the redbrick two-story. White trim outlined the windows, and the arched front door was also white. An interesting gabled roofline mirrored the smaller pointed roof over the porch.

Ran pushed the doorbell, and the sound echoed through the residence. Violet took a moment to straighten the wool jacket she wore with a long navy skirt and a pair of sturdy boots.

With his short dark hair and brown cargo pants, Zane stood with his back straight, a pistol in the shoulder holster beneath the brown bomber jacket he wore over a beige sweater.

He sliced Ran an unreadable glance as footsteps sounded on the opposite side of the door. This was all new to Zane. Ran inwardly smiled. This could turn into a very interesting evening for his newest team member.

The door swung open and Eve St. Clair stood in the opening. She was taller than Violet, maybe five-six. Violet was thinner, a willowy woman, while Eve was slender, but with attractively feminine curves. She was wearing a pair of stretch jeans and a light blue sweater. Glossy dark hair curled just past her shoulders, the shifting ruby highlights even more compelling than he had imagined.

Ran smiled. "Dr. St. Clair? I'm Ransom King. This is Violet Sutton and Zane Tanner. They're part of our team."

Eve smiled, her whole face lighting up. Ran felt a kick that was completely unexpected.

"I'm Eve. Thank you for making such a long journey. Please come in."

They stepped into the entry beneath an old-fashioned frosted glass chandelier, and Eve closed the door behind them. Ran noticed her hands were shaking.

"I'm not sure how all of this works," Eve said. "On the phone you said I should call you Ran."

"We're going to be working together, so yes, absolutely."

"Would you like a tour of the house, or shall we go into the living room, where we can chat?"

"There's no hurry," Ran said. "Let's sit down and talk for a while, maybe get to know each other a little."

"All right."

As Ran moved farther into the entry, he noticed a staircase down the hall, a living room off to the right, and a dining room off to the left. A philodendron spilled over a blue china pot in a plant stand near the door, and leafy plants in pots lined the hall.

Eve led them into the living room, furnished with a burgundy settee and two matching wingback chairs, protected here and there with delicate, white crocheted doilies. An old mahogany rocker sat by the fireplace. Burgundy flocked wallpaper covered the walls, and a brass lamp hung from the center of a molded ceiling.

Aside from the seating area in front of the hearth, the room was almost completely filled with antique furniture. In addition, there were knickknacks in display cases and bookshelves around the room filled with leather-bound volumes, along with silver-framed family photos on tables and pictures on the walls.

"Please make yourselves comfortable," Eve said. "You'll have to excuse the clutter down here. I've been able to get through the stuff upstairs, but these were my uncle's most treasured possessions." She glanced at the objects in the display cases and the photos on the walls. "I'm going through everything little by little, but I'm also working, and it's a big job, not something my housekeeper can tackle."

"Not a problem," Ran said, moving toward one of the wingback chairs.

"I've given Mrs. Pennyworth the week off so you can work undisturbed."

As Violet walked farther into the living room, her gaze swept the space and she began to sway on her feet. A fine-boned hand fluttered at the base of her throat. When she took a gasping breath, Zane latched on to her arm to steady her.

"You all right?" he asked, concern lining his forehead.

Violet nodded. "I just . . . I just need to sit for a moment." Zane walked her over to the settee and urged her down.

Violet's gaze went to Eve, whose face had gone paper white. "It's all right. Sometimes when there are a lot of objects in the home . . ." Violet took a slow, calming breath. "How do I explain it? You see, everything in our world is made up of energy. I'm sensitive to many different forms. There is a lot of energy in this room."

Eve frowned. "Are you . . . are you saying there are ghosts in here?"

Violet shook her head. "No, it's nothing like that. I just feel the weight of the things around me. The older they are, the more energy they store." She managed to smile. "It's nothing to worry about."

"I wonder if that could be the reason I . . ." Her words trailed off and she glanced away.

"The reason you what . . . ?" Ran prodded.

"Sometimes I feel as if the air in the room is pressing in on me. My chest clamps down and I feel light-headed. A couple of times, I actually thought I was going to faint. That's the reason I've been working so hard to get my uncle's items sorted and put away. I thought maybe the dust or mildew or something was the problem."

"What was your home like in Boston?" Ran asked.

"In Boston, I lived in an apartment. The décor was minimal, sleek and modern, plenty of windows to let in sunlight. As a psychologist, I deal with people's emotional baggage. Sometimes I get caught up in it. The simplicity of my surroundings helped to keep me balanced."

Ran stored the information. He knew too much clutter visibly affected Violet. Perhaps Eve had sensitivities she didn't yet understand.

Eve smiled again, a little brighter this time. "Would any of you care for something to drink? This is England. Perhaps a cup of tea?"

Zane started to shake his head, but Violet touched his arm. "It was a long flight over. Tea would be lovely." Giving a person something to do helped relax them and build rapport, a lesson learned long ago.

Zane joined Violet on the sofa, and Ran settled back in his chair. A few minutes later, Eve returned with a silver tea tray holding a flowered teapot and four delicate cups and saucers. Violet and Ran declined sugar, while Zane took two lumps. Ran had a feeling Zane wasn't much of a tea drinker.

Eve handed the tea around and her hand brushed his as he accepted the cup. A zing of awareness shot up his arm. Eve's eyes met his and the surprise in them said she had felt it, too.

"Thank you," Ran said, balancing the saucer on his knee as he leaned back in the chair. His gaze followed Eve, who sat down in a matching wing chair at the opposite end of the settee. With her ivory complexion, high cheekbones, and the slight bow at the top of her full pink lips, Eve was a beautiful woman.

She was also a client, he reminded himself.

His gaze went to Zane. Ran wondered what the investigator was thinking as he sat stiffly on the settee. Zane was way out of his comfort zone. He didn't believe in any of this. Ran wondered if he thought Violet was faking her reaction to the clutter in the house.

"So what do we do now?" Eve asked.

Zane flicked Ran a glance, leaned over, and set his cup and saucer on the coffee table. "I'll take a look around outside, make sure everything is secure." There had been recent reports of crime in the area, one of the reasons Ran had brought Zane along.

Ran just nodded. As Zane left the house, Ran took a drink of his tea. Though he was basically a coffee drinker, Earl Grey was his favorite.

His gaze returned to Eve. "Why don't you tell us about the voices," he suggested. "That's the way you described them when we spoke on the phone. You said it sounded like someone was speaking out in the hall."

"Whispering," Eve corrected. "Like two people whispering, or kind of murmuring. Sometimes they grew angry, sometimes it sounded a little like laughter, only not the good kind." She rubbed her hands up and down her arms as if she were cold, though the coal fire in the hearth actually made the room a little too warm.

"Did you recognize either of the speakers?" Ran asked. "Could it have been someone you know?"

"No, definitely not. I'd never heard the voices before I moved in. And they aren't always the same. Some nights it's as if there are several different speakers. Usually it sounds like two men talking, but once I thought I heard the voice of a woman."

Beginning to get used to the weight of the clutter around her, Violet rose from the sofa. "Do you mind if I wander a bit? It would help if I could get a feel of the house."

Eve rose from her chair. "I could show you around."

"I'd rather take my time and just stroll," Violet said. "If you don't mind."

"Of course. Please go ahead."

Violet smiled. "Ran can keep you company while I'm gone. I won't be long."

It was dark outside the windows. Unease trickled through Eve as the hour grew later. She glanced across the living room to the tall man sitting opposite her, making her uncle's burgundy wing-back chair look small. Ransom King. *Ran*, he had insisted during their FaceTime call.

Needing a diversion, Eve rose from her chair. "I think I'll move around a little before Violet comes back."

Ran nodded, but his gaze remained sharp. Eve started for the hallway, passing the dining room on the opposite side, which had tall, old-fashioned doors that slid open on long brass runners.

She wandered toward the mahogany Chippendale table in the middle of the room, draped with a Belgian lace cloth. Eight matching chairs upholstered in patterned burgundy velvet surrounded it. A mahogany sideboard rested against the wall.

The room was much less cluttered than the living room and hadn't been used in years. Once Uncle George had loved to entertain, but that had been long ago. They had grown apart after she had gone away to college. She was glad she had spent precious time with him before he passed.

Eve returned to the hallway, a central corridor with stairs leading up to the second floor. She'd started back toward the living room when she heard the murmur of voices. She hadn't met King until tonight, but she'd spoken to him on the phone, and this voice wasn't his. A second male voice began speaking, the tone harsher, bolder.

Goose bumps rose on her skin. Her pulse increased, began to pound in her ears. The whispering grew louder, an argument of some sort, then abruptly ceased. Freezing air rushed into the hall though the doors and windows were closed. Icy air stalled in her lungs and suddenly she couldn't breathe.

Light-headed, her heart hammering as if it tried to escape her chest, she leaned against the wall, knocking a porcelain vase off an ornate pedestal, sending the object crashing to the floor.

King appeared in the hall, took one look at her pale face, and strode toward her. Her knees went weak as he reached her, and he caught her around the waist before she hit the floor. He turned her into his arms, and Eve desperately hung on.

"I'm right here," King said. "Just take it easy."

She swallowed, tried to control her racing heart. "The dining room . . ." She pointed in that direction. "Let's . . . let's go in there." It was the place downstairs she went when she needed a break from all the clutter.

She leaned against King as he guided her into the room, pulled out one of the dining chairs, and urged her down in the seat.

Violet appeared in the doorway. "What's happened? What's going on?"

Eve took a steadying breath and forced a wobbly smile. "Everything's all right. I just . . . I heard them. I heard the voices."

Violet looked at King.

"Did you hear them?" he asked her.

"No, but I was upstairs. I didn't feel or hear much of anything."

King looked down at Eve, his blue eyes intense.

"Did you hear them?" Eve asked, praying that he had, for the first time admitting how worried she was that the voices were only in her head.

King's fierce blue gaze didn't waver. "Actually, I believe I did."

Eve closed her eyes and gripped her hands together in her lap. "Thank God."

"God or the devil," King said. "At this point, there's no way to be sure."

CHAPTER FIVE

BACK AT THE HOTEL, RAN DECIDED ON A CHANGE OF PLANS. UNLESS it was an elaborate hoax, there was something formidable in Eve St. Clair's house, something that had sapped her strength.

Ran had felt it, too, but he had been working long hours and under a good deal of stress over an upcoming merger. Or maybe some of what he thought he had heard was the result of the long flight and the time change.

Eve had said she was prone to low blood sugar and dehydration. She hadn't discounted that as a factor. She needed to eat something and drink some liquids, she had said, then get some sleep. Before she'd gone to bed, she had sent him an email, letting him know she was all right, but hoping he hadn't changed his mind about returning.

Her email had ended,

Whatever it was, it felt terribly dark and disturbing. I was glad you were there and I wasn't alone.

The words touched him. Clearly, she needed someone to help her. He hadn't felt needed by a woman since Sabrina had died. He blocked the painful thought and pondered the voices he had heard in the hall. But the encounter was so brief, he couldn't be sure it had actually occurred.

Violet said the upstairs was quiet and very clean, and she hadn't picked up anything of concern. Still, the sound of muffled voices remained lodged in the back of his mind.

Ran had canceled the arrival of the rest of the team and gone back to the hotel. Tomorrow night they would return with their research equipment, currently being stored in Jesse's hotel room.

The gear included sophisticated full-spectrum 6k cameras; ultraviolet and various colored lights, infrared night vision; and EMF meters to measure fluctuations in electrical magnetic fields.

Temperature-reading devices, some of them handheld, could register intense cold spots indicating the possible presence of spirits. Microphones and EVP meters recorded electronic voice phenomena.

Katie and Jesse handled the technical aspects of the investigation. Aside from the graphs, video, and audio recordings the equipment provided, validating what had been seen, felt, or heard, Ran was only mildly interested in what the data showed. The connection between this world and the world on the Other Side was what he found fascinating.

It was the reason he had formed the team, the reason he continued to fund investigations. It wasn't just a circus act to prove ghosts existed. Ran had come to believe in the importance of the work they were doing. Not just exploring psychic phenomena but helping earthbound spirits find their way home.

After a good night's sleep and a hearty English breakfast of eggs, sausage, toast, tomatoes, and juice, Ran took a walk along the shoreline to clear his head. The crash and roll of the waves against the rocks and the beauty of what seemed an endless sea calmed his mind and helped him focus.

Katie and Jesse were upstairs rechecking the equipment, while Zane prowled community resources in search of information on the house and its former occupants. Zane was looking into the archives of the *Echo,* the local newspaper, dating back to the twenties, which he had confirmed as the date the house had been built.

Though Violet preferred going in with only basic background information, allowing her to keep an open mind, the research would be important later to verify what might be learned. To-night, Violet would try to make initial contact, see what sort of energy she could be facing.

With luck, tonight they would find out more of what was happening in the house.

Ran joined the team downstairs for supper in the hotel restaurant, the Cast Iron Bar and Grill, a bright, cheerful place with windows looking out at the ocean across the street.

"You're right on time," Katie said as Ran walked up to the table. "The server just brought menus."

He sat down in one of the chairs and settled back in the seat.

"I liked her," Violet said. "Your Eve has a very interesting aura."

Ignoring Violet's reference to Eve as belonging to him, Ran spread his white linen napkin over his lap. "So you don't think she's a charlatan?" His instincts said Eve was for real, but he wanted Violet's opinion.

"On the contrary. I think she may have gifts she isn't yet willing to accept."

Ran nodded. "I had that thought myself."

The waitress returned and took their orders. They talked until the food arrived; then all of them dug in.

"Everything's ready to go," Jesse said around a mouthful of fish and chips. "No damage from the plane ride. Gear's all checked out and in good condition."

"Once we get there," Katie added, "we'll be set up and running in less than an hour."

Ran nodded. "Good to hear."

"We're excited." Katie swallowed a bite of seafood salad. "From what Violet told us, Eve had some kind of reaction last night."

Ran took a drink of the cola he had ordered. In England, most people drank whiskey, ale, or tea. The team had a no-alcohol rule that lasted until after they were finished for the night. Even then, drinking was moderate. No one wanted the results of their study to be questioned.

"I don't know exactly what happened," Violet said. "But when I got downstairs, Eve was white as a sheet. I thought she was going to pass out."

Zane turned to Violet. "What do you think caused that reaction? If she'd fainted, she could have taken a bad fall and gotten seriously injured."

Violet toyed with her food, pushing succulent grilled cod around on her plate. "Apparently, Eve felt a burst of energy. It manifested itself in what she heard as voices."

"I believe Eve feels a strong sense of danger," Ran said. "That's the reason she got in touch with us in the first place. It's the reason I decided to wait until tonight to go in with our equipment. I wanted to give her time to recover from her experience. Having all of us there as backup should be a big help."

"Safety in numbers," Zane said.

"In a way, I guess."

They finished their meal, all of them eager to get started. Ran shoved back his chair and rose from the table. "Check's taken care of. Everyone ready to go?"

"Absolutely," Jesse said, rising. He was a few inches shorter than Ran, built like a brick house, thick muscles bulging beneath his ebony skin. He was also mentally strong, determined in whatever goal he pursued.

Jesse had come aboard as a skeptic like Zane, but it hadn't taken long for him to become convinced. He was an audio genius, loved gadgets of any kind, and with Katie handling the video equipment, they were both real assets to the team.

Ran led them out of the restaurant, through the lobby to the front door. The white Bentley limo waited outside. Jesse and Katie loaded the gear into the trunk and joined Ran, Violet, and Zane, settling themselves in the deep red leather seats across from each other.

Since the house was close to the East End and not far from the docks, the limo dropped them off, along with their gear, and the driver headed back to the hotel.

With the reported increase in neighborhood crime, a Bentley stretch parked on the street late at night might pose too much of a temptation. Ran would call the driver when they were ready to leave.

Carrying their equipment, the group walked up the brick path to the front door. Ran knocked, stepped back, and waited as the sound of light footsteps approached.

Smoothing the dark gray slacks she wore with a pearl-gray sweater, Eve answered the knock at the door. Her pulse kicked up as she checked the peephole and spotted the team waiting on the porch.

Eve pulled open the door and smiled up at Ransom King. "Thank you again for making the trip all the way to England. Please come in." She eased back to let the group walk past her into the house.

King paused in the entry. "You remember Violet and Zane."

Eve nodded. "Of course."

"This is Kathryn Collins and Jesse Stahl. They're members of the team."

"It's Katie." The pretty blonde smiled and extended a hand Eve shook. For an instant she wondered if King and the blonde were together, but there seemed to be only a professional connection between them.

"Nice to meet you," Jesse said, also shaking her hand. He was a very attractive black man with keen dark eyes. His bright smile immediately put Eve at ease.

"Zane has been looking into the history of the house and the people who owned it," King said. "He may have something that'll help explain the dark feeling in the house last night."

"And the voices?" Eve asked.

"Violet may be able to help us with that. We should know more later."

She managed to smile. "I made a trip to the market this afternoon, bought some soft drinks and snacks. Would you like something before we start?"

"We've already eaten," Ran said. "But I think we could use a cold drink. Why don't I help you get them?"

She walked down the hall to the kitchen on the left, feeling Ran's tall, broad-shouldered presence behind her as they stepped through the doorway. The big, open kitchen had been remodeled over the years, but with its small white fridge, Formica countertops, and a typically British AGA cast-iron range cooker, it retained a sense of another era.

Setting out a tray, she took cans of Coca-Cola Light, a can of ginger ale, and bottles of water out of the fridge, then opened a cupboard to take down some glasses.

"Cans are fine," Ran said. Picking up the tray, he carried the drinks into the living room and set the tray down on the walnut coffee table. Katie, Jesse, and Zane each grabbed a bottle of water, while Violet took the ginger ale. Ran popped the top on one of the cola cans and took a long swallow. Eve tried not to notice the corded muscles in his throat moving up and down as he drank.

Eve quickly glanced away.

They all sat down in the living room, giving everyone a chance to get comfortable before they went to work.

"Let's talk about the house," King said, taking the same wing-back chair he'd commandeered before. "Last night, Violet was upstairs while you were downstairs. Tell me what you felt in the hall."

Eve smoothed a hand over her lap as she thought about the voices that seemed more and more demanding. "It's difficult to explain. Thinking about it now, I'd say it was an overwhelming sense of darkness. Absolute despair. It's happened before, but last night was the worst. I think whatever it is, it's getting stronger. I felt as if things were spiraling out of control, and I had no power to stop it."

Ran took a long swallow of his soft drink. His gaze found hers across the distance between them. "We're all here tonight. That should make you feel a little safer. Violet will be opening herself up more to what might be happening, so perhaps we'll get some answers."

"We're here at this moment for a reason," Violet said with conviction, seemingly convinced the entire world and beyond was part of some grand design. "Maybe tonight we'll find out why we've been brought here."

Eve hoped so. The less time she spent with Ransom King, the better. She didn't like the unfamiliar feelings he sparked in her.

After her unhappy marriage and subsequent divorce, she wasn't interested in a man on any level.

On the other hand, she felt safer with Ran King in the house. She had no idea why, but it was true.

King rose from his chair, picked up the tray, and left to return it to the kitchen. As he passed, the confident way he moved caught her attention.

Eve ignored it.

She needed every ounce of calm she could find to deal with whatever was lurking in the shadows of the house. Tonight, perhaps King and his team of investigators would help her figure that out.

CHAPTER SIX

*R*AN RETURNED TO HIS SEAT IN THE LIVING ROOM. KATIE AND Jesse stood near the doorway, ready to set up their gear. Zane was outside keeping watch. Ran had left on purpose, giving Eve a chance to get comfortable with the team. She was talking to Violet, who had asked her why she continued to stay in the house when she was clearly uneasy being there.

"After my divorce," Eve said, "I sold everything I owned to move here and start a new life. I can't afford to move again. I'm just starting to rebuild my practice as a psychologist. Plus, the house has been in my family since the late nineteen twenties. It's where I spent the best days of my childhood. The house holds cherished memories for me. It's an important part of my heritage."

"No one in your family ever mentioned anything unusual happening here?" Ran asked.

"No, and I can't imagine why Uncle George never said anything."

"You mentioned spending a great deal of time here as a child," Ran said. "You didn't notice anything unusual while you were growing up?"

"No, I . . ." Eve fell silent. "Now that you ask . . ." She frowned. "I'm not exactly sure. . . . At the time, it didn't seem unusual. But now . . . considering what's been happening, maybe it was."

"Go on," Ran encouraged.

"I remember when I was young, I had this invisible friend. Other kids have them. It didn't seem odd at the time."

"What did your friend look like?" Violet asked.

"He was a little boy, maybe four or five. We played together sometimes. It didn't go on for long. Uncle George discouraged it, and I wanted to please him. In time, I made other friends, and I guess I just grew out of it."

"Do you remember anything about the boy?" Violet asked. "His name, perhaps?"

Eve shook her head. "No, I'm sorry, I don't—" She broke off, her hazel eyes widening in surprise. "Wally," she said. "Walter, but he called himself Wally. I never knew his last name, but I . . . I remember he wore funny clothes."

Eve closed her eyes for a moment, working to summon the memory. "Wally's pants were more like knickers than trousers. Navy blue, ending just below the knee, and a waist-length matching jacket. And there was this little navy-blue hat with a tassel on the top. Like a miniature sailor's suit." Her eyes found Ran's across the room. "Good Lord, I can't believe I remember that."

"We'll check it out," Ran said. "But if I recall my history correctly, that sounds like something that might have been worn by a child in the Victorian era."

Eve nodded. "Yes, I think that's right."

"Too early to be the ghost of someone who lived in a house built in the nineteen twenties," Jesse reminded them.

Eve's shoulders drooped. "You're right."

Violet leaned forward on the sofa. "Unless something else is going on."

Eve made no comment.

"Our capabilities change over the years," Violet explained. "Perhaps as a child you hadn't learned to block your perceptions yet. As you grew up, you ignored them. Now that you're older, they're coming back, more finely tuned than they were before. You notice things that no one in your family had the awareness to feel."

"Or simply pretended not to notice," Ran added.

Eve's grateful glance moved over him and the members of the team. "Well, you're here now," she said. "Perhaps you can figure out what's going on."

With Eve's permission, Katie and Jesse headed off to set up the cameras, audio and video recorders, temperature-sensitive instruments, and other miscellaneous gear.

Violet requested the equipment be focused in the back portion of the hall, where Eve had heard voices and had suffered such a strong physical reaction.

While Jesse and Katie worked, Zane checked in, then went back outside to wander the area around the house, continuing to ensure there were no security problems. As time slipped past, Ran took a walk through the house, including the rooms upstairs.

There was a bathroom at one end of the hall. He passed three bedrooms, all furnished with antiques, but less cluttered than downstairs. The main bedroom had its own bathroom with an old-fashioned clawfoot tub. Lovely glass perfume bottles with the names of Parisian designers—Chloé, Chanel, Yves Saint Laurent—sat on the dresser.

As he crossed the bedroom to the door, his glance strayed to the pink satin comforter and throw pillows on the bed. He smiled at the feminine décor.

Eve presented a solidly professional appearance, but deep down, he had no doubt she was a very feminine woman.

It was the living room, he realized as he walked in, that continued to project an eerie disquiet, though it might have simply been the power of suggestion. It occurred to him as he glanced around that all of George St. Clair's many possessions represented a sort of museum dedicated to the St. Clair family, as well as a showcase for all his collectibles.

Ran glanced over at Eve, who sat quietly on the burgundy settee, her hands gripped in her lap. Eve disliked clutter. So did Violet. As a sensitive, Violet felt things at a different level than most people. She felt the vibrations of energy collected over time.

Ran sat down next to Eve. "You doing okay?"

"I'm getting nervous. I think I'll go outside for a while, clear my head before you're ready to begin."

"Come on." He took her hand. "We'll both go out." He looked down at their joined hands and his body stirred.

Ran let go of her hand.

Outside the house, the air was chilled by a wet breeze that blew in off the ocean. "You have an office on the property?" Ran asked.

"Yes, it's next to the garage. It was added a few years back."

"No voices? Nothing like that?"

"No." Eve wrapped her arms around herself against the chill. It was dark out, just a sliver of moon showing through the clouds.

Ran draped his jacket around her shoulders. "We should probably go back inside," he said.

Eve nodded. "I'm ready." She looked up at him, her hazel eyes green now and crystal clear. "I don't like the feeling I'm getting in there. I'm glad you're here."

The words touched him. There was something about Eve St. Clair that drew him, an inner light that seemed to shine through the darkness around her. Perhaps it was the reason the energy in the house was attracted to her. The reason he had been drawn to her since the first time he had spoken to her on the FaceTime call.

"Be interesting to know what Zane found out about the history of the house," Ran said as they walked back inside. The air felt overly warm in the entry after being out in the cold, and there was a heaviness in the atmosphere he hadn't noticed before.

Too many things, Violet would say. *Too many memories attached to too many objects.*

"I asked Zane to wait until we were finished before he gives us his findings," Ran said. "Violet prefers it that way."

Ran felt the opposite, that knowing as much as possible about the past gave him an advantage.

Katie walked toward where they stood in the entry. "Everything's ready."

"We can do this two ways," Ran said to Eve. "You can stay out of it and let Violet do the work by herself. Or you can join us, watch things unfold. The choice is yours."

"I need to be there," Eve said without hesitation.

Ran nodded. He had guessed that would be her reply. Jesse had positioned the equipment along both sides of the hallway and aimed some of it up the stairs. He'd placed one of the dining chairs in the hallway farther down the corridor facing the rear of the house. Violet took that chair.

A few feet behind her, Jesse set chairs for Eve and Ran. Katie and Jesse were busy adjusting the cameras and equipment.

"One thing you need to know," Ran said, taking the seat beside her. "Not all ghosts are spirits, but all spirits are ghosts."

"I don't understand."

"Ghosts were once in human form. Spirits, who were also once in human form, may be a type of energy, something invisible that can express feelings or sensations."

"You mean they can project their anger or despair, things like that?"

"That's right. And sensations like heat or cold, pain, pressure, touch. Spirits may have the ability to be visible, but they may not want to be seen."

"Maybe that's why I haven't actually seen anything."

"Yet."

"Oh, dear, I'm getting even more nervous." She glanced down the hallway past where Violet sat a few feet in front of them. "So what do we do now?"

"Now we wait," Ran said. It was the hardest part of the investigation. Waiting. Waiting. And more waiting. Sometimes nothing happened all night. Or ever. Other times, the air seemed to fill with sensations so strong, everyone could feel them.

Jesse turned off the lamps in the living room, leaving the house in darkness, then turned on the infrared lights, filling the hall with a dull, eerie red.

Everything was ready.

All they needed now was for Violet to find a connection with whatever phantoms might wish to reach out to her from the Other Side.

Eve checked her wristwatch. Two hours had passed with only a break here and there. As time dragged and the house grew darker, quieter, Eve's nerves continued to build. Jesse changed the lighting, and the hallway went from foggy red to bilious green.

Eve blinked.

"Night vision," Ran said to her quietly.

Katie adjusted her camera to handle the difference in the light and sat down in the chair she had dragged over next to her lens half an hour ago when her feet started hurting.

Periodically, Violet tried calling to the spirit, or spirits, speaking quietly, reaching out, hoping they would answer. Finally, discouraged, she got up and moved around, heading first into the living room, then the dining room, then turning around and walking past her chair, farther down the hall toward the kitchen.

Violet had almost reached the kitchen door when the sound of breaking glass shattered the quiet. Eve jumped, and her heart started pounding. Turning, she saw the blue flowerpot near the front door had crashed to the floor and broken into a dozen pieces.

Her gaze went to Ran. "What . . . what's going on?"

Ran reached over and took hold of her hand. The warmth seeped into her, and her heartbeat steadied.

"Let's wait and see," he said softly.

As Katie and Jesse quietly checked their equipment, Eve heard the sound of approaching footsteps. The noise rose into the thunder of a dozen running feet. Not adults. More like children. She prayed Ran and Violet could hear them, too. She wanted to ask, but her mouth was too dry to speak.

Eve started to tremble. Ran's big hand squeezed hers. Then she heard them, two men arguing, both of them angry. She didn't realize she had risen from her chair.

"What do you want?" she heard herself ask. "Why are you doing this?"

Icy air enveloped the hallway. Eve felt it in every muscle, bone, and joint. Katie made a sound in her throat. Jesse went to work on the temperature recording device.

The brass chandelier hanging in the entry began to sway, moving back and forth. She saw the red light on the camera go on and knew it was running. Eve tried to imagine what, if anything, would appear on the video recording.

Violet returned to her chair a few feet in front of Eve. "Let us help you," she said.

Eve felt the cold as it deepened, grew icy, seemed to envelop her. "What . . . what do you want?" she asked again, still standing. A dense, thick pressure seemed to surround her, pressing so hard on her chest it was difficult to breathe.

Make! Them! Leave! The harsh demand was slightly muffled but loud enough to make out the words. Eve started to tremble. She felt Ran's hand wrap around her arm, urging her back down in her seat.

"We just want to help you," Violet said, but whatever it was seemed focused on Eve.

You!

There was such hostility, Eve gasped for breath. She couldn't get enough air, and the room began to spin. A little sound came from her throat as she swayed on her feet, and her wild gaze went to Ran.

"That's enough!" he shouted, shooting to his feet. "Hit the lights!"

Jesse flipped on the hall light, and Katie turned on the lights in the brass chandelier in the entry. The bright illumination after the eerie red jolted Eve from what felt almost like a trance. She sucked in a badly needed breath of air.

Ran's arm slid around her waist to steady her, and Eve leaned back against him for support.

"Pack it up," Ran said to Jesse. "We're done for the night. Put everything back where it belongs."

"Man, that was something," Jesse said, grinning.

"I can't wait to go through what I caught on camera," Katie said.

Eve looked up at Ran, his warmth easing some of the tightness in her chest. "Do you . . . do you think we'll actually be able to see something?"

"I don't know what we'll get," Katie replied. "I've got hours of video to go through. With any luck, I'll find something." The pretty blonde went back into the hall to take her camera off the tripod and pack it away.

With the lights back on inside the house, a quick rap came at the door and Zane walked in, a gust of air trailing in his wake. For a moment his glance went to the broken blue pot spilling dirt on the floor. He frowned but didn't ask how it wound up broken.

"Looks like you're finished in here," Zane said.

"For tonight," Ran said.

Eve's gaze went to his. Ran and his team were planning to come back. Eve wasn't sure she could handle it. Then again, aside from giving up her home, what other choice did she have?

CHAPTER SEVEN

As they stood in the entry, Eve felt Zane's searching dark eyes skimming over her, where she still stood in the protective circle of Ran's arms. It felt good to be there. Too good. Eve flushed and moved away.

"How did it go?" Zane asked.

Ran pulled out his cell. "We're just getting ready to discuss it." He pressed one of the contact buttons. "We'll need the car out front," he said, presumably to his driver.

Eve was grateful for the moment to compose herself.

"Jesse has the chairs back in place," Ran said. "Why don't we all sit down at the table in the dining room?" His hand settled at Eve's waist as he guided her into the room, clearly remembering this was the place she felt safest downstairs. Seating Eve to his right, Ran sat down at the end of the table. Zane and Violet also sat down.

Ran sent Eve a reassuring smile, then turned his attention to Violet. "Interesting evening," he said. "What do you think?"

The lines around Violet's mouth tightened, creating little puckers. She shook her head. "I don't like it. Whatever's going on, it's very dark and ominous, and considering what happened to the flowerpot, there's a chance it could be dangerous."

Zane's dark eyes widened. "The ghost did that?"

"Something did," Ran said.

"There's another problem." Violet sat up a little straighter. "I wish I didn't have to say this, but whatever energy is in the house, it seems to be fixed on Eve."

Silence fell.

"How can that be?" Eve asked. "I've only been living here a couple of months. My uncle never had any problems."

"That you know of," Ran added, repeating what he'd said before.

"That's true, but I was here every summer, Christmas, and spring break. Wally never reappeared, and nothing else happened."

"You never noticed anything out of the ordinary?" Ran asked.

Eve forced herself to think about those days long ago. "I don't know. Whenever I was here, I was always busy. I had friends in the area. As I grew older, I was immersed in the world of being a teenager, mostly worried about being accepted and thinking about teenage boys."

Ran's mouth edged up in amusement.

"Your uncle was here when you came for a visit," Violet was saying. "Perhaps he was a mitigating factor."

"In what way?" Ran asked.

"The spirits were used to him." She looked over at Zane. "I'm making assumptions here, Zane. Eve said her family owned the house for generations. Am I correct in assuming George St. Clair lived here all his life?"

"That's right. The house was originally constructed in 1921 by a banker man named Reginald Maitland. He owned all the land around here. Two years after he and his family moved in, Reginald contracted pneumonia and died. His widow sold the house to Arthur St. Clair. After that, it passed down through the eldest son until George St. Clair willed it to Eve."

"Find anything in the family history that might have relevance to whatever is happening in the house? A violent death? Murder? An unexpected illness that resulted in death? Those are the kinds of things we normally encounter that can keep a spirit earthbound."

"There were deaths, of course," Zane said. "Aside from Reginald

Maitlin, who died in the hospital, George's father, James St. Clair, died in his bed upstairs, but he had been ill for some time. I didn't see anything that stood out."

Zane glanced down at the notes he had made on his phone. "One more thing. Just before I headed back to the hotel, I ran across the mention of another house previously constructed in this location. Over the years, it fell into disrepair, and Maitland tore it down to build the one Eve is living in now."

Ran's gaze swung to Eve, and she could read his thoughts. *Another house was here before.* The tempo of her heart picked up as she considered the possibilities.

"When was the first house built?" Ran asked.

Zane shook his head. "I don't know. I need to do a little more digging, take a look at records stored in a different location. As I said, I only stumbled across a mention of it at the end of the day."

"Tomorrow, then," Ran said. His gaze went to Eve. "Perhaps what Zane finds out will explain your friend Wally."

"What? You think Wally is real?"

That intense gaze didn't waver. "What do you think?"

Her heart was still beating a little too fast. "That . . . that isn't possible. I mean . . . Wally seemed real when I was a child, but . . ." Her hand came up to her throat. "Oh, my God."

"The question isn't what's real or what isn't. Not at this point," Ran said. "The question is, what do we do to make sure you're safe in the house?"

Her chin firmed. "I live here. I'll be fine."

"One of us could spend the night," Ran suggested.

"I could stay," Katie offered. "I could sleep downstairs on the sofa, and you wouldn't even know I was here."

Eve shook her head. "Please don't worry. As I said, I'll be fine."

"You could stay at the hotel for a couple of days until this all gets sorted," Ran pressed.

Eve dug in even deeper. "I have several clients scheduled for tomorrow. I'll need to prepare. Besides, I'm not letting any invisible, intangible—something—force me out of my own home."

Ran smiled. "I'm glad to see your spirit returning—if you'll allow me the pun." He turned. "Violet?"

"As Eve said, she's been living here for a while. I think we were the catalyst for what happened tonight."

Eve forced a faint smile. "It's settled, then." She rose from her chair. "I'll be looking for all of you tomorrow night."

Ran stood up, too. "The car should be here by now. Katie and Jesse are finished packing up. If you need anything, I'm not far away." He handed her a business card. "My personal cell number is on there. Don't hesitate to call."

Eve just nodded. In minutes, King and his people were gone.

Though the house was dark and quiet, she didn't feel any of the fierce emotions she had felt before. Perhaps Violet was right, and it was having strangers in the house that had caused such a wild disturbance. They were gone now. She should be fine.

She glanced around. Nothing moved in the shadowy corners of the living room. No sound of voices down the hall. She blocked thoughts of other nights in the house, the reason she had contacted Paranormal Investigations in the first place.

She had to admit it gave her a sense of comfort knowing that Ran and his team would be coming back. Maybe together they could figure out what was happening and find a way to make it end.

Eve prayed it would be so.

Ran phoned Eve the following morning. "It's Ran," he said. "You have any more trouble last night?" It bothered him that he'd left her alone. Someone should have stayed to be sure she was all right. He'd wanted to be that someone, which was the reason he hadn't offered.

His attraction to Eve was a complication he didn't need.

"I told you I'd be fine," she said. "And I was."

"Did you get any sleep?"

"I've been sleeping on the sofa, but after last night, I . . . umm . . . moved back upstairs. It was nice and quiet. Now that Violet explained the energy contained in the clutter downstairs, I think that could be part of my problem."

"Could be." But it wasn't the only part. "Any chance you could make time for lunch? There are some things we need to discuss."

"I . . . don't know. I have a client scheduled for two o'clock."

"We could eat at noon, if that would work."

"Wherever I am, I guess I have to eat."

"Good. I'll send the car for you. It'll be outside at quarter till."

"All right, that sounds good."

Was that interest he heard in her voice? Problematic as it was, he hoped so. "I'll see you at noon."

Ran hung up and relief trickled through him. Eve was all right. Nothing out of the ordinary had happened after he'd left her last night.

He leaned back in the black mesh chair at the desk in his suite. They'd had several cases where their intervention had made the disturbances worse. Suspected poltergeist activity in a house in Connecticut—items moved from place to place, glasses broken, writing on mirrors in the bathrooms—had worsened after the team had gotten involved.

At one point a butcher knife had flown across the kitchen and slammed into a wall. Fortunately, it soon became clear the poltergeist activity was being generated by the single mother's two teenage boys, who were practically at war with each other over a girl in their high school class.

Once the kids realized the danger they were creating—unbeknownst to them—they talked things out, settled their dispute, and the poltergeist activity ended.

Only once had they tackled a truly evil spirit, the ghost of a man who had murdered four women before he'd been shot by police. The woman who had moved into the house where he had lived before his death had suffered an attempted strangulation in the middle of the night and a brutal sexual assault by her invisible attacker.

The force was so powerful even the members of the team were frightened. In the end, Ran had gone to a friend for help, Lucas Devereaux, a former priest.

A full exorcism had resolved the problem. The demon who

had possessed the man was purged and banished to whatever fate awaited him.

Ran thought of the energy it had taken to move the glass flowerpot, thought of the malevolence in the voice they had heard, and vowed that until this case was resolved, Eve wouldn't be spending another night alone in the house.

CHAPTER EIGHT

*R*AN WORKED ON SOME OF THE HOTEL MERGER FILES HE'D BROUGHT with him, a task that took longer than he'd expected. He needed to check in with his executive assistant in Seattle, but the time difference made that impossible until later in the afternoon. When he glanced at his Rolex, he realized it was almost time for lunch.

Changing out of his sweats and T-shirt, he dressed in dark blue jeans and a light blue button-down shirt and headed downstairs. By the time he reached the lobby, the Bentley was pulling up in front.

Ran made his way down the front steps and opened the rear passenger door. Eve took the hand he offered and slid out of the limo. Her narrow skirt rode up and he noticed a terrific pair of legs, trim ankles, and narrow feet.

"You look nice," he said, liking the fit of her apricot linen skirt suit and printed white blouse. Gorgeous ruby highlights glinted in the thick dark hair curling around her shoulders. His fingers itched to find out if it felt as silky as it looked.

"I'm glad you came," he said. "But you didn't need to dress up."

Eve smiled. "Business lunch calls for business attire."

She looked even prettier in the sunlight than she had in the dimly lit interior of her home. Ran offered his arm and she took it, let him lead her up the front steps into the lobby, down a carpeted hallway into the restaurant.

The hostess smiled. "Your table is ready, Mr. King. Mrs. Sutton is already here. If you'll pleasc follow me."

The tension in Eve's shoulders relaxed. He wondered if she thought the luncheon was just an excuse to get her alone.

Irritation trickled through him. He made it a point not to mix his business and personal lives. But his interest in a woman was usually returned. Apparently that wasn't the case with Eve. The thought did not sit well.

They joined Violet at a table in front of the windows. Outside in the distance, the ocean crashed against the rocks along the quay. Though the sun still shined through the clouds in places, ominous thunderheads lurked in the distance, signaling the approach of a storm.

Ran pulled out a chair for Eve, seated her, then sat down in the chair between the two women.

"Ran told me he spoke to you this morning," Violet said. She wore her usual slacks and sweater, her silver hair pulled into a neat twist at the back of her head. "So you slept all right last night? No problems at all?"

"I had a bad dream, but I don't remember it."

"Whatever it was, dreams don't usually come true," Violet said. "Although some people have a gift for using them clairvoyantly."

Eve made no comment. Ran could see she was desperately trying to work all of this out, and he had a feeling her discomfort was only beginning.

A server arrived to take their orders: seafood salad for Eve, clam chowder for Violet, fish and chips for Ran. He spread his linen napkin across his lap and looked over at Eve, his gaze lingering on her delicate jaw and interesting hazel eyes. Beyond her looks, there was a glow about her that he'd seen in few other women.

"Thank you for coming," he said to her.

Eve shrugged. "The timing worked, so it wasn't a problem. Have you seen the video or heard the audio from last night?"

Ran swallowed a crispy bite of fish, enjoying the malt vinegar tang. "I have. That's one of the things I wanted to talk to you about. I looked at the video outtakes with Katie this morning. Jesse sent me the audio clip via Dropbox, and I listened to it before I came downstairs."

"What did they show?"

"The video shows flashes of light in the infrared light, mostly down the hall in the area just past the kitchen. Something was definitely there. I think you'll find it interesting."

"And the audio?"

"You can make out three words. *Make. Them. Leave.* They were muffled but discernable. It sounds a little like whoever is speaking is talking from inside a box or something. Whatever it was also said the word *You!*"

"I want to hear it. I want to see the video," Eve said. There was excitement in her voice, touched by a hint of trepidation. She was going to see actual proof that her experiences were real.

"We'll go up to my suite after lunch and I'll play them for you."

The wariness crept back into her eyes. Damn it, he wasn't some kind of stalker. "Violet can join us if that would make you feel more comfortable."

Eve flushed. "I'm not afraid of you, Ran."

Then perhaps it was something else. Perhaps the attraction was mutual, and she was fighting it just as he was.

"Good, then we'll go up and take a look," he said. "We're here to help you. If we get lucky, maybe we can also help whoever is stuck here move on to the Other Side."

Eve looked up at him. "I never thought of it that way."

Violet reached over and set her hand on top of Eve's where it rested on the table. "That's an important part of what we do. In cases like this, the spirit is often confused. We help them figure things out and show them the way to the light, which will take them to the place they belong after death."

"Heaven? Is that what you mean?"

"We don't really know," Ran said. "The answers to questions like that are what all of us are looking for."

They finished their lunch and Ran escorted Eve upstairs. His suite was light and roomy, the bedroom completely separate from the living room. Eve seemed to relax.

"The clips Katie sent and the audio excerpts are on my laptop. You're welcome to watch the recordings made of the entire evening, but nothing much happens earlier. I can tell you our temperature gauges all went crazy just before the lights started flashing and again when we heard the voices. It's a shame we weren't set up that first night."

"I suppose. But you're coming over again tonight, so you must think it'll happen again."

"Why don't we take a look at what we got and you can tell me what *you* think."

Ran seated Eve in the desk chair in front of his laptop computer screen, then dragged up a chair for himself. He pulled up the video file and hit the start button. About sixty seconds passed before the light show began.

A flash of white at the end of the central hallway started moving toward the front door. The white light grew larger, brighter, shot forward past all the chairs, then retreated.

"That was when the blue pot got broken," Ran said.

"It's hard to tell what's going on. Just a quick flash of light."

"The camera can detect images that can't be seen with the naked eye. That's the reason we use infrared and night vision."

Next there was a shower of small white lights that seemed to be coming from an area below the hallway, rising through the floor, then disappearing.

"That correlates with the footsteps we heard," Ran said.

Now two white lights moved, flashed, one on each side of the hall. "The voices," Ran said. "Two men arguing."

"I spoke to them," Eve said. "I asked them what they wanted. I asked them why they were there."

"Watch what happens next." One of the lights darted past where Eve was standing, soaring upward before it disappeared.

"That's when the chandelier in the entry started swinging."

Eve's gaze remained on the screen. A bright white light flashed, then disappeared.

"That's when the voice said, 'Make! Them! Leave!'"

A few minutes later, the light flashed again; then it was gone. Eve sat back in her chair. "I can't get my head wrapped around it."

One more quick light flashed, and then it was over.

"Wait till you hear the audio. I'll play you the end result, the audio recording combined with the video showing the light flashes. It'll make more sense."

Leaning over, Ran brought up the file and clicked the start button. As he backed away, he caught the scent of Eve's soft perfume and desire slipped through him. Ran swore a silent curse as he sat back down in his chair.

On the EVP—electronic audio recorder, a graph with a line that moved up and down showed the decibel level of the sound it was recording. There was also a light bar that went from green, yellow, orange, to red.

"The instrument is set to a very sensitive level," Ran said. "You can see what happened when Violet started speaking."

The equipment captured the sound of Violet's voice, which showed a rising line on the graph and turned the light bar from green to yellow and then orange with the different tones of her voice.

"You see how it works. Now I'll play the video on the left side of the screen and the audio on the right side."

Eve watched as Violet spoke quietly, trying to make some sort of connection with whatever was in the house. A white flash streaked down the hall toward the front door. At the same instant, the sound of breaking glass, the flowerpot, shot the light bar to red.

Silence followed, then the sound of running feet matched a shower of small white lights that came up from below and disappeared. The sound of two men's voices, arguing loudly, matched the two white lights in the hallway opposite each other.

"What do you want?" Eve's voice asked. "Why are you doing this?"

One of the white flashes shot past her and the chandelier started swinging. Then the light grew in diameter and strength. *Make! Them! Leave!* The light bar glowed red.

Then a last flash of light. *You!*

The word sent a chill down Eve's spine.

Ran's voice came at the end. "That's enough! Hit the lights!"

Ran leaned over and closed the audio/video files. "The rest is just us talking before Jesse turned off the recorder."

Eve said nothing, just sat there staring at the screen.

"You okay?" Ran asked.

She looked up at him with big hazel eyes that had changed from green to a brown so dark they looked nearly black. "It's real, isn't it? The ghosts? Everything that's happened. It's not my imagination or some kind of illusion."

"From what we've seen and heard, it looks like there's some kind of entity there. We like to be absolutely sure that what's happening isn't some kind of physical phenomena that can be rationally explained."

"Such as?"

"Fungal spore activity in old buildings, for instance, can cause hallucinations. Or they can be caused by frequencies too high for the human ear to perceive."

"And, of course, there's the possibility of mental illness," Eve said dryly.

Amusement touched Ran's lips. "Something that you, as a doctor of psychology, would be well aware of."

"Yes."

"In this case, we have physical evidence of paranormal phenomena. Which you have just witnessed. Now we need to find out what it is."

She looked back down at the screen, then back up at him. "What do we do next?"

Before Ran could answer, his phone rang. He pulled it out, saw it was Zane. "Have you got something?"

"I do."

"Are you in the hotel?"

"Just got here."

"Come on up." Ran disconnected, turned to Eve. "Zane's got something for us."

When the knock sounded, Ran walked over and let Zane into the suite. "You found something?"

"I did." Zane was neatly dressed in khaki cargo pants, a pullover, and sneakers. His bomber jacket was draped over one shoulder. "Hi, Eve," he said as he walked into the living room.

"Hi, Zane."

Ran rose from the chair he'd pulled up to the computer. "Why don't we all get settled and you can tell us what you've found."

They seated themselves on the comfortable cream sofa and chairs arranged around the coffee table. "There are soft drinks in the fridge if anyone wants something," Ran said. Eve shook her head, but Zane walked over and grabbed a cola before sitting down in one of the chairs. He popped the top and took a swallow.

"So what have you got for us?" Ran asked.

"Last night I told you Eve's house wasn't the first one built in that location. Today I went to several other sources to collect information—the General Register Office and the Sunderland Historical Commission, which sent me over to look at records stored in the public library."

Ran found himself sitting forward. "And . . . ?"

"A couple of interesting things. To begin with, the original structure in that location was an alehouse called The Pelican. I saw references to it as far back as the late seventeen hundreds."

"I had no idea," Eve said.

"Eventually, The Pelican burned down, and the land was sold to a guy named Edward Warrington. Warrington built a three-story Victorian-style house on the property in 1867."

Zane looked down at his notes. "Descendants of the Warrington family lived there until the early 1900s, but the house was not treated kindly. It fell into disrepair and the last of the Warringtons moved out. The place sat empty for fifteen years, until the land was purchased by Reginald Maitland, who tore down what was left of the place and built the house Eve now lives in."

"I never knew so much had happened there over the years," Eve said.

"I didn't see any reports of mysterious deaths, nothing like that," Zane continued. "Not to say those things couldn't have happened. But one thing stood out. Though The Pelican was destroyed, the original cellar beneath the tavern was still intact when Warrington bought the property. It was made of mortared stone and must have been in very good condition, because Warrington just built his residence on top of it."

Ran leaned back on the sofa. "Interesting. Any chance Reginald Maitland did the same thing?"

Zane took a swallow of his drink. "I saw no mention of it, but in the twenties, there were no building codes, no permits required, so I don't think it would have been a problem. Would have saved money and provided good storage."

Ran's gaze fixed on Eve. "You didn't mention a cellar."

Eve shook her head. "There isn't one." She paused. "If Reginald had used the old cellar, he would have needed some sort of access—"

Ran nodded. "That's right."

Eve started frowning. "Wait. I just remembered something. When I arrived one summer, I noticed Uncle George had removed one of the doors in the hallway. It was a door that was always kept locked."

"Could it have been a door to the cellar?" Ran asked.

"I'm not sure. I was never allowed to go in there. He never told me why, but when I got there that summer, the door had been removed and the wall rebuilt so the two sides of the hallway matched. Even the wallpaper had been changed. It's the burgundy flocked paper you see there now."

Eve's eyes flashed to Ran. "The footsteps," she said.

"They were coming up from the cellar," he finished.

Zane looked intrigued by the prospect, but unconvinced. "The cellar would have been really old by then. Maybe the door was just locked because your uncle thought the stairs were unsafe or something."

"Maybe," Ran said. "Or maybe Uncle George was having some of the same problems Eve has been facing."

CHAPTER NINE

Seated on the sofa in the living room of the suite, Eve read Ran's intentions in his compelling blue eyes. "You can't be thinking I should open up the wall."

"The cellar would become part of our investigation," Ran said mildly. "Paranormal Investigations would take care of any costs incurred."

Eve mentally went over the events of last night, the eerie sounds, the angry voices. The rush of running feet. "You really think the footsteps we heard were coming up from the cellar?"

"We can replay the audio, but it sounded very much like multiple small feet running up or down a set of stairs."

That was exactly the way it sounded. Eve had thought that the first time she'd heard the noise several weeks ago.

She looked at Zane. "You didn't . . . find any connection to children who might have lived in the first house, the Warrington house? Or had a connection to the tavern?"

"Not so far," Zane said. "No one was killed in the fire at The Pelican, at least there was nothing mentioned that I could find. I can go into some of the Warrington family genealogy, check out Maitland, and dig into early St. Clair family history. One thing about the Brits. They keep records that go back hundreds of years."

"First, we need to know if the cellar is still there." Ran turned his attention to Eve, pinning her with those penetrating eyes.

"What do you say? You were probably planning to do a little re-modeling sooner or later. How does new paint and wallpaper sound?" He smiled. "Say yes and we'll pay to paint and paper the whole downstairs."

She had told him she couldn't afford to make another move and start over again. She intended to stay, which Ran must have remembered. He was a billionaire. He could afford it. Still . . .

"You don't have to do that," she said. "It's too much. Besides, I'm the one who contacted you."

"Researching paranormal activity is why we're here. You would be doing us a favor." He sat up straighter, making him look even taller and broader. "What do you say?"

His offer was a more than fair offer, and in truth, she wanted to see what was behind the once-forbidden door. "Fine. You can open up the wall. If the old cellar is really down there, maybe we'll get some answers."

Ran nodded. "Great. I'll call Connie. She's the team coordinator. I'll have her line up a contractor to repair the damages after we're finished. In the meantime, Jesse and I can handle the demolition."

Eve could almost feel her eyebrows climbing. "You're going to . . . what? Personally take a sledgehammer to my wall?"

A wide smile broke over his face. "You don't think I've ever done any physical labor? I put myself through college working on a construction crew."

My God, that smile. Unlike any she had seen from him before, it made him even more handsome. Her attraction climbed a notch.

She shrugged. "I just thought . . ."

"I know what you thought."

Her defenses went up. "Actually, from what I read, you went to Stanford on a full scholarship. Started a year early out of high school and graduated in three years instead of four."

One of his black eyebrows arched. "You've done your homework."

Eve made no reply. She refused to apologize for being careful.

"The scholarship paid my tuition, but there were living expenses, and car payments to make, and I valued my independence. I took the minimum. I didn't want to be indebted."

The information didn't surprise her. Everything about Ransom King spoke of self-sufficiency and determination.

"Working in construction . . . is that how you became a real-estate developer?"

"I learned a lot working with the father of my roommate, Remy Moreau. Eventually, Jacques Moreau, Remy's dad, and I became partners. Remy and I are still best friends."

Flashing another smile, he rose from his chair. "If we want to finish the job before it gets dark, we'd better get going. Plus, I promised I'd deliver you back to your office before your appointment. I'll have the car brought round to take you home. Jesse and I'll pick up whatever tools we need."

"There's a Wilko hardware store not far from here."

"Great. You handle your client; Jesse and I will tackle the wall— that is, if the noise won't be a problem."

"As I said, my office is behind the house off the garage. It has a private entrance. You won't bother me."

"All right, then. Let's go."

The hour Eve spent with her client, Donny Beck, seemed to drag. Faintly, she could hear the hammering and pounding going on inside the house. Curiosity at what the men would find made it hard to concentrate.

Donny shifted nervously on the blue padded chaise on the other side of her desk. "The days just seem so long, you know? It's either dull and boring or things are just too stressful to handle."

At twenty-five years old, blond and fair, Donny suffered from both depression and anxiety. He lived with his mother a few blocks away. Judith Beck had brought her son to Eve for help. Eve believed his estranged parents were the biggest part of his problem.

"Everything's always up in the air," Donny said. "It's hard to stay positive, ya know? Like you're always telling me I should do." With an inheritance from his grandfather, Donny had never had to work. He was spoiled and selfish. Which he freely admitted. It only made his problems worse.

Eve tried not to look at the clock. The session had ten minutes to go. She dragged her gaze back to her patient's narrow face. It wasn't fair to Donny not to give him her full attention.

"I met this girl named Amber," Donny was saying. "She's a former addict, but she's been sober for nearly five years. I really like her."

A recovering addict was probably not the best choice for Donny. "Take your time, Donny. Get to know her a little. Don't rush into anything. Did you talk to the man at Iceland Foods who offered you a job?"

Donny surged to his feet. "I don't need a fooking job!" He strode up to her desk. "Time's over," he said darkly. "I'll see you next week." Donny stormed out of the office and slammed the door so hard the glass panes rattled.

Eve sighed. It was typical Donny behavior. She wished they were making more progress.

The hammering continued, drawing her back to the activity inside the house. Her other appointment had called to reschedule later in the week, for which Eve was grateful. She tidied up her office and locked the door behind her, made her way up the back stairs into the mudroom.

As she crossed the old-fashioned kitchen and stepped through the door leading into the hallway, she spotted the gaping hole in the wall. Ran and Jesse, both in jeans and low-topped leather boots, were tearing away big pieces of drywall.

Jesse's T-shirt, wet with sweat, clung to his muscular body. But it was Ran's physique that captured her attention.

She knew he stayed in shape. She'd had no idea his wide-shouldered, narrow-hipped build would be as hard muscled as Jesse's. Damp white cotton outlined solid pecks, six-pack abs, and biceps that bulged whenever he moved.

Billionaires were *not* supposed to look like that!

Ran tossed aside a jagged piece of drywall. "You're just in time. The cellar's definitely down there. We just found the entrance.

An old wooden staircase is on the other side of what was once a door."

Eve forced herself to ignore both men and made her way through the debris to the opening they had found in the original wall.

"Be careful not to step on a nail," Jesse warned.

Eve reached the opening and stared down at the black hole below. "It's too dark to see. I need to go upstairs and change so I can get down there."

"We're almost done with the demolition," Ran said. "We just need to clean up this mess; then we'll be ready to take a look. We each brought a change of clothes. Any chance we could borrow your shower?"

"Second floor, end of the hall. There are plenty of clean towels in there."

"Thanks." Jesse flashed his trademark grin.

Eve took a last glance at Ran, felt a slide of heat that made her abdomen tighten, quickly turned and headed upstairs.

By the time she had changed into a pair of stretch jeans and a pale-blue knit sweater, the trash was gone from the hall, presumably dumped in the outside bin, and Ran was gone, probably upstairs in the shower. She didn't let her mind wander in that direction.

Jesse was in the kitchen wearing clean jeans and a navy T-shirt that read:

GHOST HUNTER
IF YOU SEE ME RUNNING
TRY TO KEEP UP

Eve pointed at the shirt and couldn't stop a laugh. "That's the way I felt last night."

Jesse grinned. "It's definitely an interesting job."

A few minutes later, Ran appeared in black jeans and a black T-shirt. She had never seen him really dressed down until today. It revealed a totally different side of him. Not Ransom King the billionaire, but Ran King, the man. Even more appealing and even more dangerous, because he was way out of her league.

He was carrying a pair of wet towels. "I'll put these in the laundry room."

"Thanks." She had definitely pegged this man wrong.

"You ready to take a look?" he asked when he returned.

Eve nodded. "More than ready. I've been wondering what was behind that door since I was four years old."

Ran took one of the flashlights he had brought and shined the light into the dark room below, but it barely illuminated the interior.

"I'll go first," he said. "I need to rope up before I try the stairs. No way to know if they'll hold my weight." He looked over at Eve, must have noticed the worry that pinched the skin between her dark eyebrows.

The room had been sealed for years. The question was why?

"It's only a precaution," Ran explained. Tying the rope around his waist, he handed the other end to Jesse, who anchored the rope around the newel post at the bottom of the stairs in the hall, then ran it below his hips. He braced his legs apart, giving him the leverage he needed to hold Ran's considerable weight.

There was a landing at the top of the old wooden staircase, but most of the railing was gone. Flashlight in hand, Ran tested the first wooden step. "Feels solid enough." The beam of the flashlight reflected off gray stone walls. Eve caught a glimpse of the stone floor that seemed a mile below, and fresh worry slipped through her.

Ran went down a couple more steps, tested the railing, tested a few more stairs. Halfway down, the railing ended, wood creaked loudly beneath his feet, and he froze. Eve's pulse increased.

"I got you, boss," Jesse said.

Ran took another step. The wood groaned beneath his weight but held. He had almost reached the bottom when the wood stair snapped beneath his foot, sending him smashing down to the next step, which split in half, and he dropped the last couple of feet. It would have made a jarring landing if Jesse hadn't kept the rope taut, stopping his descent. Carefully, Jesse lowered him the last several feet to the rough stone floor.

"You okay?" Jesse asked.

"I'm good." Ran slipped the rope from around his waist. "I was afraid this would happen. We're going to need another way to get down here." He panned the flashlight, giving Eve a look at the room around him.

The cellar wasn't empty. It wasn't as cluttered as the living room, but there were piles of old newspapers, a stack of empty paint cans, a wooden ladder with broken rungs, and two steamer trunks.

"I need to get down there," Eve said. "I want to know what's in those trunks."

"Ran figured the stairs might not hold, so we got plenty of rope," Jesse said. "We can knot it and you can hand-over-hand down to the basement." He looked her over, taking in her slender figure. "Or maybe not."

"I can do it." Eve smiled. "I was a Girl Scout when I was a kid back in Boston."

Jesse grinned. "All right, then."

Ran prowled while Jesse created a chain of knots in the thick rope. As he had before, he secured one end across the hall around the newel post.

"Are you sure it'll hold?" Eve asked.

Jesse put all his weight on it, had to be close to two hundred pounds. The newel post held fast.

"It's good and solid. It'll hold." He grinned. "Besides, you only weigh about half as much as I do."

A little more than that, she thought, but a smart woman never divulged her secrets, so she kept her mouth shut.

"You go ahead," Jesse said. "Ran'll be there to catch you if you fall."

"I'm not going to fall." She looked down at Ran, thought of those big hands wrapped around her waist, and her breathing went shallow. She walked over to the landing, sat down with her legs dangling over the side, reached down and grabbed the rope.

"Wrap the line around one leg as you descend," Ran coached

her. She remembered how to do it, was glad she was wearing snug-fitting stretch jeans instead of looser clothes that might get in the way.

The rope steadied her and gave her the confidence to keep going down. She'd played tennis back in Boston, hoped to continue here, knew the muscles in her arms and legs were strong. She was a few feet from the bottom when she felt Ran's hands settle at her waist.

"You can let go. I've got you."

She let go of the rope but instead of setting her on the ground, he swung her up in his arms. The hard chest she had admired earlier pressed against the side of her breasts and desire hit her so hard she felt dizzy.

"You can . . . you can put me down now."

His eyes met hers. "Right. Of course. Sorry." He set her on her feet and turned away, fixed his gaze on the wall in front of him. He seemed so intent, Eve couldn't help wondering if he had felt the same rush of heat she had felt. If he had, what was he thinking?

CHAPTER TEN

"W<small>E NEED AN EASIER WAY TO GET OUR PEOPLE AND EQUIPMENT</small> down here." Ran walked over and looked up to where Jesse stood next to the rough opening in the hall.

"Phone the manager over at the Wilko store," Ran called up. "Name's Fred Rosen. Tell him we're going to need that ladder he showed me. Tell him we'll pay double if he can deliver it this afternoon."

Ran turned back to Eve. "I told him we might need more supplies. He's got my credit card on file. I don't think it'll be a problem."

"You're very efficient," Eve said.

Ran grunted. "Sometimes it's a curse."

"Really? No matter what I'm doing, I never seem to have enough time. You make everything look easy."

"Maybe. But sometimes I wish I didn't have to think so much. I wish I could just go with whatever impulse hits me at the time. You know, be more spontaneous." At the moment, he'd like to forget he was in charge, forget Eve was a client, and act on the impulse to carry her upstairs to her feminine pink bedroom and spend the night in her bed.

"If you'd been less efficient, you probably wouldn't have accomplished all the things you have."

"Probably not." He turned, looked up as Jesse ended his call to the hardware store, and walked closer to the opening they had made.

"Ladder's on its way. I had them send a couple more flash-lights. I'll toss you this one."

Ran moved to catch it, grabbed the light as it arched down from above. Turning, he spotted Eve across the room, kneeling beside one of the steamer trunks, a big, square, beautifully con-structed oak box with heavy brass bands and ornate hinges.

"It's locked," she said.

"What about the other one?" A camelback trunk with molded metal inserts that probably dated to the mid-1800s.

She headed over. "Same thing."

"Don't worry, we'll get them open. They're nice pieces. We don't want to do anything to destroy their beauty or their value. Let's see what else is down here."

Shining the light in front of him, he walked the perimeter of the room, aiming the light along the walls. Dark green moss grew between the stones, which were various shades of gray.

He took a quick look through the stack of old newspapers. They dated from the twenties. Mostly they dealt with WWI, but he didn't see anything that pertained to the house.

Farther back and off to one side, the light illuminated what looked like haphazard layers of wooden boards nailed one on top of another.

"What the hell . . . ?" He moved closer. The wood was old, but the nails were round, not square, so probably the work was done after 1900.

Eve hurried to join him, her gaze going over their unexpected find. "Maybe the wall was crumbling and they tried to repair it."

"I don't know. Maybe."

"What else could it be?"

He moved closer, shined the light on the boards, trying to look between them, see what was on the other side. Making no progress, he walked back to the opening and looked up at Jesse. "Toss me that claw hammer we were using earlier."

"You got it." The hammer arched down and Ran caught it by the handle.

He walked back over to the wall and used the claw end to start pulling off the outer boards.

"You want some help down there?" Jesse called to him.

"I've got it covered. Keep an eye out for the hardware truck. We need that ladder."

"Will do."

As Ran pried off a few more pieces of wood, Eve flashed him an uncertain glance. "If that wall is in disrepair, pulling off those boards might bring the whole place down on top of us."

"I don't think that's the problem." He had a hunch it was more than just crumbling stone that was hidden behind the boards. "I'll be careful," he said, just to make her feel better.

He swung the hammer, sank the claw end into another board, heard the squeak of an old nail as it reluctantly let go, and yanked it away. He pulled off a few more pieces of wood, getting down to the first layer, then grabbed one of the flashlights and shined it through a hole between the boards.

"That's what I thought," he said.

Eve moved up beside him, her soft perfume replacing the moldy smell in the basement. He forced himself to concentrate.

"What is it?" Eve asked.

"A tunnel."

"A tunnel?" Eve bent to peer into the darkness between the boards, following the light Ran shined, illuminating the blackness a few yards into the cavern. "Wow. I didn't expect to see something like that down here."

"It's been boarded up, but it's definitely not a natural phenomenon." He shined the light around the edges of the opening. "It looks like the tunnel was originally sealed off with bricks. When they began to crumble, someone did a haphazard closure with wood."

"No wonder Uncle George didn't want me coming down here."

Ran picked up the claw hammer and pulled away more boards, exposing a hole in the old crumbling brick wall. He tossed the boards into a pile next to the tunnel opening and stepped back so Eve could see.

She looked up at him with excited eyes as green as the moss between the stones. "I wonder where it leads?"

"We need to find out. We've got to identify the ghost or ghosts we're dealing with. To do that we have to figure out who those voices belong to. Simply put, we need more information."

"Like who dug the tunnel in the first place and what it was used for."

Ran nodded. "I'll text Zane, see if he can dig up some info on the tunnel. If we do our jobs—and if we get lucky—somewhere in the past, the names of the spirits who were here last night are going to turn up. It's almost impossible to clear the energy causing the disturbance until we know who we're dealing with and why they're still here."

He wasn't sure if it was doubt or interest that crept across Eve's face. Ran turned back to his work, prying off another couple of boards, allowing him to shine the light farther into the tunnel. The interior was taller than he was, about six and a half feet high and almost as wide, a man-made cavern shored up on the ceiling and sides with wooden timbers.

"Are we going in?" Eve asked.

He shook his head. "It was boarded up for a reason. I'll have a structural engineer take a look. If we get a green light, we'll go in and find out where it leads."

He checked his wristwatch, not the Rolex but the waterproof Omega Seamaster he wore when he went sailing. "Katie and Violet are due in an hour. They'll be bringing our equipment. We need to get that ladder and get it set up."

Eve glanced over at the old wooden chests. "You think you can get one of those open?" She gave him a look. "I mean, without tearing it to pieces."

He thought of the destruction he had wrought in the hall and the boards stacked up in the basement. Ran chuckled and held up the hammer. "Your chests are safe, I promise."

But opening them wasn't as easy as he'd thought. Using a clothes hanger that Jesse tossed down, he was eventually able to pick the lock on the big square oak trunk, which appeared to be the older of the two.

Eve knelt in front of it, her face glowing with excitement. This was her family home. She had to be wondering what secrets the chests might be keeping.

Ran heard Jesse's footsteps overhead, walking down the hall to the front door, then the door swinging open. "Sounds like the ladder is here. I'll be right back." He climbed the rope hand over hand, pulled himself up on the landing, and went to help Jesse.

He thought of Eve and wondered what different sort of ghosts she might find hidden in the trunk.

From the style of the clothing inside, which dated to the Victorian era, the old oak trunk must have belonged to the Warringtons, the owners of the house at that time. The big chest was only half full. Several prim, once-white, now aged-to-yellow nightgowns, each with a high-neck, ruffled front, and long sleeves that buttoned at the wrists, sat folded on the top of the pile.

There was a wide-brimmed straw hat with faded artificial flowers that had seen far better days. The flowers disintegrated as Eve lifted out the hat, and a trace of sadness slipped through her. What had happened to the woman who had worn the hat so long ago?

She picked up an ivory lace fan and spread it open, couldn't resist fanning herself. Off to one side at the bottom of the trunk, a pair of brown leather high-button shoes with scuffed toes and worn heels sat next to a pair of ice-blue satin slippers that would have been worn for evening.

Pieces of a lavender parasol that had fallen apart rested in the bottom of the trunk. Sentimental value? she wondered, since it had clearly been useless before it had been stored away.

She felt an excited thrill at the blue silk ball gown with its silver-trimmed bodice, voluminous skirt, and silver organdy overskirt. Lifting the dress out and holding it up, she saw that the woman who had worn it was only a few inches shorter than she was.

Eve thought of the small running feet she had heard in the hall and hoped there was no connection between them and the woman who owned the clothing in the trunk.

She felt Ran's presence before she saw him, appearing next to where she knelt beside the trunk. She glanced up, amazed a man his size could move so quietly, a talent she had noticed before.

"Find anything interesting?"

"Just a few old clothes and miscellaneous feminine items that must have belonged to one of the Warrington women." She picked up the ivory fan and spread it open. She touched it reverently and felt the quick flash of tears. "I wonder what special memories this held for her?"

Ran leaned down and skimmed a finger along her cheek, picking up a drop of wetness she hadn't realized was there.

"I think I understand why the spirits are reaching out to you. You have a very sympathetic nature, Eve. They must believe you can feel their pain."

Eve brushed aside the notion and rose from the cold stone floor, not realizing she would be standing just inches from Ran's broad chest. She looked up at him, realized if she went up on her toes, she could press her mouth against his. Because it was exactly what she wanted to do, Eve forced herself to move away.

She managed to smile. "No ladder yet?"

"They're unloading it as we speak." His gaze held hers for a long, silent moment before he turned and walked toward a commotion near the rough opening in the hallway above.

Jesse directed two Wilko employees carrying a sturdy aluminum ladder; then the three of them started sliding the ladder into the basement. Ran reached up and caught the object, helping to ease its descent. Once the adjustable metal frame was locked in place, getting down to the lower level would be manageable.

Eve caught the sound of more voices, recognized them as belonging to Zane, Katie, and Violet.

"You got that pulley system rigged?" Ran called up to Jesse.

"We're loading the bucket right now." Jesse and Zane set the cameras and audio gear, bubble-wrapped for protection, into a big, empty bucket and lowered it down to the space below. Ran emptied the bucket and sent it back up.

The second load carried what Eve had learned was a thermal imaging reader—a cold-spot detector; an EMF meter—which measured fluctuations in electromagnetic fields, and Lord only knew what else.

Jesse and Zane carried a stack of newly purchased metal folding chairs down the ladder and set them up, providing places to sit. Katie carried down the last chair. It was cold in the basement, the stone floor and walls keeping the temperature in the low fifties. A damp draft blew in through the hole that led into the tunnel.

"I hope you all dressed warmly," Ran said.

"I relayed the info about finding the tunnel," Jesse said. "I told everyone it was going to be as cold as a witch's—" He broke off at Ran's look of warning.

"I told them it was going to be damned cold down there."

Ran nodded.

"I need to run up and get a wrap," Eve said, grasping the chance to be away from whatever emotions she was feeling in the cellar, as well as from Ran King's imposing presence.

The ladder felt sturdy beneath her feet as she neared the top. Hearing a noise in the living room, Eve detoured down the hall in that direction and spotted Violet on the settee, a paperback novel open in her lap. The older woman took off the half-glasses perched on her nose and smiled as Eve walked into the room.

"How are you holding up?" Violet asked. She was dressed in slacks and a brown turtleneck, her feet encased in a pair of flat-heeled boots.

"This has certainly been an education," Eve said. "As well as the history of the house, I'm learning about my family and the other people who once lived here."

"So no matter what happens, none of this will be a waste of your time."

Eve frowned. "You don't think we're going to find the ghosts?"

"I didn't say that. But it's been my experience that what we're doing often shines a light on other things as well, things that could end up being even more important."

She thought of Ransom King and the attraction she hadn't expected to feel. Surely that wasn't what Violet meant.

"I'm going up to change," Eve said. "I won't be long."

But she took her time returning. Ran and his team would be busy setting up their equipment. Zane would be checking security outside, and Violet seemed to be enjoying her book.

Unable to put off her return any longer, Eve made her way

back downstairs. In a dark green Boston Celtics sweatshirt, carrying a fleece jacket, she carefully descended the ladder, not really surprised to see Ran standing at the bottom in case she slipped and fell. He had a protective streak, she'd discovered, one more thing about him that appealed to her.

"Zane's got some news," Ran said, leading Eve over to one of the gray metal folding chairs, urging her to take a seat. He returned for Violet, helping her down the last few rungs of the ladder, guiding her to the chair in front, then taking a seat next to Eve.

"Zane?" Ran encouraged.

There were enough lights in position to illuminate the cellar. Zane stood next to the hole in the wall.

"To begin with, turns out this isn't the only tunnel in this area. At one time, there was a whole maze of them down here. Most have collapsed or been filled in. Others just fell out of use and people forgot they were there."

"When were they built?" Ran asked.

"No idea how long ago the first ones were constructed, but they were still in use in the late eighteenth century."

"Back when the tavern was here."

"That's right," Zane said.

"What were the tunnels used for?" Eve asked.

"Smuggling. Mostly tea, silk, French wine, and brandy. The occasional shipment of Belgian lace. Smugglers brought the goods ashore in the middle of the night, moving the supplies in from the coast through caves or ravines in the cliffs along the beach that connected with the tunnels. Before this turned into an industrial area, the shoreline was a lot different than it is today."

"Nobody ever got caught?" Katie asked.

"The whole town closed its eyes to what was going on, which was a way of avoiding the customs house tax—as high as thirty percent."

"I can understand the temptation," drawled Ran, the businessman.

"Where'd the goods end up?" Jesse asked.

"They were passed through holes in the floors of the houses

the tunnels went under, or in this case, into the cellar below the tavern. I'm guessing back in its day, The Pelican would have been a prime destination for smuggled merchandise."

Ran glanced up as if he could see through the floors to the old tavern that had once sat in this location.

"That's all I've got on the tunnels so far," Zane said. "I'm still working on Warrington and St. Clair family genealogy."

"Anything of interest so far?" Ran asked.

"Edward Warrington had two wives. In 1875 he married a young woman named Priscilla Stanton. She died in her late twenties, no offspring. His second wife, Mary Salter, was older, early thirties when he married her. The union produced two boys and a girl."

"Either of the kids die at an early age?"

Eve realized Ran was thinking of Wally, who would have had to die as a very young boy.

"None of Mary's children died young, not from what I read. The house passed down through the eldest son." Zane smiled. "I never used to like history, but I have to admit, this stuff's got me hooked."

Eve caught the hint of amusement that touched Ran's lips. "Glad to hear it," he said.

CHAPTER ELEVEN

*I*T WAS BLACK AS PITCH AND DEAD QUIET IN THE CELLAR, DANK AND smelling of mold now that the tunnel had been opened. Zane was outside, keeping an eye on the neighborhood around the house.

As before, Jesse and Katie had set up their equipment to capture any movement or activity. Several cameras, mounted on tripods, were aimed in different directions, and Katie moved periodically between them. Infrared light turned the stone walls a hellish shade of red.

Violet sat in a metal folding chair facing the tunnel, with Ran and Eve a few feet behind her.

The longer the silence stretched out and the quieter it became, the more the sounds of nighttime activity increased in the tunnel. The drip, drip, drip of water somewhere deep underground. The scurry of rodents making their way through the debris in search of food, tiny clawed feet scratching along the walls.

Ran sat close enough to feel the faint shudder that went through Eve's body. He reached over and caught her hand, gave it a reassuring squeeze.

"You don't have to stay," he said softly.

"I'm okay. It's just . . . I hate rats."

"They aren't my favorite, either." But in situations like this, the small furry creatures were the least of his worries. It was the dark energy that lurked in the shadows that sent chills down Ran's spine.

It was after midnight when the lights on the EMF meter began to dance, indicating fluctuations in the electromagnetic field. The hair stood up on the back of Ran's neck as icy cold swept into the room. Jesse flicked him a glance as the thermometer reading dropped out of sight. Beneath his wool sweater, goose bumps rose on Ran's skin.

Sensing an unknown presence, Violet sat back in her metal folding chair. "We're glad you came," she said softly. "We're all friends here. We've come to help you."

Something shimmered in the dense infrared light.

"We can help you if you'll let us."

The shimmering light intensified, began to take the vague shape of a person. Ignoring Violet, the figure floated toward Eve, then hovered a few feet in front of her.

Ran's pulse accelerated. He wanted to reach for Eve, let her know he was there if she needed him, but interfering was exactly the wrong thing to do.

"Who are you?" Eve asked, the strength in her voice surprising him.

The figure shimmered and floated, the image fading, then strengthening.

"I'm Eve," she said. "My family has lived in this house for a very long time."

Through the opaque, fog-like image tinged red by the light, Ran could make out the stone walls of the cellar.

"What's your name?" Eve asked.

The spirit made a reply, but the sound was indistinct, something that sounded vaguely like Hay or Kay, or perhaps it was May. Ran wondered if the spirit could be that of a woman.

"Do you live here?" Eve asked.

No answer.

"Is there something you want to tell us? Is that why you're here?"

The figure hovered and floated but made no reply.

"Why are you here?" Eve asked more directly. "Is there something you want us to know?"

Ac-ci-dent.

The word was garbled but clear enough to make out.

"Something bad happened," Eve guessed. "But it was an accident. Is that how you died?"

The ghostly form snapped into a brilliant ball of white light, then violently streaked across the room—a hostile and definite no.

Ran saw the tremor that passed through Eve's body and one of his hands unconsciously fisted. Though Eve was frightened, her voice remained calm.

"Not you, then. Someone else. Someone else died in an accident."

The light returned to hover in front of her and didn't move away.

"Who got hurt?" Eve asked. Her face revealed little emotion, but the hands in her lap gripped tighter. "A child?"

Ran thought of the small, thundering footsteps they had heard and figured his thoughts mirrored Eve's.

Another bright white light appeared, this one pulsing. It began to dart around the room at a furious speed, the energy building, making the presence of a second spirit clear.

The second light swelled to twice the size of the first, clearly indicating some sort of dominance. The more powerful light moved into Eve's space and Ran started to rise, his fear for Eve overriding his thirst for knowledge. The slight pressure of Eve's hand on his thigh had him sinking back down in his chair.

The light grew in ferocity. *Get . . . out!* A man's voice, the words indistinct but vibrating with anger.

Eve began to tremble. "Someone else has joined us. Who are you?"

Instead of a reply, one of the boards Ran had pried off the entrance to the tunnel lifted into the air and shot across the room, missing Eve's head by inches. A cry escaped as the board crashed against the stone wall, rusty nails gleaming like blood in the eerie infrared light.

"That's enough!" Ran surged to his feet. The infrared light went off and Jesse flicked on one of the heavy, long-handled flashlights, while Ran turned on one of the lights on the floor. "Everybody out. Be careful going up the ladder."

Jesse took Violet's arm, while Ran set a hand at Eve's waist, urging her toward the metal stairs leading out of the cellar.

"What about the equipment?" Katie asked as Jesse made sure Violet got safely up the rungs to the landing, then waited for Eve to climb to the top.

"Leave it for now," Ran said. "We'll be back. We're not done here yet." He waited until everyone was safely out of the cellar, then climbed the ladder to join them, feeling drained and at the same time wildly exhilarated.

Each ghostly investigation they had dealt with as a team had been distinctly different, each a story all its own. Though there had been certain similarities, nothing close to this had ever happened. Ran fiercely wanted to know more.

He glanced down into the cellar, dark now with the lights off again, and eerily silent. They had made contact, all of it recorded, though nothing had gone as they'd planned. Ran looked up and spotted Zane standing next to the opening in the hall, his brown eyes wide and uncertain. Ran noticed the brass chandelier in the entry had been turned on.

"So I'm guessing you caught at least part of what happened down there," Ran said to the investigator, his hand firm at Eve's waist, keeping her close beside him.

"Yeah," Zane said. "I don't know exactly what to make of it."

Ran felt a trickle of amusement. "No matter how long you do this, that doesn't change." He turned to the others. "Why don't you wait for Eve and me in the dining room? We'll join you in a few minutes. Jesse, call for the car. I think all of us are ready to pack it in for the night."

He urged Eve out the front door and closed it behind him. Though the sky was overcast, the temperature chilly, it was warmer on the porch than it had been in the frigid cellar.

"You were amazing in there tonight," Ran said. "I've never seen anything like it. You handled that as if you'd communicated with spirits a dozen times."

"To tell you the truth, I was scared to death. But I could feel at least one of them reaching out to me. I had to let them know I was there if they wanted my help."

"You made it look easy, and that isn't the way it works. Most people wouldn't have been able to handle it."

"My job helped. I'm used to being in tense situations with a patient. I've learned to control my emotions, not show what I'm actually feeling."

Ran nodded. "For whatever reason, the energy in the house seems drawn to you."

"I just want them to leave. I'm a psychologist, not a sensitive, or a psychic, or whatever it is you call them. I'm not like Violet."

Ran's gaze held hers. "At this point, I'd say that remains to be seen. For someone totally new to the experience, you seem to have a unique connection."

She glanced up at the sky as if she searched for answers among the stars mostly hidden by the layer of gloom. "I thought Violet was going to be the one to talk to them."

"That was the idea. Unfortunately, the spirits seem to have picked someone else. Namely, you."

Eve made a little sound in her throat. "What if I just go somewhere else and let Violet take over?"

Unable to hold back any longer, Ran reached out and ran a finger down her cheek. "We can try that. But from past experience, I think you're the one they've chosen. Violet hasn't been able to develop a rapport, and I don't think that's going to change."

Eve's eyes found his in the sliver of moonlight that appeared through a break in the clouds. "Maybe I should call the whole thing off."

The muscles in Ran's jaw tightened. "I wish it were that simple. If I'd had any idea this would happen . . ." He scrubbed a hand over his face, suddenly feeling the heavy weight of responsibility across his shoulders. "Even if you moved out of the house, at this point there's a chance the spirits would follow you."

"What?"

"They can attach themselves to a person the same way they attach themselves to a house, a church, a cemetery, or whatever it might be. I never would have let you get involved if I'd known you had that kind of talent."

Eve stiffened. "You think being able to communicate with dead people is a talent? Like a carnival act or a comedian? That's what you think?"

Ran could feel the anger welling inside him, the acid taste of guilt washing into his mouth. "You want to know what I think? I think it's not just a talent—it's a gift. One that comes with grave responsibilities. You have no idea how much I wish I could reach out the way you can. How much I ache to know my wife and child are safely on the Other Side. I'd give anything to be able to talk to them one last time. Anything, to know they're happy wherever they are." Ran turned away, shocked at the depth of emotion he had allowed Eve to see, fighting for his usual iron control.

He felt the light touch of Eve's fingers gently settling on his shoulder, turning him to face her. "I'm sorry. If I could, I'd reach out to them for you. Maybe you're right and it is a gift. I don't know. None of it makes any sense to me."

Ran took a deep, steadying breath and slowly released it. "In a way, this is new for me, too. Nothing like this has ever happened before. No one we've ever worked with got caught up in the situation the way you have. Unfortunately, now that you're involved, we have to deal with it. *You* have to deal with it. You don't have any other choice."

A slash opened up in the clouds. A spill of moonlight turned Eve's face a ghostly shade of pale before the darkness closed in again.

Ran eased her into his arms, and Eve's palms flattened on his chest. "Whatever happens, all of us will be here for you. We aren't leaving you to face this alone."

"You're not . . . you're not including yourself, are you? You must have countless obligations. You can't possibly mean to stay here until this is over."

"That is exactly what I mean to do."

Eve stared up at him. Ran told himself to let her go and step away. Instead, he drew her closer, bent his head and lightly brushed his lips over hers. When she didn't resist, he took more, found the taste of her both sweet and sensual, just as he had imagined. The soft scent of flowers enveloped him, making his desire for her swell.

He thought she would pull away, do the sensible thing and let him know he was out of line. Instead, she leaned into him and her arms slid around his neck, encouraging him to take the kiss deeper. The slender curves of her body softened against him and her nipples hardened, flooding him with hungry need.

Surprised by the intensity of his arousal, Ran let the moment spin out longer than he should have, then forced himself to ease away. Eve's eyes were big and round, still glazed with desire—and the same hint of surprise he was feeling.

"That probably shouldn't have happened," he said. "But I'm not sorry it did."

Eve's gaze remained on his face, and he wished he could read her thoughts, which, he had discovered, she was more than adept at hiding.

He ran a finger over her damp bottom lip. "Before we go back inside, there's one more thing."

"Tell me it's not about the ghosts."

Amusement slipped through him. "Not exactly."

"What then?"

"I don't want you staying alone in the house. You saw what happened down there. If that board had been a few inches over, you could have been hurt or even killed. I'll book you a room at the hotel. You can stay there until this is over." He didn't tell her he had no idea how long that might take. He didn't want to upset her more than she was already.

Eve started shaking her head. "This is my home. I have a patient appointment tomorrow. I'll . . . I'll be all right."

He didn't want to argue, but he wasn't backing down. "You're sure that's what you want?"

She managed a nod, but it wasn't very convincing.

"Okay, you can stay. But if you do, I'm staying with you. That's not up for debate. I can sleep on the sofa. If things get spooky or you just can't sleep, you can come downstairs, and we'll share a cup of tea or maybe a brandy." His mind filled with a dozen different ways he could make her fall asleep. "Whatever it takes."

Color washed into Eve's cheeks and she glanced away. After their heated kiss, there was no doubt what he was thinking.

Eve smoothed her features. "I couldn't possibly ask that of you."

He had considered having Katie stay, but the happenings in Eve's house were way above her pay grade. And the truth was, he didn't trust anyone but himself to keep Eve safe. Or at least be there to get her out of danger.

"As I said, we're in this together. Tomorrow, the engineer is coming over to inspect the tunnel. Maybe finding out where it leads will shed some light on what's going on."

CHAPTER TWELVE

*E*VE SPENT A MISERABLE NIGHT IN HER EMPTY BED WHILE RAN SLEPT in one of the guest rooms down the hall. She had stubbornly refused to let him sleep in the living room on the settee, which was a good foot too short for him.

Instead, she'd helped him settle in upstairs, causing her to think about him half the night, to remember his kiss and imagine what might have happened if the kiss had resumed once the rest of his team had returned to their hotel.

After her divorce, Eve had rarely thought of her unfaithful husband, Phillip. Understandable since their marriage had been more about companionship and career opportunities than love. Phillip Markham, a renowned psychiatrist, had simply appeared in her life one night at a conference in New York. They had enjoyed a drink together at the bar, dated briefly, then married.

Two years later, he had met someone else and continued his upward climb, leaving Eve with little more than a shadowy recollection of the time they had spent together.

Reclaiming her maiden name had severed their ties altogether. Phillip was a distant memory, while Ran King had swept into her life with the force of the storm that continued to build outside. One kiss and she was sure he would be imprinted on her mind for the rest of her days.

She shouldn't have allowed it, no matter how much she wanted to, no matter how his muscled chest pressing into her breasts made her ache for more. She didn't dare open herself to a man like King.

Ran's ambitions, which had made him mega rich, came with a heavy load of responsibilities. Like Phillip, he would be there one moment, gone the next, only this time she wouldn't be able to dismiss her feelings so easily.

More and more, Eve's fascination for this man she barely knew continued to build. Even now, a single sweeping glance from those amazing blue eyes could make her body yearn for the kind of physical satisfaction she had imagined but never actually experienced.

Beyond that, the grief in his voice when he spoke of his wife and child touched a place deep inside her. He hadn't meant to let her in, she knew. Nor had he meant to kiss her. When Ran had finally pulled away, Eve had the distinct impression he was as shaken as she.

Exhausted, she finally fell asleep a little before dawn, then awakened to discover she had slept far later than usual. She hurriedly showered and changed into dark brown slacks and a summerweight, peach knit sweater, suitable attire for her eleven o'clock appointment with her patient Bethany Parsons.

The sound of banging hammers pulled her down the stairs, where a crew of men in sawdust-covered jeans and sweat-stained T-shirts worked in the hallway. Ran looked more presentable, striding toward her in crisp blue jeans and a sky-blue short-sleeve button-down.

Eve forbade her mind to remember the feel of those thick biceps beneath her fingers last night, or the softly coaxing demands of a kiss that had aroused her as nothing ever had.

"What's going on?" she asked as he strode toward her, careful to keep her thoughts from showing on her face.

"We're putting the wall back up—at least temporarily. There'll be a door for access to the basement and a reliable staircase. All of it can stay or go once this is over. That'll be up to you."

"A door isn't going to keep the ghosts confined."

"No, but it'll keep out some of the cold blowing in through the tunnel."

"True." She studied the group of men, some of them hammering furiously, others carting lumber back and forth down the hall. A saw buzzed somewhere in the basement. She wondered what ridiculous amount Ran was paying them to work so feverishly.

"They'll be done by late afternoon," he said.

Eve wasn't surprised. "So we'll be picking up where we left off last night?"

"That's right." He pulled her out of the path of a lanky, thin-faced man wearing overalls and a baseball cap, a hammer in his hand.

"How did you sleep?" Ran asked. "I didn't hear anything unusual. I was hoping you didn't, either."

Eve didn't tell him it wasn't ghosts that had kept her awake; it was reliving his kiss. "Everything was quiet. Or at least it seemed so."

He nodded. "Good."

Her gaze held his. "What about you?" she couldn't resist asking. "I hope you slept well."

His lips twitched. "I had something far more pleasant to think about than spirits."

Her face heated. She was usually a master of hiding her emotions. Somehow this man seemed able to see past her defenses.

"I have a patient at eleven," Eve said. "I need to be ready when she arrives."

Ran checked his heavy black wristwatch. "Then you better get going."

Weaving her way around the workmen, Eve headed down the hall to the kitchen, out through the mudroom, to her office next to the garage. Fifteen minutes later, her eleven o'clock appointment arrived right on time.

Bethany Parsons was the opposite of cocky, arrogant Donny Beck. At fourteen, she was painfully shy, with very pale-blue eyes and a halo of curly red hair around her face, making her look a little like Orphan Annie.

Bethany had suffered an abusive childhood, run away from

home at thirteen, and spent two weeks on the streets before a kindly woman had spotted her huddled beneath a hedgerow in front of her terrace house and brought her in out of the rain.

Mrs. Halston, a widow, had gone to the police, who had arrested Jilly Parsons for child abuse when it was discovered she had been selling the girl to a string of "boyfriends" who frequented her house.

With Bethany's birth mother dead and her father nowhere to be found, eventually Mrs. Halston had managed to get custody, but there was still a long road ahead for the girl to make a full recovery.

At the timid knock on her door, Eve walked over and pulled it open. She smiled. "Good morning, Bethany. Come on in."

The teen stood there shyly, a worried look on her face. "You aren't moving, are you? I saw a lot of men going in and out of your house."

"I'm not leaving." Eve thought of the brawny workers in the hall. After her ordeal, Bethany wasn't comfortable with men. "I'm just having some repair work done. The house has been here a very long time, you know."

Bethany's thin shoulders relaxed. "I know. Mrs. Halston says it was here when she was a girl. Before that there was a big old Victorian house, but it got torn down."

"That's right." Eve led Bethany over to the pale-blue leather chaise on the other side of the desk, and Bethany sat down.

"Mrs. Halston told me her nana was glad when the St. Clair family bought the property. She said the old house was really scary, all boarded up the way it was."

Eve thought of the spirits still lingering in the house and fought the shiver working its way up her spine. "I'll bet it was." She sat down behind her desk. "So how are you doing? Any more bad dreams?"

Bethany lowered her eyes to stare at the hands she clasped in her lap. "Not as bad as before."

"Want to tell me about them?"

She looked up. "Do I have to?"

"You don't have to. But talking about things makes people feel better. That's why you're here."

Bethany swallowed. "I know, but it's hard."

"I know it is."

Bethany smoothed the front of the baggy jeans she was wearing with a loose-fitting top. She didn't like to draw attention to herself. Eve understood why.

"I had another dream about the man with the floppy brown hat," Bethany said. "He made me do things to his friends, just like before. I don't remember what the men looked like. I always kept my eyes closed."

Eve wished she could hold the girl's hand, but she had to remain professional. Attachments at this stage weren't necessarily good.

"Maybe one of these days you'll be ready to open your eyes and look those bad men straight in the face."

Bethany shook her head. "I would rather forget them. I don't ever want to see their faces again."

"Whether you decide to face them or forget them, in time, if we keeping working together, the choice will be yours."

Bethany's shoulders relaxed. "I hope so."

Eve thought of the spirits trapped in the house. Maybe as Ran had said, helping them was the right thing to do. In some ways, it wasn't much different from helping one of her patients, someone like Bethany.

A trickle of fear arose at the memory of the heavy chunk of wood that had shot across the room and barely missed hitting her in the head. Ran was right. What they were doing was dangerous. She had no idea what these entities were capable of.

Still, she had chosen her path when she had sent the email asking for help. Now she had no choice but to proceed. Her resolve strengthened. Maybe with all of them working together, they could find the answers that would send these otherworldly beings on their way.

For the first time, Eve felt ready to face the night ahead.

CHAPTER THIRTEEN

RAN STOOD NEXT TO ROBERT HAWTHORNE, A STOCKY, BARREL-chested man who looked more like one of the guys in the construction crew than an engineer.

He was wearing a miner's hard hat over his salt-and-pepper hair, a clipboard tucked under one arm. "We've done a great deal of preliminary work. As much as we could at this juncture. As I said, our current theory is that smugglers added on to the tunnel several times. There's also quite a strong possibility it branches off in several different directions down there."

Though a copy of the drawing Hawthorne had found in local historical archives wasn't available, apparently the map showed the earliest portion of the tunnel dating back to 1750, a section leading inland from what had once been a cave in the cliffs.

"At this point," Hawthorne continued, "physically traversing the interior is the only way to ascertain more."

"If you think it's safe—"

"That is not what I said. Indeed, what I'm trying to say is, the only way to know exactly how much of the tunnel still exists or where it leads is to go in and take a look. The thirty-yard section I examined was in passable condition. My guess is parts of it were still in use even after the Warringtons bricked up the entrance. I dare say, if other sections are indeed still intact and have been maintained at least to some degree, you might be all right to risk going in."

"There's always some element of danger in exploration."

"True enough. If you feel it's worthwhile, you can always shore up the passage as you go along. It would take a good bit of work, of course. I would be happy to help you develop a plan."

Ran made no reply. He needed more information, and he wasn't willing to wait weeks or months to get it.

Robert checked his watch in the overhead fluorescent lights the workers had installed in the basement. "At this point, I have nothing further to add. I'll have my report sent to the email address on your business card, along with a bill for my services."

Ran nodded. "I'll forward it to my accountant. Thanks for making yourself available on such short notice."

Since he was receiving double his usual fee, Hawthorne just smiled. He extended a hand Ran shook. "No need to trouble yourself further. I can see myself out."

A rough wooden staircase, complete with handrails, had already been completed. Hawthorne climbed to the top and disappeared into the hallway. Ran looked up to see Eve coming down the wooden stairs. She had changed into jeans and a long-sleeve pink T-shirt.

She looked good, like cotton candy or raspberry sherbet—good enough to eat. He forced himself not to remember the kiss on the front porch last night and blocked the direction his thoughts were leading.

"I gather that was the engineer," Eve said, dragging Ran's mind back where it belonged.

"Robert Hawthorne. Hawthorne and Longworth Engineering has a solid reputation in the area."

"So what did Mr. Hawthorne tell you?"

"Robert gave the tunnel a fairly good report card, considering. He went in about thirty yards and took a look around. He thinks portions of it were still in use even after the Warringtons bricked up the entrance to the basement."

"I wonder what they were using it for?"

"Good question. Who was using it? And what were they using it for?"

* * *

Eve stood by as Ran's cell phone signaled a text.

"Jesse," he told Eve, reading the message on his screen. "He's on his way back with some of the items I sent him to get."

"What kind of items?"

"Miner's hard hats, shovels, spare flashlight batteries. The area around Sunderland is known for mining, so the hats shouldn't be hard to find."

Excitement poured through her, along with a good dose of nervousness. "When are we going in?"

Ran's gaze shot to hers. "Jesse and I are going in. It could be dangerous. I'd rather go by myself, but it's a dumb move, and Jesse wants to be included."

"Well, I want to be included, too. Just because I'm a woman—"

"It's not that. At least not exactly."

"I don't care why you don't want me to go. I'm going with you. This is my house, therefore my tunnel. I started this. I'm going to finish it."

A muscle jerked in Ran's cheek. She figured it was rare that someone went against him. He took a deep breath, clearly fighting to hang on to his temper.

"Have you thought about what we're going to find in there? You said you hate rats. I guarantee there are going to be dozens, probably hundreds of them in there."

Eve shuddered, but she had already figured that out. "I'll deal with it."

"Fine. The house is yours. The tunnel begins on your property. I'll admit that gives you the right to go in, if that's what you want. You can go in—just not with me."

"Wait a minute."

"If I take you, I'm the person responsible if something goes wrong. I'm not willing to take that chance."

Irritation trickled through her. "You may think you're responsible, but you're not. If something happens, the consequences are the result of my decision. It has nothing to do with you."

The lines of his handsome face tightened. It occurred to her that the single most traumatic event in his life had been the death of his wife and child. He blamed himself for the car accident that had killed them. Suddenly Eve understood.

She reached up and rested her palm against his cheek. "I know you're trying to do what's best." She smiled into his dark, brooding features. "How about a compromise?"

His black eyebrows drew down. "A compromise," he said darkly.

"That's right. I know it's not a word you commonly use, but—"

"What sort of compromise?"

"I'll go in with you as far as it looks safe. With luck we'll see enough to know if the tunnel has anything to do with the spirits in the house. If you really think we shouldn't continue, we'll come back. Deal?" She held out her hand, and his features finally softened.

Ran took her hand in his but didn't let go. Instead, he slowly drew her toward him, until her breasts rested softly against his chest. Lowering his head, he settled his mouth over hers.

Heat poured through her, slid out through her limbs. The gentle kiss lingered, expanded, deepened into something hot and urgent. Eve moaned when he pulled away.

"Deal," he said softly, his amazing blue eyes on her face.

Eve just nodded. That was the second time she had kissed him when she knew she shouldn't. "You have to stop doing that."

A black eyebrow arched. "What? Stop kissing you?"

"Yes . . ."

"Why? We're both unmarried adults. I like kissing you, and we both know if you'd wanted to, you could have stopped me with a single word."

"Maybe. Or maybe not. I don't have the kind of experience it takes to handle a man like you."

A corner of his mouth kicked up. "A man like me? You think I'm a player? I'm not gaming you, Eve. I rarely date, if you want the truth. When I socialize, it usually involves something to do with my business dealings."

She frowned. "You're a man. You must have needs."

"And you don't?"

Eve made no reply. Until she'd met Ransom King, she hadn't given sex much thought. It was just part of being married, more a way of feeling close to her husband than experiencing any real pleasure.

"I have a few women friends," Ran continued.

"Friends with benefits," Eve guessed.

"That's right. We get together on occasion, but it's nothing serious for either one of us."

"Is that what you want me to be? Another of your friends with benefits?"

"I don't need any more friends."

Eve mulled that over, unsure exactly what he meant. "Why me?" she asked.

"I can't really explain it. You're different. I'm attracted to you. The fact is, I want you. I'm the kind of man who goes after what he wants, so if you aren't interested, now is the time to say so."

Eve swallowed. "I don't . . . I'm not . . . I don't think . . ."

"Maybe if I kiss you again it'll help you figure it out."

Desire curled through her, along with a rush of fear. She had told him the truth. She had no idea how to handle a man like King.

Eve stepped back so they were no longer touching. "We . . . umm . . . have work to do. I want to see what's in the tunnel—we both do. But the afternoon is slipping away, and I certainly don't want to go in after dark."

His mouth edged up. "It's already dark in the tunnel."

"It's not the same."

Before he could reply, Jesse appeared at the top of the stairs. "Got everything we need, boss, and a few little extras." Jesse hauled several big plastic bags down the newly constructed stairs to the cellar.

"Katie wanted to go with us," Jesse said. "She's pouting. I told her you wanted her to work on the camera footage from last night, but she said she was already done. Violet is taking her over to Sunderland Castle. It's a local tourist attraction."

"And Zane?"

"He's keeping an eye on the surrounding area. Zane's worried there might be outside entrances to the tunnel we don't know about."

"Good thought." Ran's gaze swung to Eve, then back to Jesse. "Eve's going with us—at least as far as it's safe."

"I figured," Jesse said. "I brought her a hard hat."

Ran crossed his arms over his chest. "Well, hell."

Eve couldn't stop a laugh. "Thanks, Jesse."

"Yeah, thanks a lot," Ran said sarcastically. He walked over and began to sort out the gear, which included disposable plastic rain slickers with snaps on the front to keep out any water dripping from the ceiling. There was a size small miner's hat with a lamp on the front among those Jesse had brought, along with a compass, folding shovel, and various miscellaneous items.

"I got us something I think you're gonna like." Jesse held up a device about five inches long and a couple of inches wide that looked like a camera. "Night vision range finder. Works up to a hundred fifty yards in the dark."

Ran smiled his approval. "It'll need a target object in order to calculate the distance, but if it works, it'll beat the hell out of a measuring tape."

They were planning to map the tunnel. The more they knew about it, the safer they would be.

Ran turned to Eve. "You need some better shoes. Have you got any hiking boots, something sturdier than sneakers?"

Eve nodded. "I'll go put them on."

"All right, then. We'll go in as soon as you get back." His eyes widened when she walked over and kissed him on the cheek.

"Thanks for the compromise."

Instead of a smile, hunger flashed in those brilliant blue eyes. Eve's stomach contracted. Ran had warned her. She knew what he wanted. The question was what did *she* want? And how much was she willing to risk in order to find out?

CHAPTER FOURTEEN

RAN TURNED ON THE HEADLAMP MOUNTED AT THE FRONT OF HIS hard hat. Jessie and Eve did the same. They were all dressed warmly and wearing their thin plastic rainslickers to protect against water seeping down from overhead. Ran carried a heavy, long-handled flashlight—which could double as a weapon—and a coil of half-inch rope looped over one shoulder. Eve carried a smaller flashlight, and Jesse wore a backpack with the folding shovel strapped across it.

"Last chance to bail," Ran said to Eve.

"I'm going."

No surprises there. He was coming to admire her more and more. "We ready?" Ran asked.

"Ready," Jesse said.

"Ready," Eve agreed.

"I'll lead. Eve, stay close behind me." Ran's headlamp shined into the darkness as he started into the tunnel. He had no idea how far it went, but he was determined to find out.

He had a feeling the answers to at least some of their questions lay in the looming blackness ahead of them.

"Take a reading with the range finder," Ran said to Jesse. "We'll use it as a baseline starting point."

Jessie turned on the device, including the night vision feature, and sighted through the eyepiece. "Nothing dead ahead. If I use the wall as the target, it reads a hundred and twenty yards."

"That's close to the maximum range. So we know the tunnel goes at least that far, but it could be blocked at that spot or change course in some way. Let's go."

They took it slowly, moving a few steps at a time, searching the illuminated circle in front of them, shining their lights on the walls and ceiling as they went along. He'd been right about the rats. They raced around in small furry clusters, fleeing the path of the light, their skinny, hairless tails twitching from side to side behind them. Their tiny feet made scratching noises in the dirt.

Ran turned toward Eve. "You doing okay? It's not too late to turn back."

"They're rodents, not monsters. I'm fine."

His admiration grew. The women he knew wouldn't be caught dead in a rat-infested tunnel. Well, except for Katie. She was definitely the adventurous type.

They had gone only about twenty yards when the tunnel began to narrow, shrinking in width from six feet to four, the height dropping down a few inches, just enough that his six-foot two-inch frame could no longer stand completely upright. Hawthorne had warned him.

"Everybody okay?" Ran asked.

A quiet murmur of assurance was his reply.

Ran bent his head a little and continued. He'd gone spelunking in Missouri with Remy when they were in college. Tight places weren't his favorite, but they didn't freak him out the way they did a lot of people.

So far the tunnel had continued in a straight line. Ran shined the big flashlight in front of him, then above and along the walls. Timbers were spaced at ten-foot intervals, and the ceiling was shored up with five-inch boards.

He kept going, heard Eve's soft footfalls behind him, wished he could have left her at the house. He came to an opening in the wall off to his right. "Looks like it splits right here."

Eve and Jesse both moved forward to join him. Jesse used the range finder to chart the distance they had come, then flipped open his notepad and logged the information.

"Stay here. I'm going to take a look."

"Don't go too far," Eve said, and Ran could hear the concern in her voice.

"Sounds like you're worried about me," he teased, hoping it was true.

In the light, he watched her chin tilt up. "I just don't want to have to go look for you."

He smiled. "I'll make sure that doesn't happen."

The trip down the narrow spur didn't take him long. Thirty feet in, the roof of the secondary tunnel had crumbled and collapsed years ago, blocking it completely.

"Dead end," he said when he returned.

They moved forward. As they made their way deeper into the tunnel, water dripped between the boards overhead, splashing down on their plastic slickers. Shining his flashlight ahead of him, Ran had just started forward when he heard Eve's muffled scream.

His body jerked to a stop. Ran hurried the few steps back to her. "Are you all right? What is it?"

"I'm all right. It just . . . it took me by surprise." She shined her light on the floor of the tunnel. "It's a person. Or at least it used to be."

Now it was just a lump of paper-white bones.

Ran shined the light along the floor until he located the skull. From the length of the thigh bones and the size of the skull, it appeared to have been a good-sized man.

Jesse's light joined his. "Holy shit. You think that's our ghost?"

"No." Eve's voice, without a hint of hesitation. She shook her head. "This man is gone." In the harsh light from their helmet lamps, her features looked ashen and grim. She gazed up at Ran. "I don't know how I know that, I just do. There's nothing left of him here, nothing but his bones."

Ran didn't doubt her. Eve might not want to acknowledge the talent, or gift, she had been given, but that didn't mean it didn't exist.

He crouched to examine what had once been a man. There

was no flesh on the bones. The rats would have feasted on the meat long ago. There were remnants of clothing, a piece of faded plaid flannel, what looked like denim material, most of it in tatters, the rest carted off to make nests for the rodents.

Ran turned back to the skull and bones and found himself frowning. In the bright LED light, the bones didn't appear as brittle and weathered as he imagined old bones would look.

"How long ago do you think he died?" Jesse asked, voicing the same thoughts.

"I don't know, but we need to find out. We'll call the authorities as soon as we get back. In the meantime, let's find a spot and take a break."

"I've got some water in by pack if anyone's thirsty," Jesse said.

"Let's keep going," Eve said firmly.

Ran caught the hint of urgency in her voice. "All right. Jesse, you okay?"

"I think Eve's right. Let's get to the end of this thing and get the hell out of here."

Ran started forward, moving a little faster than before. A shaft of light appeared ahead, a circular opening that led to the surface. He could stand to his full height in the middle of the opening, and though the sky was overcast, he could smell the pungent sea air.

"At least we'll have an escape route if we need one," Jesse said.

Ran shined his light up the shaft. It was reinforced with wood and there was a channel near the surface that diverted water away from the hole. "Good point and probably why it was put here."

They moved a little farther forward, the sound of their footsteps mingling with the *drip, drip, drip* leaking down from above.

"There's another split in the tunnel," Ran said.

"We need to go to the right," Eve said.

"The main tunnel heads left. Most likely connects with the cave Hawthorne mentioned that leads to the sea."

"We need to go right," Eve repeated, already turned in that direction as if she knew what lay ahead.

Ran didn't hesitate. "Right it is," he said, allowing Eve to follow the pull of her senses. The tunnel narrowed again and the ceiling dropped down a few more inches. Ran shined the light over the walls on both sides, noting it was in about the same condition as the portion of the tunnel they had traversed so far.

Bending, he led them through the darkness, a wave of furry rodents fanning out ahead of him. The circle of light picked up a giant cobweb that formed an eerie, translucent barrier. Eve made a sound in her throat when a big spider raced toward the center of the web, daring them to cross its path.

Ran used the long-handled flashlight to tear the web apart, and the spider scurried into a crack in the wall.

Eve had moved up behind him and he could feel her trembling. He turned, slid an arm around her waist, and drew her close. "I gather you don't like spiders any more than you like rats."

"Or snakes," Eve added.

Jesse groaned. "Don't even tell me."

"The adder is the only poisonous snake in this country," Ran said. "They aren't all that common."

"I'd still rather not run into one," Jesse said. "Especially not down here."

Ran shined his light ahead. "There's something farther down the tunnel. Put the range finder on it."

"Eighteen yards to a barrier of some sort. Looks like it might be the end of the line."

"Let's hope so," Ran said. Reluctantly, he let go of Eve and started forward. The tunnel flared, growing to the size it had been before. Ran straightened to his full height and took a deep breath. The air smelled damp and moldy, but at least he could stand up again.

It turned out the barrier wasn't a barrier; it was a carefully constructed stone wall, the far side of a cellar much like the one under Eve's house, only bigger.

"We made it." Jesse sighed as they stepped out of the tunnel into the stone-walled room. Water dripped off their rain slickers. Jesse peeled off his slicker and unslung his backpack.

Ran dropped the coil of rope he'd been carrying on his shoulder, pulled off his slicker, and looked up at the timbered ceiling. Near the top along both sides of the room, thin slivers of gray afternoon light seeped through a row of boarded-up, horizontal windows.

"What is this place?" Jesse asked.

When Eve made no comment, Ran turned to look at her. She was staring straight ahead, her breathing slow and deep, as if she were in some kind of trance.

Ran fought the urge to reach out to her, bring her back from wherever she had gone.

"Wally . . . ?" Eve asked softly.

Ran felt a chill.

"Wally, is that you?"

As a small wavering figure appeared, Jesse's eyes widened.

"It's Evie," she said in a voice that sounded like a little girl. "I didn't know you were still here."

Jesse reached into his backpack and pulled out a handheld EVP recorder. As he raised it, hoping to record Eve's voice, his foot connected with a rusty old bucket, the sharp ring eating through the silence.

"Wait!" Eve said. "Don't go!"

But the mood was broken, and Eve's body sagged. Ran caught her as her knees buckled. Jesse popped the snaps on her rain slicker and peeled it off, and Ran turned her into his arms.

"It's all right, honey. I've got you. Everything's okay."

Her arms went around his waist and she rested her cheek on his chest. He could feel her trembling. She fit neatly under his chin, and a surge of protectiveness washed over him. It was unlike anything he had felt since his wife and daughter had died.

He frowned at the unsettling thought.

"Sorry," Jesse said. "I just . . . when I saw him, I kind of lost it. I thought he might say something and I wanted some proof. I can't believe I actually saw a ghost."

As a member of the team, Jesse had encountered a lot of unusual occurrences, but only Violet and Katie had ever seen a fully manifested ghost.

"Tell me what you saw."

"It was a kid. Little boy, maybe four or five years old. He was wearing this miniature sailor suit and one of those flat round hats with a fluffy ball on the top."

"It's called a tam," Ran said, though he hadn't seen the spirit himself. He thought of the years he had spent searching for some sign of his wife and child, but the comfort that finding them would have brought continued to elude him. Perhaps helping Wally would make up for some of that disappointment.

"The kid looked exactly the way Eve described him," Jesse said.

Eve stirred against him and lifted her head. Her eyes were no longer glazed, and her breathing had returned to normal.

"You all right?" Ran asked.

"I'm . . . I'm okay."

He let her go but stayed close by in case she needed him again. It was a feeling he had missed, he realized. On the other hand, being needed by someone, then losing them could bring a world of pain.

"Where are we?" Jesse asked, scanning the stone walls and timbered ceiling. The remnants of a decaying wooden staircase offered no escape.

"I don't know," Ran said, "but unless we want to brave the tunnel again, we need to find a way out."

CHAPTER FIFTEEN

"*I*'M NOT LIKING THIS PLACE," JESSE GRUMBLED.

Eve took a deep breath. She studied the interior of the cellar, which was mostly empty except for a decaying wooden wheelbarrow, a workbench, and some old wooden carpentry tools. Everything was covered with a layer of dust.

She turned, noticed the stone walls were in better condition than the ones in the cellar beneath her house, the grout between the cracks not crumbling or falling out.

The Pelican's cellar was built in the late 1700s. She didn't think this one was quite that old.

Beside her, Ran looked up at the boarded-over windows and pulled out his phone. "We've got cell service down here. I'm calling Zane. He shouldn't be far away. With luck he can track my phone and figure out where we are."

"Good idea," Jesse said, clearly eager to escape the dungeon-like atmosphere. In less than ten minutes, a tall figure became visible through the cracks in the boards over the horizontal windows.

Ran's cell phone rang. He flicked a glance at Eve and put the phone on speaker so she and Jesse could hear.

"That you outside the windows?" Ran asked.

"It's me," Zane said. "Glad you're all okay. It took me a while to find you. This place is big and it's old. I tried the doors, but they're all securely locked. Windows are boarded up. Looks like going out through the ones in the cellar is your best bet."

"All right." But the horizontal windows would provide barely enough room for them to squeeze through. "I've got plenty of rope. Get those boards off and we'll break the glass if we need to."

Pulling the workbench under the windows, Ran climbed up and tried to open one of them, finally gave up, and Zane kicked out the glass. Ran passed Zane one end of the rope, and he secured it to a tree next to the building. Once they had a secure line, Ran climbed out, hand over hand; Eve followed, using her Girl Scout technique; then Jesse pulled himself up and out.

Bad weather had been threatening for days and the storm had finally arrived. A stiff wind swept papers along the empty streets, and the clouds overhead were heavy and damp. Once they were breathing fresh air again, they walked through the grass, around to the front of the building.

Eve gazed up at the bleak, intimidating, two-story structure, once red brick, now gray with age. Built in the Italian mode, it featured a three-story bell tower above the entry. Arched paned windows with peeling white trim stretched the length of the first floor, while water-damaged second-story windows were covered with so much grime they were no longer transparent.

Half a dozen chimneys poked through a roof missing many of its slate shingles, while bushes and hedges grew out of control, hiding some of the boarded-up windows. The place was ghastly and grim, in total disrepair.

Over the entry in the tower, a weather-beaten plaque read:

House of Mercy
Orphan Asylum
1861

Asylum. A chill settled deep in Eve's soul. She thought of Wally. Had the little boy been one of the children in the orphanage? As a child she hadn't paid much attention, but she remembered his little sailor suit had always been spotlessly clean.

She felt Ran's presence beside her and turned to look up at him. "We have to go in," she said.

He just nodded. "I know. We'll find out who owns the place and get permission."

"We could break in," Jesse helpfully suggested.

"We've already trespassed on the property and broken out a window," Ran reminded him. "Breaking in again is trouble we don't need." He glanced from Jesse to Zane. "In the meantime, let's head home. We've had enough excitement for today."

Ran had called for the car as soon as they had escaped the basement. They could have circled back to the house, but a heavy mist was falling and the clouds could open up at any time.

Which happened just minutes after they were safely back inside Eve's house. Thunder cracked, rain pelted the roof, and wind battered the paned-glass windows.

While everyone warmed up and got something to drink, Ran phoned the local police to report the human remains they had found in the tunnel. Eve caught only snatches of conversation, but Ran turned to her as soon as he hung up the phone.

"Someone from the coroner's office will be coming to examine the body. With the storm, the police are short-handed. They'll call in the morning to set up a time."

Eve sighed. "Now that I know he's in there, morning seems a long way off."

"I know what you mean," Jesse said.

"The car's waiting," Ran said to him. "You and Zane head back to the hotel. I don't want Eve here alone, so I'll be staying in the guest room." He glanced at Eve as if she might argue, but after the things she had seen today, that wasn't going to happen.

"Check on Violet and Katie when you get back," Ran continued. "Make sure everyone gets something to eat. The rest of the night you're on your own."

"What's on for tomorrow, boss?"

"Nothing, until the coroner deals with the remains and we get the permission we need to go into the asylum."

Eve suppressed a shiver. She prayed the interior would be in better condition than the outside or what they had seen of the basement.

But she didn't hold much hope.

After Zane and Jesse both left for the hotel, Ran ordered pizza from the English version of Domino's while Eve went up to shower. Ran had showered down the hall, grateful to be rid of the odor of a day spent in a dank cavern alive with rodents.

By the time the pizza arrived, both of them were comfortably dressed, Eve in soft gray yoga pants and a pink sweatshirt, Ran in worn jeans and a long-sleeve navy Henley. They were sitting in the living room in front of a smokeless coal fire when the doorbell rang. Ran answered the door, paid the courier, and carried the pizza into the kitchen.

"Pizza is one of the few things I missed when I left Boston," Eve said, getting down plates and napkins, which she set on the square oak kitchen table. "But the Domino's here is great, so I don't have to miss it anymore."

They sat down and helped themselves to slices. "Delicious," Ran said, savoring the spicy pepperoni taste, but as he watched Eve tilt her head back to catch a long golden string of cheese, he thought that it was the woman seated across from him who whetted his appetite.

He swallowed another bite, followed it with a drink of beer from the bottle Eve had brought him. He wouldn't drink much. Not tonight. Not in a house with so many dark secrets.

"You know, there is something we could do tomorrow," Ran said, steering his mind back to the moment and not where it wanted to go. "We can get a locksmith over here and open the other trunk downstairs."

Eve made no comment, just reached for her beer and took a swallow.

"What is it? I thought you were eager to get in and take a look."

"I was. I mean, I am. I just . . . I don't know. I have this feeling there could be something really bad in there."

"You won't know until you look."

She sighed. "After seeing Wally again, I'm not sure I'm ready."

Ran mulled that over. They needed as much information as they could get, but giving Eve a little more time wasn't a bad idea, and there were other things that had to be done.

"I'll tell you what. We'll deal with the coroner while Zane tracks down the owner of the asylum and any other information he can find. That may take a while. If we still have time, we'll take a ride somewhere, get a little fresh air."

She looked up at him with eyes that shifted from brown to an interested shade of green. "It'll probably still be stormy."

He shrugged. "What's a little rain? We'll see how the day plays out. Maybe we can make it happen."

Eve smiled and he could see the notion pleased her. "All right."

"No patients tomorrow?" he asked as he finished the last of his meal.

"At the moment, I only have three of them. I just moved here a couple of months ago, and I spent most of my time trying to put this place in order. I'm hoping to build my practice, but I'm in no hurry." She smiled. "So unless there's an emergency, I don't have an appointment with Donny or Bethany till the end of the week. Mrs. Michaels, another of my patients, is visiting her son. She's going to call me to make an appointment when she gets back."

"Good. Then we'll make something work." But tomorrow they would have to deal with the bones of a dead man. Then, with any luck, they would get permission to visit the derelict asylum.

Ran was certain the House of Mercy Orphan Asylum was connected in some way to the spirits in Eve's house. Before they could help the spirits move on, they needed to understand how the pieces of the puzzle fit together.

He glanced over at Eve, who was boxing up the leftover pizza and putting it in the fridge. As she bent over, her soft gray stretch pants left little to the imagination.

His groin tightened. He was a man, after all, and this was a woman he wanted. Still, he had to tread carefully. He wanted Eve's trust as much as he wanted her body. He wanted to be certain she would be okay when they parted.

An unwelcome tightness settled in his chest. He didn't want to think of giving Eve up when they had barely begun to know each other.

"You must be tired," he said. "Maybe you'd better go up and get some sleep."

Her eyes met his across the distance between them. "I suppose I should."

Or I could kiss you the way I've been wanting to since you came back downstairs, he thought with a surge of desire far stronger than he had expected.

But he didn't say the words and the moment was lost as Eve moved past him out of the kitchen into the hall. Ran followed, noticing her pause as she glanced at the newly finished door that closed off the basement.

"We're making progress," he assured her. "Eventually, this will all be over, and the house will be yours again."

"Does what you do always work?"

"Not always. But we have to start with that belief. Sometimes we ask other people for help. I'm hoping that won't happen here."

Eve looked as if she wanted to ask more. Instead, she turned and headed up the stairs. Ran followed. When Eve paused at the door to her bedroom, every male instinct he possessed urged him to lift her into his arms and carry her over to her big pink bed.

"Is there anything you need?" she asked.

You, he wanted to say. But the time wasn't right. Not after a day like today.

"I'm fine. I'll see you in the morning."

Eve hesitated a moment more and he hoped she wouldn't test his restraint too long. "Good night, Ran."

He managed to smile. "Good night, Eve." At the sound of her door closing softly behind her, he padded farther down the hall to the guest room. Arousal burned through every pore. It was going to be a long time until morning.

CHAPTER SIXTEEN

*E*VE TOSSED AND TURNED, UNABLE TO FALL ASLEEP, MOSTLY LYING awake and staring at the ceiling. Her mind was spinning with thoughts, scrambling over details, rethinking what she had seen in the basement of the asylum, trying to make sense of it all.

Thoughts arose of Ransom King and her mixed emotions where he was concerned. Along with a bit of regret that she hadn't invited him to spend the night in her bed.

Ran had made his desire for her clear. Ransom King was a man who made no effort to hide his intentions, not when there was something he wanted.

Eve didn't fall asleep until well after midnight. When she slept she dreamed. A vision slipped in of little Wally, of the two of them as children. She remembered him well now, remembered the sound of his childish laughter. How he loved to visit her when she was playing on the grass in the garden.

She could almost hear him saying her name, calling her Evie, as he always did. His giggling laugher awakened her. Eve cracked open her eyes and surveyed the room, quickly realizing she wasn't dreaming at all.

Or perhaps she was.

Wally stood at the foot of the bed in his little blue sailor suit. *Come and play with me, Evie. Let's go out and play.*

Her mouth went dry. She sat up a little straighter, propping her back against the headboard, certain the image would vanish and she would truly awaken. Instead, Wally floated several inches above the floor, a wide smile on his round, freckled face.

"Wally . . ." She could barely force out the word.

The little boy motioned for her to follow him. Eve couldn't move.

Come on, Evie. . . .

The fierce beating of her heart pounded in her ears. She wanted to believe she was still sleeping, that this was just her imagination. But the red numbers on the digital clock read 2:10 a.m., and she could hear the storm blowing outside the window.

The chair in front of the vanity moved several inches, scraping across the floor, and a second figure appeared in the room. Eve's head spun.

Wally floated toward the chair. *This is my friend, Herbert.*

He was taller than Wally, maybe a year older, starvation thin, with shaggy dark hair and sunken features. His brown twill knickers and coarse linen shirt hung like sacks on his skinny, undernourished frame.

Herbie lives in the orphanage.

Oh, dear God. Eve's heart broke for the little boy and the life he must have led. She forced herself to smile and wondered if a ghost could see it. "It . . . it's nice to meet you, Herbie."

She realized she was gripping the front of her high-necked white cotton nightgown and managed to loosen her fingers. She wished Ran were here. Ran would know if any of this were real or if her mind was slipping.

A movement at the door caught her attention. Not Ran. Something she couldn't quite see. A man's voice she recognized boomed into the room, his attention fixed on the boys.

Get back where you belong! It was one of the men she had heard arguing. *Go! Now!*

Wally and Herbie both disappeared. One moment they were there; the next they had vanished. Eve sat frozen.

The voice became the sphere of light that had confronted her that night in the hall. The light hovered, swelled, shot from one side of the room to the other, shot back again.

Eve trembled. She remembered the board with the nail in the end. She wasn't sure who had sent that warning, but she didn't want to chance an incident like that again.

She eased out of bed and began inching her way toward the door. Her hairbrush went flying off the vanity and crashed into the wall a few feet in front of her.

Eve squared her shoulders, determined not to show her fear. "What do you want?"

They! Are! Mine!

The voice was loud and violent and sent a sweep of nausea into Eve's stomach. The bedroom door crashed open and Ran stood in the hallway, barefoot, bare-chested, wearing only his jeans, the long-handled flashlight in his hand.

The sphere of brilliant light raced around the room, increasing its speed until the light was just a brilliant circling blur; then it streaked past Ran and shot out into the hallway. Ran stepped into the bedroom and the door slammed violently closed behind him, jarring the perfume bottles on the dresser.

"Ran!" Eve raced toward him. Ran tossed the flashlight aside, opened his arms, and swept her against his chest.

"I was afraid something like this might happen," he said against her hair. His hold tightened. "He's gone. I'm here now. Everything's okay."

The heat and strength of him seeped into her. Eve took a moment to absorb the courage his solid presence gave her.

She eased back to look at him. "You saw it?"

"I heard the voice. I was afraid he might hurt you. I saw the light when I opened the door."

"Whoever he is—*whatever it is*—it was here before."

"Yes, that night in the hall."

Her knees felt weak. She leaned against him, pressed her cheek against his bare chest, held on a few seconds longer than she should have, finally forced herself to move away.

"Wally was here," she said. "He brought a friend named Herbie."

He caught her shoulders. "You could see them?"

"Yes."

Ran swore under his breath. "There's nothing easy about this place."

"You think they'll be back?"

He raked his fingers through his wavy black hair. "Probably not tonight. In my experience, manifestations as powerful as the ones we're dealing with require a great deal of energy. They'll need time to recharge."

She frowned. "Like a battery?"

When his mouth edged up, a little curl of heat replaced the nerves in her stomach.

"Not exactly," he said. "But energy is energy. The principle's the same." His eyes ran over her prim little nightgown and she wished she were wearing sheer red lace.

"I'll get you a glass of water," he said, but she didn't move away.

She didn't want him to go. The day had been long and exhausting, the night pure hell. She didn't want to be alone.

"I don't need any water." She flattened her palms on his chest, felt the sculpted ridges of muscle beneath her hands. "I don't want you to go. I want you to stay with me."

His big frame stiffened with tension. She told herself to be brave, take the risk. Eve slid her arms around his neck, went up on her toes, and pressed her mouth over his.

Ran didn't hesitate. Just tightened his hold and took control of the kiss, his hand sliding into her hair to hold her in place as he kissed her one way and then another, kissed her until she could barely think.

"I'll take good care of you," he promised, his mouth on the side of her neck. "I'll make you forget all of the unpleasantness you've seen today." Ran tipped her chin up and pressed hot kisses along her jaw. He framed her face between his hands, tipped her head back, and claimed her mouth, just sank in and tasted. Every move he made went straight to her core.

Heat and need, hungry desire unlike any she had ever known, tore through her. A little sound escaped that she didn't recognize as coming from her throat.

Ran pulled the ribbon on the front of the cotton nightgown

she had worn as some kind of barrier against her own desires and shoved the fabric off her shoulders. He traced a finger over her skin, over her nipple, making it tighten. His mouth followed, opening to capture her breast, teasing and tasting until her legs began to tremble.

"I want you," he said. "I didn't lie about that. I'm just afraid this won't be enough."

Eve whimpered. She didn't know exactly what he meant, but she felt it, too. That being with Ran tonight wouldn't be enough, might never be enough. She wanted more, clung to him when he lifted her into his arms and carried her over to the bed, stripped off the silly nightgown.

This man wouldn't settle for any sort of barrier between them. He was going to strip her naked clear to her soul. She could feel it in every cell in her body.

Naked, he joined her in bed and the heat of him enveloped her. Hot, wet kisses rained down on her, his mouth moving with the kind of expertise that said he didn't do anything halfway, the kind of determination he'd employed to make himself a billionaire. She wondered if there had ever been anything at which he had failed.

The thought arose of the single moment in his life when he had been powerless, unable to save his wife and daughter. She tried not to ache for him and what he must have suffered.

She felt his mouth and hands skimming over her body, moving lower, giving her the pleasure he had promised. The first wave of climax struck so hard she shook all over.

"Ran . . ." His name came out as a plea. She wanted to feel him inside her, prayed he could hear the need in her voice that hadn't gone away.

"Not yet. Not until you're ready."

She moaned as he started all over again, driving her up, teaching her things about her body she had never known. It wasn't until his heavy length filled her and he began to move that she felt the wildness, the hunger that rose like a tide inside her. The rhythm increased, pounding, pounding, forcing her over the edge one more time as he followed her to release. Only then did the wild-ness subside, the hunger finally ebb and slip away.

Ran kissed her deeply one last time, and she rejoiced in know-ing she had pleased him. Time spun out. Ran curled her against his side and pressed a soft kiss on her temple. For the first time in days, Eve drifted into a deep, peaceful sleep.

CHAPTER SEVENTEEN

*R*AN LEFT THE BED AT FIRST LIGHT. HE NEEDED TO ESCAPE, NEEDED time to deal with the unexpected emotions he was feeling. And the guilt.

It had nothing to do with the sex, which had been spectacular. It wasn't the fact he had slept with a beautiful woman. He was a man and his wife had been dead five long years.

But as he'd told Eve, his women friends had simply filled a need. A night of uninhibited sex had satisfied that need for both of them. Desire, not emotion was involved.

Last night was different. He hadn't felt that kind of closeness to a woman since Sabrina had died, didn't deserve to after putting his wife and child in the grave.

Sitting at the kitchen table, Ran scrubbed a hand over his face. He needed to take a step back, make sure Eve understood the limits of their relationship. They had enjoyed each other, but taking things further would be a mistake. He couldn't let it happen again.

The thought made his stomach churn.

He wanted her still. He wanted her in a bone-deep way he didn't understand. It had taken all his will to leave her bed this morning when he wanted so badly to make love to her again.

Ran had known a lot of women. What was so different about Eve St. Clair? Eve was smart and intriguing and in a subtle way, sexy as hell. But he had known other smart, sexy women.

But how many women had he known who could reach into the soul of the universe and speak to those on the Other Side?

Perhaps whatever light burned in Eve was the same light that drew him. He didn't know. He just knew his conscience was riding him hard, reminding him that he had no right to feel the things Eve made him feel.

He would talk to her, make sure she understood how much he had enjoyed spending the night with her. At the same time, let her know they couldn't continue. He wasn't interested in a relationship. In a few days' time, her house would be cleared, and he would be heading back home.

It occurred to him that perhaps Eve felt the same. Perhaps she'd be relieved to know he wouldn't be pressing her for more nights like the one they had shared.

His hand tightened around the coffee mug. The notion did nothing to improve his dour mood.

In the end, he decided to postpone the inevitable a little while longer. There was too much going on. Too many things could easily spin out of control. First and foremost came Eve's safety. The team needed to resolve the dangerous situation in the house. To do that, they needed more information.

Ran went up to shower and dress. By the time he'd returned downstairs, Eve was busy in the kitchen making a pot of tea. She turned as he walked into the room.

Silver teaspoon in hand, Eve just stood there, looking beautiful and uncertain, clearly dreading the usual "morning after" conversation. It was a conversation Ran had never had. He made sure his intentions were out in the open before he took a woman to bed, and he never spent the night. He always left when the party was over.

"I . . . umm . . . heard the shower running down the hall," Eve finally said. "You must have a million things to do."

There was only one thing he wanted to do. He wanted more of Eve St. Clair—a lot more.

"I always have plenty to do, but after what happened last night, I didn't want to leave you alone in the house."

Her uncertainty faded and her chin went up. "*What happened last night?* Are you referring to the ghosts? Or the night we spent in bed?"

Amusement touched his lips. "I was worried about your angry spirits. Regarding the night we spent together, if I had my way, we'd still be up there. But more of the same isn't a good idea. I have a life back in Seattle. You're building a life right here."

A hint of sadness passed over her face. "You don't have to explain. I've known that from the start. Last night was special for me. I don't regret it. I doubt I ever will."

His chest squeezed. The night had been special for him, too. That was the problem.

Ran moved before he could stop himself. He turned her to face him and pulled her into his arms. For an instant, Eve resisted. Then her body softened and when he kissed her, Eve kissed him back. He could feel her heart beating, matching the speeding rhythm of his own.

Reluctantly, Ran let her go. He ran a finger down her cheek. "What happened last night . . . I don't regret it, either."

Eve returned to the stove, her hand trembling as she poured tea from the gold-rimmed china pot into her cup. "Would you like to join me?"

"I had coffee. I'm fine."

"You should eat something. I've got bagels, croissants, yogurt, and juice."

He should go, but he really didn't want to. "Whatever you've got would be great. In the meantime, I'll call the coroner."

Some of the color leached from her cheeks. "I hadn't forgotten. I wish I could."

Ran made the call. Eleven o'clock worked for everyone.

Eve set out breakfast, and they sat down across from each other at the kitchen table, both careful to keep the conversation light.

Then Zane called. "A guy named Milton Carlisle Stanhope III owns the building," he said. "Apparently, he's retired, lives in the south of France."

"Give me his number."

Zane rattled off the +33 area code and number. Ran considered having his executive assistant make the arrangements, but the time change in Seattle posed a problem and he wanted the matter settled.

"See what you can find out about the history of the place. Look for any connection to the St. Clairs."

"Will do."

Ran ended the call, then dialed Stanhope's number and waited impatiently for the line to pick up. The call was answered by a woman named Marie Dupre, Stanhope's personal secretary. She had a lovely French accent and the voice of an older woman.

"My name is Ransom King. I'm the owner of King Enterprises out of Seattle, Washington. I'd like to speak to Mr. Stanhope in regard to a property he owns in Sunderland, England."

Her accent was pronounced. "I am afraid Mr. Stan'ope is unavailable at this time. Per'aps there is something I could do to 'elp you, Mr. King."

"Perhaps there is. The building I'm interested in is empty and very old. I'd like to take a look inside while I'm in the area."

"You are interested in the property as a real-estate investment?"

Not exactly, but he could hardly tell her he was there in search of ghosts. "I might be." And as he thought about it, maybe he was. He hated to see a historical structure failing into ruin. "Currently, it's in extreme disrepair. I was hoping Mr. Stanhope would have an estate agent in the area who could let me in and give me some time to investigate the possibilities."

"I can speak to 'im, but Mr. Stanhope is in very ill 'ealth. I will 'ave to phone you back."

"That's fine. You have my cell number."

"*Oui.*" Ms. Dupre rang off, and Ran shoved the phone into the pocket of his dark blue jeans. He'd cleaned his low-topped leather boots as best he could and put them back on. No choice since he'd be tramping around in the tunnel again. Not a pleasant thought.

Ran phoned Jesse and filled him in, told him to update the rest of the team, then checked his wristwatch.

"The coroner should be here any minute," he told Jesse. "I'll be back in touch after I speak to the owner of the asylum."

Ran was in the living room checking the messages on his phone when the knock came at the door. Eve appeared in the hallway, and they went to the door together.

Oswell "Ozzie" Townsend was a frail-looking older man, silver haired and slightly bent. The man beside him, brown haired, midthirties and good-looking, wore a tweed sport coat and brown slacks. The way he filled the sleeves of the jacket said he stayed in shape.

"Mr. King, I presume," Townsend, the coroner, said.

"Yes, and this is Dr. St. Clair. The house belongs to her."

"I prefer Ozzie, and this is Detective Inspector Daniel Balfour of the Sunderland Town Police. Until we establish whether the bones are historic or contemporary, the tunnel is a crime scene."

"Understood," Ran said, having already figured that out.

Eve stepped back to allow them into the entry. "Please come in. Would you like something to drink, a cola, perhaps, or a bottle of water?"

Ozzie shook his head. "We have more people on the way. Better to just get on with it."

Detective Balfour made no comment. His attention was fixed on Eve. His dark eyes swept her from head to foot with obvious interest, and Ran's jaw went tight.

Several government vehicles pulled up in front, and a man and a woman dressed in white coveralls got out. Appropriate, Ran thought, for the toxic atmosphere of the tunnel.

"Shall we wait for the rest of your party?" Eve asked.

"We'll take a look first," Ozzie said. "Then bring them in."

"All right," Eve said. "If you'll just follow me." Eve led them down the hall to the newly installed basement door, still just rough, unpainted wood.

"We're doing some remodeling." Ran pulled open the door, revealing a staircase that smelled like new wood. "Why don't I lead the way?" He didn't wait, just headed down the stairs, not surprised to hear Eve's softer footfalls behind him, followed by the coroner and the detective.

"We marked the location of the bones about forty yards down the tunnel. I'll be happy to show you the spot."

Ozzie and Balfour both walked past him into the tunnel, took a look around, then returned.

"Dodgy place, that's for sure," the detective said. "I'll bring the others and get my gear."

Ran turned to Eve. "I know better than to ask if you're coming with us."

She smiled. "Actually, I've decided to stay behind. I have every faith you'll be able to find the bones and leave them securely in the hands of our local constabulary."

Ran returned the smile, glad to see her taking it all in stride. "Smart girl." It appeared she had forgiven him for this morning. His smile faded. Or maybe she didn't care enough to be hurt.

Twenty minutes later, a clean, disposable slicker over his clothes, Ran led the coroner, the detective, and the two people on the forensics team into the darkness stretching in front of him. They all wore miners' hard hats and carried lamps. According to what Ozzie had told him, they would photograph the location and do the primary forensics, then bag the bones and bring them back out through the cellar.

Ran was more than a little interested in finding out exactly how old the mystery bones were. And what had been the cause of death.

CHAPTER EIGHTEEN

Worried about the people working in the dilapidated tunnel, Eve's anxiety began to build. She escaped to her office, planning to work while she waited. Seated at her desk, she reviewed Bethany Parson's file, adding a couple of fresh thoughts to the notes she had made during their last session.

Her concentration faltered. Concern for the people in the tunnel mingled with thoughts of Ran and the harsh ending to their brief affair.

Whatever Ran had felt, last night was one of the most incredible moments of Eve's life. Ran had made her feel precious, almost worshipped. She had hoped it had been special in some way for him, hoped she wasn't just another of his women. This morning in the harsh light of day, Ran had made it clear that was nothing but a beautiful illusion.

She didn't blame him. She had been the seducer, not the other way around. Her behavior might have been an embarrassment, but instead, she replayed every moment she had spent with him again and again.

Eve checked the time and went back to the house in case the police had returned from the tunnel. At the sound of heavy footfalls on the stairs, she turned off the tea kettle and stepped into the hall just as Ran topped the landing.

He was carrying his boots and the damp rain slicker he'd been wearing, his big feet encased in a pair of white athletic socks. A few drops of water glistened in his heavy black hair.

Eve curled her fingers into her palms to keep from reaching out to touch him.

"The police are still working," he said, heading for the mud-room. "Ozzie says they'll need at least another hour. I'll clean these up and be right back."

He was wearing his boots when he returned, minus the mud, and they walked into the kitchen together.

"I could use a drink of water," he said.

Eve pulled a plastic bottle out of the fridge and handed it over, watched him crank off the lid. Ran tilted his head back, the muscles in his neck working as he swallowed, so male and sexy her abdomen clenched.

She grabbed a bottle of water for herself and sat down across from him, drank her fill just to get her mind back on track.

"How did it go?" she asked.

"It was interesting. We were right about the bones belonging to a man. The coroner thinks the remains are only a few years old. He'll need to do some testing, but he says there are rodent teeth marks on the bones. That's the reason they were stripped so clean."

Eve shivered.

"There was something else."

Her hand tightened around the plastic bottle. "What?"

"When we found the bones yesterday, we were careful not to touch or move anything. If we had, we would have seen a bullet hole in the back of the skull."

"Oh, no, the man was murdered?"

"Looks that way."

"So whoever killed him used the tunnel to dispose of the body."

Ran just nodded and took another long drink of water.

Eve thought of all that had happened since Ran King and his team had arrived. "I don't think that man has anything to do with the ghosts."

"That was your impression the first time you saw him. I think you're right. His death was recent. The phenomena we're investigating point to something that took place years ago."

"Yes. If Herbie was a friend of Wally's and Herbie lived in the orphanage, whatever happened to them happened after 1861, when the orphanage first opened."

"We need to get in there." He pulled out his cell phone to check for messages. "No service in the tunnel." He scrolled through. "Here it is. Stanhope's personal secretary, Mrs. Dupre, left a message. Says to call an estate agent named Tom Mason to set up an appointment. She left a number."

"Are you going to tell him we're hunting for ghosts?"

"I'll have to play it by ear, try to get a read on him. He might like the idea. You never know." He smiled, and for the first time she noticed the tiny dimple next to his mouth.

Her stomach dropped out. It simply wasn't fair for a man to be so attractive. Memories of the night before sent heat rushing into her face.

Of all the men she could be attracted to, she had to pick one who didn't want her. Or at least not anymore.

Ran walked away to make the call and returned a few minutes later. "Mason can let us in today at four o'clock."

"You think the police will be finished with the bones by then?"

Ran nodded. "As you can imagine, they were anxious to get out of the tunnel. It shouldn't be much longer."

Eve took a deep breath. "Okay, then. If you don't mind, I have some work to do. I'll be ready to go when you are." She started to walk away, but Ran caught her shoulder and turned her to face him.

"I wanted to take you for a drive."

Her lips tightened. "Past tense. Don't worry about it. I understand."

"Damn it, Eve, that's not the way it is."

"It doesn't matter. We're both adults and it was only one night. As you said—you have your life and I have mine."

She heard noises in the cellar, then footsteps on the stairs. "The police must be finished. I need to make sure they have everything they need." Eve turned and walked out of the kitchen.

The sky was still overcast, but there was a lull in the storm. The weather forecast said the bad weather would continue for at least several more days.

At exactly four p.m., Eve stood in front of the House of Mercy Orphan Asylum. Ran stood a few feet away, speaking to the estate agent, Tom Mason, a burly man with a fringe of gray hair around his bald head.

Mason unlocked the front door, then handed Ran the key. "Yer welcome to stay as long as ye like. As ye said, place's in fierce condition. Ol' man Stanhope would likely entertain any sorta reasonable offer."

"Thank you, Tom. I'll have the key brought back to your office tomorrow morning."

"Ye've got me card. Ye need anything, ye know where to find me."

Ran just nodded. Mason walked back to his car, a light blue-gray Vauxhall, started the engine, and drove away. The car Ran had rented and had delivered before they left the house, a silver BMW, sat a few feet behind it.

Eve had offered to drive him in her little Ford Focus or let Ran borrow it, but he had refused.

"The other members of the team need transportation," he had said. "And I'm tired of being at the mercy of a driver. From now on, I'll have my own vehicle. I'll drive us over and back. That way we won't get wet if it starts to rain."

"You're comfortable driving on the left-hand side of the road?"

"I spent some time over here when we were getting the UK King's Inn chain up and running."

Eve's gaze followed the estate agent's car as it turned the corner and disappeared. "What did you offer Mr. Mason to get him to be so cooperative?"

"I gave him a hundred-pound note for his trouble and dangled the possibility of a sales commission in front of him."

"You wouldn't really buy the building, would you?"

He shrugged his muscled shoulders. "I'm always open to possibilities. At the moment, I'm more interested in discovering the past this building is hiding." He checked his heavy wristwatch. "Violet and the others will be here any minute. Why don't we take a quick look inside before they get here?"

Returning to the car, he grabbed the long-handled flashlight he had been using in the tunnel. Eve grabbed a smaller flashlight and they returned to the asylum. When Ran pulled open the tall, ornately carved front door, Eve froze in shock.

She had expected the place to be in bad condition, but the interior was far worse than anything she could have imagined. The wallpaper in the entry was shredded and water stained, the plaster crumbling into moldy piles on the floor, exposing the rotted wood underneath.

Most of the tiles on the entry floor were missing or broken, barely visible beneath several inches of dirty rainwater. But it was the graffiti on the walls—bloodred Satanic emblems, pentagrams, the painted head of a goat—that made it look like something out of a horror movie.

Dear God. Eve thought of the spirits, of Herbie and Wally and their possible connection to the asylum, and the flashlight fell from her nerveless fingers. She felt Ran's firm grip on her arm, holding her upright.

"Let's wait outside for the others," he said.

Eve opened her mouth, then swallowed her objection. Ran King's protective nature had surfaced. He wouldn't allow any of his people to put themselves in harm's way. Last night notwithstanding, that seemed to include her.

He led her outside and the heavy door closed behind him. "It's worse than I thought," he said. "If you can't handle it, we'll come at it from a different direction."

What that could possibly be, she had no idea. It didn't matter. This was her problem and she intended to see it through.

"I'll be all right. I should have been better prepared."

"Hard to prepare for something like that. What you saw was only the entry. It may be worse upstairs."

How could it possibly be worse? Then she realized he meant up where the orphan boys had been kept, and her stomach violently knotted. She loved kids. Had always wanted a family of her own, a notion she had given up after her divorce. That everything happening seemed to revolve around children made the whole situation worse.

You can do this, she told herself.

The white Bentley arrived and Violet, Katie, Jesse, and Zane all climbed out.

In loose jeans, a sweater, and sturdy boots, her silver hair pulled back in a twist, Violet walked over and hugged her, sensing, perhaps, how much being there disturbed her.

"That bad, is it?" Violet asked.

"Worse," Eve said. "And we only got as far as the entry."

Violet squeezed her hand. "Well, all of us are here now, and we make a formidable team."

Eve found herself smiling. "I know you do. I'm glad you're here."

"That *all* includes you," Violet said, and Eve realized it was true. They would have made a lot less progress if it hadn't been for her.

Katie walked up, honey-blond hair swinging forward as she leaned in and gave Eve a hug. "I have a hunch tonight is going to be very interesting."

Jesse walked up next to Eve. He tapped his EVP audio recorder. "Whatever happens, we're going to make sure we have proof." He and Katie disappeared into the asylum with an armload of equipment.

Zane was the last to join them, a manila file under one arm. "I got some intel on the asylum. I figured you'd want to know."

Ran had said Violet preferred to go in cold, just see what she and the rest of his team could pick up. Apparently the situation had changed.

"What have you got?" Ran asked.

"As the sign out front says, the orphanage was opened in 1861. For hundreds of years, Sunderland was the biggest shipbuilding town in England. The asylum was opened to provide an education for the male orphans of seafaring men, both legitimate and illegitimate."

Zane's gaze shifted from Ran to Eve. "The boys were taught seamanship and wore a naval-style sailor suit as a uniform."

Eve thought of Wally and felt a sweep of nausea. Wally had been an orphan. That was how he knew Herbie. Ran's hand settled at her waist, silently lending his support.

Violet gave Eve a soft smile. "So now you know where your little friend came from."

Wally and Herbie had both been orphans. Wally had died when he was a little boy. Her throat tightened. After all these years, he was still imprisoned here on earth.

Determination welled inside her, replacing the sadness. If there was any way she could set the boys free, she wouldn't stop until it was done.

CHAPTER NINETEEN

"*T*HIS WHOLE THING JUST FEELS SO SURREAL," EVE SAID AS THEY stood in front of the ornate wooden front door.

Ran looked at Zane. "The place is in terrible condition. When did it close?"

"There isn't a lot written about it. It was definitely still in use in the late 1890s. Even after it closed as an orphanage, the building was used by community groups. The military used it in World War Two, and it wasn't completely abandoned until several decades after that. That's all I've got so far."

"That's all we need." Ran walked over and pulled open the front door. "We might as well get on with it."

"I'll keep watch out here," Zane said.

Violet walked inside. Ran took hold of Eve's hand as she walked past, and together they continued through the entry into what must have been the main salon, where Katie and Jesse stood waiting. Though the windows were partially boarded up, enough light filtered in through the filthy glass for them to see.

Dirty water sloshed over Jesse's boots as he turned to survey his surroundings. "This place is raw, man. The perfect place for a haunting."

Ran cast him a dark look. The old asylum was terrifying enough without Jesse making comments like that.

"We need to figure out where to set up," Ran said. "Eve, Violet, and I are going to take a look around."

Violet would be opening herself up to any sensations she might feel. Eve had no idea how to do that, so she just tried to let herself relax into the moment.

Ran laced his fingers with hers. Whatever he might or might not feel for her, in this situation, she was glad he was there.

They started with a walk through the main rooms on the first floor, the main salon, the dining hall, what must have been several offices. All were in the same horrible state of destruction and decay as the entry. The last place they discovered on the lower floor was what had once been a small chapel with several rows of pews on each side of a central aisle. There was a stained-glass window below the peak of the roof with several of the colored glass panes broken out.

The chapel was in the same terrible condition as the rest of the asylum, with some of the pews turned upside down, others broken apart, and red graffiti sprayed on the walls behind the altar, where a crucifix once had hung. Predictions of the end of the world, Nazi swastikas, more Satanic symbols, layer upon layer of devastation and decay over the years since the asylum was abandoned.

Though parts of the building had been remodeled since its construction, much of the original architecture remained: the manteled fireplaces, blackened from years of use, the once-beautiful wooden banister on the curving staircase leading to the second floor, smooth from years of wear.

Whatever uses it had been put to, the building still whispered the stories of the children who had escaped the poor houses and prisons, but not the loneliness that oozed from the very walls.

"Anything?" Ran asked Violet.

"Lots of things. None of them good. Mostly just a crush of violent emotions and bone-deep sadness."

"Anything specific?"

Violet shook her head.

Ran turned to Eve. Her head was pounding, her stomach churning. The disgusting smell of rot and urine made the bile rise in her throat.

"Anything?"

Not the sort of *anything* he was interested in. Certainly nothing that qualified as having to do with spirits or ghosts. "No."

They continued on, went into the kitchen, which had been updated somewhere along the way but was still far from modern. The cupboards sagged and the counter had been pulled away from the wall, but it wasn't as bad as the rest of the building.

"Look, there's a room off to one side." Eve pulled Ran across the kitchen. He set her aside as she reached for the doorknob and opened the door himself.

"Interesting," he said. "Looks like someone is still getting some use out of the place."

There was a metal desk and chairs, a cot along one wall with an old army drab wool blanket draped over it. Only a single board covered the window, allowing a good amount of light to enter the room. The walls needed painting, but there was no graffiti, and a separate entrance led outside.

Ran walked over, turned the lock, and pulled open the door. Heavy mist and gusty winds blew in before he could close and re-lock it.

Violet frowned as she glanced around at what appeared to be the only livable room in the asylum. "A homeless person living in here, perhaps?"

"I don't know," Ran said with another look around. Eve felt a clutch of emotions, but they didn't feel connected to the orphanage or events that might have happened there.

Ran urged them out of the room and closed the door. They went back to the main salon, where Jesse and Katie still waited. "I'm going to check the stairs."

Eve watched him head up, taking his time, checking to be sure the steps would hold his weight. He returned a few minutes later.

"The original structure was built far better than most of the construction today. The stairs are solid."

"I'll go on up," Violet said.

"I'm going with you," Eve said.

"We'll go up together." Ran turned back to Jesse and Katie. "I'll let you know where to set up as soon as we figure it out." Leading the way, he reached the landing halfway up and waited for the women to join him, then proceeded up to the top of the stairs, Eve and Violet a few steps behind.

The ceilings were high in the downstairs rooms, which made for a tall staircase. The hall the stairs led to took off in opposite directions. As before, rancid water stained the walls and floors in both corridors. Tattered faded curtains hung from some of the windows. An old wooden rocker sat abandoned in the middle of the hall.

Ran stayed close as they started down the corridor to the right. Eve jerked to a halt at an open door into one of the dormitories. It was a scene from a nightmare, with mold and filth, rust and decay everywhere.

Eve held back the little sound of horror that tried to escape her throat.

Ran shined the light over the dilapidated furniture in the dorm room, a row of old iron beds, some with rusted metal springs, others covered by wet mattresses with soggy stuffing coming out.

Eve started to tremble.

"What is it?"

Eve gripped Ran's arm so hard it must have hurt. She could hear children's giggling laughter, then the sound of running feet. Sobs followed. Soft moans tugged at her heart. She swayed and her head spun.

"Easy," Ran whispered. Violet came up beside her, the older woman's presence soothing. Eve thought Violet must also be hearing the heartbreaking sobs.

Eve took a steadying breath. "Wally . . . ? Wally, it's Evie. Are you here?"

She thought she heard light footsteps, but it might have been the *drip, drip, drip* of the rain on the roof.

I don't like this place.

Eve recognized the little boy's voice and her heart constricted. "Wally? It's Evie."

Violet spoke to her softly. "Tell him he doesn't have to stay. Tell him he just needs to find the light."

Eve steadied herself. She couldn't see any light, but she trusted Violet to help Wally.

"You don't have to stay here, Wally. You can leave anytime you want."

She saw him then, a small figure in blue. Wavy, like looking through water. Her legs wobbled.

"Look for the light, Wally. Can you see it? People who love you will be waiting at the end of the light."

The small figure floated toward her. *What about Herbie and the others? Can they leave, too?*

Dear God. Eve glanced at the row of empty beds along the wall. How many children were trapped in this place?

She trembled, forced a note of calm into her voice. "The others can go with you. Look up toward heaven. See if you can find the light."

Lightning cracked outside the window, so close it shook the building and rattled the cracked and broken glass panes. The roar of the wind increased until it sounded like a freight train about to crash through the walls.

They! Are! Mine!

Wally vanished. Thunder boomed and waves of torrential rain fell from the sky, slanting in between the boards over the broken windows. One of the old iron beds began to jump up and down, rattling and moving in little leaps toward the spot where Eve stood.

Get! Out! Now!

A metal spring tore loose from one of the beds and went flying across the room, another spring followed, then another, slamming into the plaster walls. A storm of flying bedsprings flew through the air with hurricane force. Ran stepped in front of Eve, shielding her with his body.

"Let's go!" he commanded.

As Violet rushed out of the room, the shower of sharp rusted metal came to an end, but Eve just stood there, unable to believe what was happening.

Ran took her arm and his voice softened. "Time to go, sweetheart."

Eve blinked and shook herself free of whatever trance-like state she'd been caught up in. Violet led the way. Ran guided Eve, following close behind. As they started down the hall, Eve realized that Jesse and Katie were also upstairs, that they had been using their equipment, making video and audio recordings.

"Pack it up!" Ran demanded. Barely slowing down, he continued toward the stairs, and they all headed down, their footsteps echoing eerily through the empty rooms of the building. Ran didn't stop until they were outside the asylum, a good distance away from the front door.

"Man, that was something," Jesse said, grinning.

"It was something, all right," Ran said darkly. "Something definitely not good."

Eve looked up at him. "You could see him? You saw Wally?"

"No, but I heard the running feet and the man with the angry voice. Same as before. Whatever it is, it's bad news. It's powerful and vengeful and now it's connected to us." Unconsciously, he reached up and touched the back of his neck. His fingers came away scarlet with blood.

"You're hurt!" Eve cried.

Ran stared down at his bloody hand. "It's just a scratch. I'll get it cleaned up when we get back to the hotel." Ran motioned toward the limo. The driver spotted him, started the engine, and pulled up to the curb.

Eve pulled a tissue out of the pocket of her jeans and pressed it against the back of Ran's neck.

"Thanks," he said, took the tissue, and wiped away the blood.

Eve worked to calm herself, but her voice shook as she thought of what had happened. "There are others trapped in there, Ran. We know about Herbie, but Wally said there were others. More children, I think."

Ran swore a soft curse. His gaze went to Jesse, Katie, and Violet. "Where's Zane?"

"I texted him," Jesse said. "He'll be here any minute."

Zane walked around the corner of the building just then. "How'd it go?" he asked.

"Dude, you shoulda seen it," Jesse said. "Beds were hopping, stuff was flying. It was something right out of a horror movie."

"That place gives me the creeps," Zane said.

"Man, you have no idea."

Ran's gaze ran over the members of his team. "You guys head back to the hotel. Jesse and Katie—I want to see what you were able to pick up tonight. Violet—I want your impressions as well. All of you get something to eat. I'll expect you in my suite at eight p.m. Eve and I will meet you there."

Eve frowned. "Wait. What's going on?"

Ran started guiding her back toward the rented BMW. "We need to strategize. We need to do it somewhere other than your house. You'll be safe at the hotel until we figure this out." He opened the passenger door. "Besides, I need a drink."

Eve agreed. After what she had witnessed in the asylum, she could use something to ease the churning in her stomach and the nerves tightening the muscles in her neck. And Ran was right. Even if he spent the night, she wouldn't be able to close her eyes if she stayed in the house.

Still shaking, Eve let him settle her in the passenger seat. His big hand brushed a breast as he clicked her seat belt in place, and her nipple tightened. Hysterical laughter bubbled up in her throat. After the terror she had felt and what she had seen, how could she possibly feel desire?

Ran walked around the hood and slid in behind the wheel of the BMW. "Everything's going to be okay." He fired the powerful engine. "We're going to figure this out."

Eve clenched her hands together in her lap. As Ran pulled out on the road, she flicked him a sideways glance. "I wish I'd never sent that email."

For a moment, Ran's gaze held hers. "Opening the tunnel definitely played a part in what's happened. But there's a chance some of this would have occurred anyway. If it did and you were living there unprotected . . ." He blew out a tired breath. "I don't even want to think about it."

Eve trembled. Her mind was still spinning with the unleashed power she had witnessed. Dear God, what if the malevolent spirit in the asylum had come after her in the house and Ran wasn't there?

Eve didn't want to think about it, either.

CHAPTER TWENTY

*T*HOUGH RAN WOULD HAVE PREFERRED DRIVING STRAIGHT TO THE hotel, Eve convinced him to stop at her house so she could pick up clean clothes and her toiletries.

While he waited downstairs in her living room, he phoned the hotel and made a room reservation. Just a few extra dollars for the inconvenience of moving the current guest, and the suite next to his would do nicely. He only wished Eve were staying with him, instead of next door.

Another call went to the estate agent, Tom Mason, asking permission to keep the key a few more days to continue his inspection of the building.

"No trouble, mate," Tom said. "They ain't linin' up to buy the old place."

"Thanks, Tom. I'll keep you posted."

Ran's last call went to his close friend, Lucas Deveraux. After a few pleasantries, Ran got straight to the point.

"I've never seen anything like it, Luke. We can't seem to get a fix on who or what it is, but it appears to be holding a number of souls captive."

"A number? More than two or three?"

"It looks that way. It was an orphan asylum for more than a hundred years. I think something must have happened. We haven't figured out what it was. Nothing shows up in asylum records, but we're still digging."

"You certainly make it sound intriguing."

"Terrifying is more like it. There's a lot more to the story, but I'd rather tell you in person. Can you help us?"

"I can try. You know I can't guarantee success, but if it's as bad as you're saying, someone needs to do something."

"Actually, there's a woman involved who is doing her best to help. Her name is Eve St. Clair. She's new to all this, but—"

"Let me guess. Pretty and smart, and you're showing her the ropes?"

Ran sighed. "Eve's all those things, but it's not like that." He only wished it were that simple. He glanced at the doorway just as Eve appeared, an overnight bag slung over her shoulder.

"I have to go," Ran said. "I'll call Constance, have her phone you. She'll arrange for the jet to pick you up and bring you here as soon as you can fit us into your schedule. There'll be a car waiting when you arrive."

"All right. Take it easy, okay? I'll be seeing you in a day or two."

As Lucas hung up the phone, Ran wondered if he'd heard a hint of concern in his good friend's voice. Luke was no longer a priest, but he was everything a priest should be, kind and caring, intelligent, and extremely discerning. Had he perceived deeper emotions when Ran had spoken of Eve?

He turned to where she stood in the doorway.

"Business?" Eve asked.

"Paranormal Investigations business. A former priest by the name of Lucas Devereaux. If you're ready to go, I'll tell you all about him on the way to the hotel." Ran took the overnight bag off her shoulder and slung it over his own.

"Remember that locksmith you mentioned?" Eve said.

"I remember."

"I'm ready to look inside the camelback trunk. Maybe there's something in there that will help us figure things out."

"I'll make some calls as soon as we get to the hotel, see if I can arrange for someone to meet us tomorrow morning."

Eve just nodded. She was still shaken, he knew, as she had every right to be. He was a little unnerved himself. They went out the front door of her house to where the rented BMW was parked. Ran opened the car door and settled Eve inside, then loaded her bag into the trunk.

The storm was building again, heavy gray clouds amassing over the town, wind whipping the leaves on the trees. The roads were slick, but the days were getting longer as spring moved toward summer. It wouldn't be dark till nearly nine p.m.

"So . . . Lucas Devereaux," Eve said, returning to their earlier conversation as the car rolled along A183.

"He's a friend of a friend. Remy Moreau, my roommate in college, introduced us not long after Luke went into the priesthood. Apparently, he'd been in some trouble as a boy, got involved in a gang, that kind of thing. Someone got killed. Luke was determined to make amends. Joining the priesthood seemed like the right decision at the time."

"You said *former* priest. What happened?"

Ran flicked her a glance as the Beamer cut through traffic. "Luke's no wilting lily. He's a good-looking man with the same sexual appetites as any other red-blooded male. To put it simply, he fell in love. Rather than break his vows, he left the priesthood. Unfortunately, his lady friend was more attracted to the forbidden love of a priest than to Luke himself. She turned down his marriage proposal and all Luke got out of it was a broken heart."

"At least he realized he wasn't cut out for the priesthood."

"In some ways he was. Lucas has a certain . . . ability. While he was still in the church, he got involved in the exorcism of a woman supposedly possessed by demons. An older priest taught him the necessary church rituals, and apparently, working together, the two of them rid the woman of the evil that possessed her. After that Luke took on other cases and he was highly successful. Even now, the church occasionally calls on him to use his abilities."

"How does that work if he's no longer a priest?"

"In certain cases, the church gives special dispensation."

Eve fell silent. Then her hazel eyes widened as the implications set in, the reason Ran had phoned one of his closest friends.

"Oh, my God. You think the voices are demonic. I don't even know if I believe in such a thing."

"I'm not sure I do, either."

"Wait a minute. You've been doing this for how long?"

"I started right after my wife and daughter died. Almost five years."

"If you don't believe in demons—"

"I've seen what Luke can do. I've used him on two different occasions. Both times, he was able to clear the house, and the problems the owner had been facing disappeared."

"What did he do?"

"You'd be better off asking Luke. He'll be here as soon as it can be arranged."

They arrived at the hotel. The clerk checked Eve into her suite and handed her a key card. Ran escorted her upstairs to the room next to his, but she made no comment. Ran carried her overnight bag through the living room into the bedroom and set it on the bed.

It was exactly the wrong thing to do. Memories of the night they had spent together burned through him and his groin tightened. He glanced to the doorway where Eve stood, and hungry need rose like a beast inside him. He might have been able to ignore it if he hadn't seen the same need reflected in Eve's pretty hazel eyes, dark now, without a hint of green.

Before he could stop himself, Ran strode over and pulled her into his arms. Sliding a hand into her thick dark hair, he tipped her head back and his mouth crushed down over hers.

The kiss was hot, wet, and deep. Fresh desire knifed through him. Eve didn't bother to pretend the kiss didn't affect her. A little sound came from her throat as she went up on her toes, slid her arms around his neck, and kissed him back.

Ran's whole body tightened. Palming her breasts, he cupped them through her sweater, remembering the exact shape and fullness, the smoothness of her skin, the way her nipples pebbled beneath his fingers.

He wanted to strip away her clothes and carry her to the bed, to taste every inch of her lithe, feminine body, then bury himself to the hilt.

"I want you so damned much," he said, kissing the side of her neck. "I've never wanted a woman the way I want you."

The words he'd never said before hit him like a splash of cold water. The guilt inside him swelled. He had loved Sabrina, his wife and the mother of his child. This was different. Eve stirred a yearning unlike anything he had ever felt before.

She gave a soft little moan as he began to ease away.

"I'm sorry," he said, tipping his forehead down to hers. "I didn't mean for that to happen. Please forgive me."

Eve's gaze found his. "Forgive you? What sin is it you think you've committed?"

Ran forced himself to turn away. He raked a hand through his wavy black hair. "I don't know. I just . . . It eats at me, the feelings I have for you, Eve. I thought we could just enjoy ourselves until it was over. But I don't seem able to do that. I feel things I don't want to feel, and I can't handle it."

Eve made no reply. He was afraid what he read in her face was pity.

"I need to go," he said. "As soon as you're settled and get something to eat, you can join us next door."

Her shoulders straightened. "I'm settled enough. I want to hear what you and your team have to say."

Ran took a deep breath. "All right. I'll call room service. Order something for both of us. If you're ready, we can go."

Eve checked her appearance in the mirror over the dresser, smoothed her hair, and applied fresh lipstick to her plump pink lips, sending his mind straight back to the bedroom. Ran didn't dare glance at the bed as she walked past him out of the room, just followed her out and closed the door behind them.

As soon as they reached his suite, he went into the bathroom and stripped off his jacket and his blue oxford shirt. Flying pieces of metal had cut into the back of his neck. There was a cut in his scalp and a gash on his cheek. Though the nicks and cuts were fairly minor, he was glad he'd had a recent tetanus shot. After soaping a rag, he was trying to clean the cuts when he looked up to see Eve standing in the doorway.

"Good heavens, its worse than I thought." She frowned. "It's almost as if the spirit was targeting you."

Ran felt the pull of a smile. "Maybe he was jealous."

"Very funny. Give me that washcloth and sit down on the toilet seat. You don't want these cuts getting infected."

"I had a tetanus shot before I went to Mexico. We were building a King's Inn down in Mérida. I figured better to be safe than sorry."

"Well, that's a relief."

Ran tried to ignore the feel of Eve's fingers sliding gently over the back of his neck, delicately washing the cut in his scalp and the gash on his cheek, but his body noticed and he went hard.

"There," Eve said. "That should do it." She tossed the washcloth in the sink, turned, and walked out of the bathroom.

Ran breathed a sigh of relief. He didn't trust himself where Eve was concerned. He was a man used to having what he wanted. He was tired of fighting himself, tired of the guilt he shouldn't be feeling after all these years. He wanted Eve St. Clair, and he knew Eve wanted him, too.

The doorbell rang, a welcome distraction. As he pulled on a clean long-sleeve T-shirt, he could hear Eve talking to the waitstaff who delivered the tray, a sandwich for him and a bowl of soup for Eve, who needed something to settle her stomach. Not surprising after what she had been through that day.

To say nothing of his untimely, unsatisfying pursuit.

For both of their sakes, he needed to do something about it. He just wasn't quite sure what that was.

As soon as they finished eating, Ran set the tray with the empty dishes in the hall. He turned just as Violet walked up, followed by Katie, Jesse, and Zane. By eight p.m., the group was seated in the living room while Jesse set up the video he and Katie had made.

"We're ready whenever you are," Jesse said.

Ran turned to Zane, who sat in one of the comfortable chairs that matched the cream sofa, sipping a can of Cola Light. "I'm almost sorry you missed the action tonight. It's something you'd have to see to believe."

Zane set his soft drink down on the coffee table. "I look forward to seeing the video."

Ran nodded. "You were with us when we walked through the asylum. You remember the room off the kitchen?"

"I do. It's in way better shape than the rest of the building. Looks like it's still being used."

"That's where you come in. I want to know who's using that room and what it's being used for."

"Okay, I'll find out."

"Not tonight. I definitely don't want you going back there tonight. And don't go by yourself. Either Jesse or I will go with you."

"I was a Green Beret. I'm not afraid of ghosts."

"In this case, it isn't malevolent spirits I'm afraid of. It's criminal activity."

Zane straightened in his chair. "As I think about that room, I see what you mean."

"We'll go back and nose around first thing in the morning."

"Yes, sir."

Ran's gaze turned to Jesse and Katie, two solid people who formed the core of his team. "All right, let's take a look at the video you two made."

CHAPTER TWENTY-ONE

*E*VE SAT ON THE SOFA, TRANSFIXED AS SHE STUDIED THE MONITOR set up on the coffee table so all of them could see. As they had done before, using the timeline of events, Jesse and Katie had paired the audio with the images on the video camera.

The film showed Ran, Eve, and Violet making their way up the wide staircase. The camera panned the destruction and decay of the second floor, then cut to Eve, Ran, and Violet in the dormitory.

The EVP recorder kicked in, picking up a rushing noise, barely audible. Eve remembered clearly the sound of small running feet. Something that could have been sobs, then moans. The audio picked up a distorted version of exactly what Eve had heard. The video showed Violet walking up beside her, there to lend her support.

Seconds later, Eve called out to Wally. Light footfalls sounded on the EVP meter. Then a child's muffled words. Wally saying, *I don't like this place.* On the monitor, only a small, cloudy image appeared that could have been dust or mist, but Eve had seen Wally standing right in front of her.

The rest of the video played out exactly as Eve remembered, the storm intensifying, thunder booming, rain beating down. When the rusted iron bed began to hop up and down, moving toward her across the warped wooden floor of the decaying dormitory, gooseflesh rose on Eve's arms.

Zane made a sound of disbelief. Eve felt the same bone-chilling fear she'd felt in the asylum as bits of broken metal bedsprings flew in every direction across the room, tearing into Ran's cheek, his scalp, and the back of his neck.

A deep, angry male voice shouted, *They! Are! Mine!* And a few seconds later, *Get! Out! Now!*

Perhaps her presence had stirred up spirits in the orphan asylum, but it didn't change the fact that whatever was happening posed a grave danger to anyone who spent time there.

The sofa dipped as Ran sat down beside her. Eve remembered the width of his broad back as she had cleaned his wounds, the feel of his muscles as they tightened beneath her fingers. She thought of the way he had kissed her, and her body grew flushed and damp. She had believed he no longer wanted her. Clearly, that wasn't true.

But Ran was still feeling a deep sense of guilt over the death of his wife and child, and fighting his conscience over the desire he felt for another woman.

Eve's heart went out to him. She warned herself that whatever his feelings for her, he could never get involved with another woman until he accepted that accidents happened, put the past to rest, and forgave himself.

Eve tried to believe that ending their untenable relationship was for the best. After her failed marriage, she didn't need another man in her life, certainly not one as complicated as Ransom King.

Still, as she felt the heat of his big, hard body beside her, the press of his thigh against hers, she remembered how good it had been when they had been together and couldn't help yearning for what could never be.

The evening had been damned interesting, Zane thought. The video certainly left him with a lot of unanswered questions. As he hadn't actually been there when the mysterious occurrences had happened in the asylum, he figured maybe there was a rational explanation.

It was late as he stood in the shadows outside the dilapidated structure, in a spot where he could watch the door into the room off the kitchen. The wind was icy and brisk, whipping the branches overhead.

Zane zipped his bomber jacket against the chill and settled in to wait. He was a detective. Getting answers was part of his job. Stakeouts were a way to get answers. King expected him to wait until morning, but odds were, if something criminal was going on, it would take place in the dark, not in the light of day.

After years as a Green Beret, Zane knew how to handle himself. At least against danger of the human variety. Ghosts—if they existed—were something else entirely. He still wasn't sure what to make of the things he had seen on the video, but he wasn't as skeptical as he had been.

Though the rain had stopped hours ago, the chill in the air urged him to find a comfortable place out of the wind. He sat down on a portion of the crumbling brick wall that surrounded the property, behind a box hedge that followed the same route.

He'd been sitting there for over an hour when a car pulled into the empty lot next to the abandoned asylum. A man got out on the driver's side, tall, very lean, and dark- haired. Another guy got out on the passenger side, similar in build with a long, dark beard. Another man got out of the rear passenger seat, shorter, with the same dark features.

Zane went on alert when the last man, tallest of the four, with shoulder-length hair pulled back and tied at the nape of his neck, reached in and dragged another person out of the back seat.

Dressed in baggy jeans and a sweater a size too large, the small figure hunched over, a woman with her arms bound behind her, swaying unsteadily. Long, tangled blond hair hung down, covering most of her face, but he could tell she was young.

And she wasn't there of her own choosing.

Clamping down on his temper, Zane slipped deeper into the shadows, disappearing from sight as he had been trained to do. He needed information, needed to be sure exactly what he was seeing.

The man with the ponytail gripped the young woman's arm to keep her from falling as she stumbled forward, staggering to keep her balance. Drunk or drugged? Too far away to tell, but Zane figured it was the latter.

Fresh anger coursed through him and one of his hands unconsciously fisted. He watched the men haul the girl toward the room. One of them used a key to unlock the door and pull it open, and the fourth man shoved her inside. The others followed and the door closed behind them.

Zane swore foully.

Providing security for Ransom King had nothing to do with the young woman who'd been dragged into that room. On the other hand, he was a Green Beret, not the kind of man who could watch an injustice being committed, stand by, and do nothing.

Zane pulled his cell phone out and typed a quick text, eased out of the shadows and moved toward the boarded-up window in the room off the kitchen.

Ran couldn't sleep. It was after one a.m. He'd spent the last two hours thinking of the woman asleep in the room next door, unable to get the heat out of his blood. Dragging on his dark blue jeans and long-sleeve navy T-shirt, he dug his feet into a pair of sneakers, grabbed his jacket, phone, and wallet, and headed downstairs. Maybe a walk on the beach would clear his head. He grabbed his car keys. Or maybe he'd go for a drive. Maybe both.

Ran took the stairs instead of the elevator, hoping to burn off some of his unwanted energy, then headed for the front door. He was surprised to see a familiar figure striding in the same direction.

"Couldn't sleep, either?" Ran asked Jesse.

He didn't bother to answer. "Zane's got trouble. I'm on my way over to the asylum."

Ran swore softly. "I told him to wait until morning." He shoved open the brass front door and they both walked into the brisk night air. "My car's in the parking lot. You can tell me about it while we're on the way."

Jesse looked relieved. They both jogged toward the BMW, and in seconds Ran was driving out of the lot toward the orphan asylum.

"What the hell is Zane doing over there? I told him I'd go with him in the morning."

"I know he wanted to check out that room off the kitchen. He said he couldn't do his job without knowing what kind of threat we could be facing, and he couldn't do that in the daytime. I got up to hit the head and heard a text come in on my cell. It was Zane. He said he was staking the place out when four guys showed up with a woman in tow. Apparently, a kidnap victim. Zane's going in to get her out. He wanted to let someone know where he was in case things went south."

"Sonofabitch." Ran stepped on the gas and the car shot forward. "He didn't consider calling the police?"

"He said he needed more information. That was the last text I got. By then I was dressed and ready to go." Jesse flashed a wide white grin. "Can't say I'm not glad you showed up when you did. Two against four isn't great odds. Even if one of us is a Green Beret."

The property wasn't that far from the hotel. Ran pulled over half a block from the asylum and turned off the engine. They both quietly got out of the car and quickly closed the doors, hoping no one had seen the interior lights go on. As they started toward the hulking dark structure looming out of the mist and began to circle around to the back, Jesse pointed to an unoccupied vehicle in the lot next to the property.

Ran nodded. Up ahead, a slice of dull yellow light seeped through a crack in the boards over the windows, easily marking their destination.

Ran motioned Jesse into the shadows along a box hedge on the side of the building. Creeping silently forward, they listened for sounds coming from inside, looking for any sign of Zane.

Out of the silence, Zane appeared like one of the asylum ghosts, face and hands blackened with mud, scaring the bejesus out of Ran. He almost smiled.

Zane tipped his head, motioning them farther away to a place where they could talk and not be heard.

"What's going on?" Ran asked.

Zane quickly filled him in on what had happened so far, adding that he'd heard enough to know the men were waiting for another party to arrive.

"If I'm right, they could be selling the girl."

"Fuck," Jesse said.

"I think it's time to call the police," Ran said.

"I would have already done it, but I was waiting for the buyers to get here. I figured the cops could round all of them up at one time."

"It's a risk," Ran said. "I don't like taking risks. Call 999 and get them over here."

Zane nodded and made the call. "No idea how fast things move in England. Police might not get here for a while."

"For that girl's sake, I hope it doesn't take them too long," Ran said.

Jesse's gaze went to the road. "There's a car coming. Not the cops."

Ran spotted a pair of headlights as the vehicle made a turn at the corner and rolled toward them.

"Get back over to the box hedge," Zane said. "We need to stay in the shadows out of sight. Jesse, you're okay, but, Mr. King, you need to put some mud on your face and hands."

An image flashed of Ran and his daughter making mud pies. It was a good memory, one he quickly tamped down.

"Sounds like fun," Ran drawled as they quietly dispersed.

A black Mercedes pulled into the lot and two men got out. Six of them now. The odds were getting worse. At least Zane was armed.

The men, one silver-haired in a perfectly tailored dark suit, the other younger, broad-shouldered, and powerfully built, clearly the muscle of the two, disappeared inside the room off the kitchen.

Zane was nowhere to be seen, but Ran knew he was close by. Ran and Jesse crouched in the shadows, waiting to see what would happen next. Ran hoped the police would arrive in time.

He wasn't sure what Zane was thinking. Good chance the former soldier was enjoying the action. Ran almost smiled.

The door opened and the silver-haired man walked out of the building. "Make sure she's secure, Evan, before you put her in the car." Clearly, he was the man in charge, the guy with the money.

"Don't worry, sir. I got her." The girl was still bound, only now she was gagged as well. Ran swore beneath his breath.

He glanced over at Jesse, who straightened, making him several inches taller, his chest expanding as he prepared to move. The moment the asylum door closed, leaving the other four men inside the building, Zane stepped out of the shadows.

A silent communication passed among all three of them. Zane pulled his weapon, a big dark semiautomatic, and Ran mentally readied himself. Moving together quietly, they let the silver-haired man, Evan, and the girl get as far as the parking lot.

"Hold it right where you are," Zane said, moving into position while aiming his gun at the younger man, the bigger threat. Ran and Jesse fanned out, taking up positions some distance apart in the parking lot. "Step away from the girl," Zane commanded. "And put your hands in the air."

The men stood frozen but made no move to comply.

"The police are on their way," Ran said. "Let the girl go and you can leave." They needed to get out of there. Four more men were inside the asylum, four more hostiles to deal with if the situation deteriorated.

Neither man moved to obey. "The little bitch cost me a fortune," the silver-haired man said in an upper-class British accent. "She leaves with me."

"Let her go, or I pull the trigger," Zane said calmly.

"I can tell you're Americans. Do yourselves a favor and stay out of this."

Zane centered the barrel of his gun in the middle of the older man's chest. "I said let her go."

"You heard him," Ran added. "This is your best option. The smart move would be to take it."

The silver-haired man looked at his lackey, who was holding on to the girl. Her head hung forward, the drugs still keeping her in line. "Do it. Let her go. A little virgin quim isn't worth all this trouble."

Evan shoved the girl so hard she sprawled on the pavement, scraping her knees, then her cheek as she fell forward. Zane cursed. Jesse hurried over to help her to her feet.

The girl swayed as she looked up at him. "*Blagodaryu vas,*" she said in what Ran thought sounded like Russian.

"*Pozhaluysta,*" Zane said, still holding the weapon. "You're welcome."

In the distance, police sirens blasted their singsong alert, growing louder as they drew near.

Zane still pointed his semiauto at the men. "This is going to get real sticky real soon," he said to Ran. "I say we let them go, take the girl, and leave."

Ran didn't want to. He wanted the bastards locked up in prison. But if the men inside figured out what was going on, the situation would escalate in a hurry, and someone could get killed. Add to that, the older man's clothes and attitude said he had plenty of money. Even if he were arrested, he could tie things up in court for months, maybe years. In the meantime, what would happen to the girl?

"You're lucky this time," Ran said to the older man. "You can leave. We have other business to attend."

The two men turned and raced toward the Mercedes. Jesse cut the zip ties binding the girl's wrists, lifted her into his arms, and they ran for the BMW.

Ran fired the engine. The last thing he noticed as he drove away was that the dim slice of yellow light was gone from the room off the kitchen. The kidnappers had left through the orphan asylum.

A dark thought entered his mind. Maybe the angry spirits would deal with them. Then again, Ran figured he probably wouldn't be that lucky.

CHAPTER TWENTY-TWO

At the sound of her cell phone ringing, Eve stirred groggily awake. She had only been sleeping fitfully, coming awake off and on. Too much on her mind, too much she didn't understand. Groping toward the bedside table for her phone, she glanced at the red numbers on the clock. Two a.m. Frowning, suddenly worried, she pressed the phone against her ear.

"Eve, it's Ran. We have a problem. We could use your help."

Her head began to clear. "Ran? What's going on?"

"We're on our way back to the hotel. I'll tell you all about it when we get there."

"The hotel? Where have you been?" Maybe she didn't want to know, she suddenly thought. Perhaps—

"Something happened at the asylum. We're bringing someone with us. A young woman. She needs a place to spend the night. We're hoping you'll be willing—"

"Of course. Whatever you need."

"We'll be there in just a few minutes. I'll explain when I get there." The line went dead, but Eve's mind was racing.

Something had happened at the orphanage. A young woman was involved. They were bringing her back to the hotel. *They*, Ran had said. Ran and who else?

Eve didn't have to wait long. Dressing hurriedly in soft brown yoga pants and an oversize sweater, she pulled a brush through her dark hair and streaked on some lipstick. A light knock sounded just as she finished.

Eve hurried across the living room and pulled open the door.

Shock rolled through her at the sight of Jesse standing in the hallway, a slender blond girl draped over his arms, her head lolling against his shoulder.

Ran moved first, holding the door as Jesse brushed past Eve and carried the girl into the suite, over to the sofa. As he settled her on the cushions, Eve ran into her bedroom and grabbed a pillow. Long, gleaming blond hair spread out as Eve placed the pillow under the girl's head.

Her eyelids fluttered open. In the lamplight, Eve could see two huge, dilated black orbs in a pair of bright blue eyes. The eyelids fluttered closed again.

"What's going on?" Eve asked, irritation beginning to surface as she did her best to understand what could possibly be happening.

"It's a long story," Ran said.

"Apparently we'll be spending the rest of the night together, so you'll have plenty of time to tell me."

Ran turned to Zane. "Why don't you give Eve a rundown."

Zane squared his shoulders. "Yes, sir."

"And by the way, after tonight, I think it's time you started calling me Ran, just like everyone else."

"Yes, sir."

Eve caught the hint of amusement in Ran's expression.

"Why don't we all sit down at the table," Eve suggested, and they headed in that direction. Zane started at the beginning, telling Eve how he had decided to go back to the asylum and stake out the room off the kitchen, hoping to discover any threat they might be facing. He described events after he arrived, the arrival of the four men and the girl, his text to Jesse, who had shown up with Ran. The story ended with the sale of the girl to two unidentified men.

"One of them was older," Ran said. "Clearly in charge. My guess, he's a guy with plenty of money, enough to purchase an innocent girl."

Eve glanced in the young woman's direction. She couldn't have been more than thirteen or fourteen, with the most delicate, perfect features Eve had ever seen. Though her face was pale, her lips were full, her nose pert, a small dent in her chin. She was slender, her legs coltishly long, young breasts just beginning to blossom.

A definite temptation, yet most men would consider her youth and, as Ran, Zane, and Jesse had, feel more protective than lustful.

"She'll need time to sleep off the drugs," Eve said. "I assume you're calling the police."

"That's part of the problem," Ran said. "On the way back to the hotel, she begged me not to bring in the authorities. I think she's here illegally."

Eve fell silent. *Dear God, could things get any worse?* "So what do you suggest we do?"

"From what Zane could understand, he thinks she's from Belarus. He speaks enough Russian to be able to communicate. Her name is Anastasia and apparently she lives with her mother. Tomorrow we'll find out where and take her home."

Eve felt a tug of sympathy. "Her mother must be frantic."

"I'm sure she is. The good news is, Anastasia will soon be safely home."

Relief trickled through her. At least the problem was only temporary.

Eve frowned. "What about the men who were sex trafficking her? We can't just let them get away with it. They'll do it again to some other young girl."

"That's part of the problem," Ran said. "If Anastasia is illegally in England and we call the police, they might deport her and her mother. I don't want that to happen."

Eve's chin came up. "You're Ransom King. You have all sorts of powerful connections. Surely there's something you can do to help them."

Ran flashed a smile. Upset as she was, Eve's stomach lifted. The man had the magnetism of a movie star.

"I'll start working on it in the morning," he said.

Eve sighed. "All right, then. Anastasia can stay here until tomorrow." She glanced up. "Zane, you'd better stay, too. You're the only one who can talk to her. If she wakes up, she's going to be frightened. You can tell her we're going to take her home."

"No problem," Zane said.

Ran leaned down and brushed a kiss over Eve's cheek. "Thanks for your help." He turned to Jesse. "I guess we'd better try to get some sleep." He flashed Eve a look that left no doubt he would rather be staying with her than sleeping alone. "I'll be right next door if you need me."

Eve could still feel the soft brush of his lips over her skin. A last long glance and Ran left the suite, with Jesse close behind him.

Eve busied herself getting a blanket out of the bedroom closet for the girl and a pillow for Zane, who planned to sleep in the chair next to Anastasia.

"I'll watch out for her," Zane promised. "Try to get some sleep."

Eve shook her head. "This whole thing just gets crazier and crazier."

"I know it seems that way." Zane smiled. "It's all in a day's work for me."

He was a really good-looking man, she realized. And kind, she thought.

"Good night, Eve."

"Good night, Zane." Eve crossed to her bedroom, part of her wishing she were safely back in her own home, the other part grateful to have Ran and his team working to straighten out this whole mess.

If that were actually possible.

At this point, Eve wasn't so sure.

The sun came out in the morning, brightening Eve's otherwise dreary mood. So much had happened. There was so much left unresolved. She glanced out the window. A calm ocean stretched to the horizon. Later in the day, it was supposed to rain, but for now sky and sea were a stunning azure blue.

As soon as she had showered and dressed, Eve went into the living room to check on her houseguests. With Zane acting as translator, Eve learned that Anastasia called herself Anya. Anya Petrova. Her mother's name was Sveta.

Mother and daughter lived in a neighborhood occupied by

other Belarusians in Newcastle upon Tyne, less than an hour's drive away. When Zane told Anya they were going to take her home, she started crying. She hugged him, then hugged Eve, holding on as if she would never let go.

Eve said a prayer of thanks that the men had been able to save her.

As a psychologist, Eve had dealt with trauma in girls Anya's age. Her current patient, Bethany Parsons, had been molested as a child. As bad as Anya's abduction had been, at least she hadn't been sexually assaulted. Zane, who had overheard part of her kidnappers' conversation, explained that along with her delicate features, blond hair, and blue eyes, part of Anya's value came from her virginity.

Healing wouldn't be easy, but the situation could have been far worse.

Jesse joined the three of them for a late room service breakfast. "The boss is on the phone with someone in his office," Jesse said. "Told me to order him some bacon and eggs."

Eve thought of the time difference. "What is it? Midnight back in Seattle?"

"More like two a.m. His staff is used to it."

Eve felt a thread of guilt. She was taking Ran away from his business, and he was doing it all for free.

While they waited for the meal to be delivered, Anya showered and dressed in a pair of Eve's yoga pants and a V-neck sweater, then sat patiently as Eve braided her still-damp blond hair.

Breakfast arrived just as Ran showed up. Anya hugged him and Jesse and cried again as she thanked the men for saving her life. As soon as the meal was over, Eve, Ran, Zane, and Anya headed down to the lobby, out to Ran's rented BMW for the trip to Newcastle upon Tyne.

With blue skies and the sun shining, the drive along A19 over the River Wear on the Hylton Bridge took them past green fields and old inns, castles, and other historic properties. Newcastle itself was a prospering city, with every sort of neighborhood, including the migrant district where Sveta and Anya lived.

A woman in her forties, Sveta was as blond as her daughter, though her once-beautiful face carried the fine lines of a life marked by smoking and stress. She was a little overweight and extremely wary, understandable since she was there illegally.

Through Zane, Eve learned that Sveta worked in a laundry not far from their apartment. She also took in sewing for extra money while her husband remained in Belarus. The joyous reunion between mother and daughter was heartfelt but didn't last long. Like all working mothers, Sveta had to get back to her job.

"Will Anya be safe?" Ran asked the woman through Zane.

Sveta explained that her daughter had been visiting a friend in Durham when she was abducted, the two girls merely walking along a country road when men in a van spotted them. Dasha, the other girl, managed to get away, but Anya had been forced into the back of the van. When Dash told Sveta her daughter had been abducted, she'd been terrified she would never see her again.

Time slipped past. Good-byes were said, hugs exchanged. It was midafternoon by the time the BMW wound its way back to the hotel. Eve felt warmed by the good they had done, a feeling she believed the others shared.

The feeling didn't last long. The difficulties Eve was facing resurfaced in her thoughts—the invasion of her home by unexplained forces, and what Ran and his team planned to do to solve the problem.

Arriving back at the hotel, Ran walked Eve up to her suite, then returned to his own. As soon as the Seattle office opened, he went to work. There were Zoom meetings with his staff, more meetings with VPs in different parts of the country. He was in the middle of a merger that would add a chain of more affordable hotels to the upscale King's Inn brand, and though the deal was progressing on schedule, there was still plenty of work to be done.

Though he had intended to be back in Seattle long before now, fate had intervened. Not only was there a fascinating mystery to solve, but Ran was also forced to deal with his unexpected feelings for Eve.

Every day he spent with her deepened the connection he felt. After watching her interact with Anya and her mother, witnessing her caring and concern, his respect had climbed another notch.

Along with his desire. His blood pounded whenever she was near. He needed Eve, and Ran believed Eve also needed him.

From the information he had gathered, the man Eve had married had been a grim failure as a husband. He had stripped away her confidence and left her feeling as if she were the one who had failed. Ran believed she needed the admiration and affection he could give her.

Planned to give her—now that he realized how mutually beneficial their relationship could be.

Though the situation continued to disrupt his life, Ran believed Eve needed his help in more ways than she realized. Unfortunately, first they had to deal with the not-so-small matter of the spirits occupying her home.

Ran phoned Eve late in the afternoon. Though they had been together all morning and part of the afternoon, they'd had no time alone. There were matters they needed to discuss, and the truth was, he simply wanted to be with her.

She knocked on his door a few minutes later and he opened it to find her dressed in a pair of beige slacks and a peach silk blouse, business attire. He wondered if she were trying to return their relationship to a less personal level.

And why she felt the need.

"I'm glad you called," Eve said. "I was hoping we could talk."

"Come on in." He stepped back out of the way as she brushed past him. The soft scent of her perfume drifted up and his body tightened. In the lamplight, her hair, clipped neatly up on the sides, gleamed like sable, and his arousal strengthened.

"I had room service send up some cold drinks and canapés," he said. "That fast-food restaurant we drove through on the way back from Newcastle didn't do much."

"I'm all right, but I could definitely use a soft drink."

He popped open a can of Cola Light, which seemed to be her

preference, added ice, and handed it over, then poured one for himself.

"Did you talk to the police?" Eve asked, the ice in her glass clinking as she took a drink.

"I called them this morning and spoke to the desk sergeant. I told him I was the one who had called in the disturbance at the old asylum last night."

"What explanation did you give for how you got the information?"

"I told him I was considering buying the place. The man in charge of my security believed something criminal might be going on and went over to check it out. I gave him the details of what Zane reported. Four men—perhaps members of a gang—were using the room off the kitchen for possible criminal activities. I didn't give him details, nothing that would involve an innocent young woman."

Until his current problems were solved, dealing with the wealthy man who'd bought Anya would have to wait. But Ran had a long memory. Though the license plate had been obscured, there were other ways of finding someone with that kind of money and those twisted sorts of sexual proclivities.

Ran took a drink of his cola. "Why don't we sit down?"

Eve seated herself on the sofa in front of the hors d'oeuvres tray, and Ran sat down beside her. Eve's gaze swung to his, her eyes more green than brown. Curiosity? Or suspicion? Ran wasn't quite sure.

"How are you holding up?" he asked. "Not only ghosts to deal with but men who kidnap innocent young women."

"I'm just glad Anya's safe."

He nodded. "With that problem out of the way"—*for the moment*—"we can focus on getting your life back to normal."

"That's what I wanted to talk to you about. I want to see what's inside the camelback trunk in the cellar."

Ran took a drink of soda and set the glass down on a coaster on the coffee table. "I made the arrangements this morning. The locksmith will meet us there whenever you're ready."

Eve shot up from the sofa. "How about right now?"

Amusement trickled through him. "I think we have time to finish our drinks. I'll text him, tell him to meet us at the house in an hour. That work for you?"

"All right." She sat back down beside him. He wondered if she felt the same simmering attraction he was feeling, the need to touch, to taste, to explore.

To reach out and grasp the pleasure they could bring each other.

Determined to put her at ease, Ran reached for a small plate and snagged a couple of canapés off the tray, hoping Eve would do the same. He'd noticed she hadn't eaten much of their fast-food lunch. As she placed several treats on a plate, he relaxed, knowing the snack would help keep up her strength.

"Are we going back to the asylum tonight?" Eve asked.

"That depends on you. I told the police we might be there for a while this evening and asked them to keep an eye on the place. I don't think we have to worry about any unexpected company. At least not of the human variety."

"That's something, I guess."

"I spoke to Violet and Katie before we left for Newcastle, explained a little of what happened last night, and told them I'd make a decision after I spoke to you. The thing is, I've heard from Lucas Devereaux. Luke will be arriving late tomorrow. If you'd prefer, we can hold off until he gets here."

Eve sipped her drink. "I want to look in the trunk. I should have done it sooner. I have this feeling . . . I don't know. I think what's in there could be important."

Ran set his drink down on the coffee table and rose from the sofa. "All right, then, let's go find out."

CHAPTER TWENTY-THREE

*T*HE LOCKSMITH, A SMALL MAN WITH A MOP OF GRAY HAIR BENEATH a faded red bill cap, arrived at the house a few minutes after Eve and Ran. Bill Moffett was his name.

"Whot ye be needin'?" Mr. Moffett asked as Eve led him into the entry.

"There's a trunk," she said. "It's quite lovely, but the lock is old and rusty and extremely stubborn. We're hoping you can get the chest open without destroying it."

"I'll do me best," the old man said. Carrying his toolbox, he followed Eve down the hall, then descended the stairs behind her. Eve flipped on the newly installed fluorescent lights as Ran reached the bottom of the stairs.

Eve's gaze went to the once-again boarded-up tunnel. A shiver went through her as she thought of the skeleton they had found. It made sense now. There was criminal activity going on in the asylum. Most likely, the man's murder was related.

She turned to Mr. Moffett. "The trunk is right over here." She led him to the humpback trunk with the molded metal inserts, and the old man dropped to his knees beside it. Setting down his toolbox, he flipped up the lid and went to work.

It took longer than Eve expected. The man was meticulous, and he seemed to respect the beauty and age of the chest. The longer it took, the more nervous Eve became.

"You all right?" Ran asked, his uncanny ability to read her emotions both irritating and comforting.

"I'm fine. It's beyond time we found out what's inside. As I said, I should have done it sooner."

"Violet would say things happen when they're supposed to. Perhaps knowing what's in the trunk would have changed what happened last night. If that had been the case, Anya might not be back home with her mother."

A terrible notion. "Perhaps you're right."

The lock grated, clattered, and clanked, finally fell open, and Mr. Moffett gently removed it. He rose and handed the lock to Eve. It felt cold in her hand, almost icy. She set the lock on the square oak trunk a few feet away, glad to be rid of it.

"All finished," Mr. Moffett said, wiping his hands on a rag, tossing it into his toolbox, and closing the lid.

"I'll walk you out and settle your bill," Ran said, and the two men headed toward the stairs.

Eve stood motionless, the sight of the old trunk filling her with dread. Another emotion intruded, a great sweep of sadness so strong it brought tears to her eyes. She swallowed. What was it about the trunk that stirred such intense emotions?

She knelt on the cellar floor and slowly lifted the lid, saw an interior lined with a beige fabric printed with teal and gold peacocks. It was faded and ripped in places, but she could easily imagine how beautiful the interior of the trunk had been when it was new.

Definitely the property of a lady.

She lifted out the upper tray, which was filled with tarnished silver buttons, hairpins, colored thread, and needles, and set it on the floor beside her. Dresses from the same period as those in the square oak trunk were the first things that caught her eye.

Eve lifted out a once-lovely peach silk day dress with rows of tucks across the bodice. The lace near the hem was slightly tattered, but the gown was still in amazingly good condition. Beneath it, a pearl-gray shantung tea dress with an apron-draped front was faded but still somehow elegant.

She carefully refolded the dresses and set them aside, looked back down into the chest. Moving an ecru muslin nightgown out of the way, she spotted a worn black velvet box not much larger than her hand. Inside, a small glass vial rested on a white satin cushion. Eve removed the bottle.

"What is it?" Ran's voice startled her. She had forgotten all about him.

Eve studied the glass vial, pulled out the tiny cork stopper, and took a sniff. "I'm not sure. I think it could be laudanum." An opiate, a painkiller, and very addictive.

"A lot of Victorian ladies used it medicinally," Ran said.

"Yes . . ." But as she held the bottle, a dark feeling rose inside her. A headache began to form behind her eyes and her stomach rolled.

"Let me have the bottle, Eve."

She looked up at Ran, saw the worry on his face. Her hand shook as she passed him the vial.

"Your face has gone pale, love. Why don't we take a break?"

"No!" Eve shook her head. "I need to know what's . . . what's in the trunk. There's something . . . I need to see what it is."

Lifting the nightgown out of the way, she set it on the floor next to the gown and spotted an old daguerreotype, the photo of a woman in a tarnished silver frame. She was midtwenties, dark haired, and beautiful.

Eve ran a finger over the picture. "I think it's Priscilla Warrington."

Ran stared down at the photo. "Looks about the right age."

Eve set the photo aside. As she removed a layer of tissue, a flash of blue caught her eye. Her breath hitched. Her heart began to throb as she recognized the clothes of a child, a little boy's knee-length trousers and matching jacket, tattered and frayed, but unmistakable. Eve started to tremble. She knew exactly who the garments belonged to, remembered seeing them all those years ago.

Her hands shook as she lifted Wally's little blue sailor suit out of the chest, and a deep burning pain unlike any she had ever felt before filled her heart.

She thought again of the silver-framed daguerreotype, and with a flash of certainty, understood.

"Dear God, Ran, Priscilla Warrington was Wally's mother." Eve could feel the young woman's love for her son. Feel her inconsolable despair when she lost him. The pain in her heart deepened. She had always wanted children. Now she knew the pain a mother felt when she lost a child.

A sob caught in her throat, then escaped as she started to weep. She barely noticed when Ran pulled her up and into his arms.

"It's all right, honey. I'm right here. I won't let you go."

Eve burrowed into him, clung to him, wept great tears into the collar of his oxford shirt.

"Easy . . ." Ran said, running a big hand up and down her back. "It's over now. It's all in the past."

"She couldn't . . . couldn't stand the pain," Eve said. "That's why she took the laudanum. After her little boy died, she didn't want to live."

"Wally?"

Eve nodded against his shoulder. "Zane said there were no children, but—"

"No natural children. Wally lived in the orphanage. He must have been her adopted son."

Eve swallowed against the ache in her throat. "I can feel her emotions, Ran. I don't know how, but I can."

"It's a gift, sweetheart. You may not want it, but it's there just the same."

Eve said nothing, her throat too tight to speak.

Ran glanced past her, into the trunk. "There's something else in there."

Eve turned, dreading what else she might find. Ran reached into the bottom of the trunk and took out a document folder of thin red leather. He opened it, held it so she could see a neatly displayed gilt-rimmed sheet of parchment with a very official red wax seal.

"We were right," Ran said, holding the folder so she could read the words. "Certificate of Adoption." Ran's gaze skimmed down the page. "Walter Augustus Reed, born May 14, 1877, son of Darius Reed, bosun's mate aboard the ship *Pegasus,* died when the ship went down with all hands, October 22, 1879. Mother deceased. Adopted this day, July 15, 1881, by Edward and Priscilla Warrington."

Fresh tears burned Eve's eyes.

"The orphanage was established to take care of the children the sailors left behind," Ran said. "According to the dates, Wally was only two when he went into the orphanage."

Eve dashed a tear from her cheek. "That would make him four when the Warrington's adopted him."

"That's right." Ran looked back down at the document. "It's signed by a man named Jonathan Murray, Director, House of Mercy Orphan Asylum."

Through the haze of tears and painful emotions, Eve's mind finally began to clear. She looked up. "That's it, Ran. That's the connection between the house and the orphanage. Wally lived in both places."

Ran nodded. "For whatever reason, after his death, Wally's spirit remained earthbound. His ghost travels between the house and the asylum. As a child, you were open to his visits and that's why you saw him."

Eve sniffed back the last of her tears. "The boy I knew was only five or six."

"He was born in 1877. He must have died in 1882 or 1883. We need to know what happened to him."

Eve went back down on her knees, dug through the last remnants in the box. The ladies' black silk gown and black jet jewelry were unmistakable. Priscilla Warrington had been in mourning for her son.

"We know who he was, but we still don't know what happened to him." Eve's heart hurt as she rose to her feet and Ran eased her back into his arms.

"We'll find out," he promised. "We'll figure it out and we'll free him to join his mother again."

CHAPTER TWENTY-FOUR

*I*T WAS GETTING LATE. AFTER THE EMOTIONAL AFTERNOON EVE HAD experienced, Ran decided it was best to postpone any efforts to contact the spirits in the house or asylum. Luke Deveraux would be arriving tomorrow afternoon. Having him there would give them all a fresh take on what might be going on.

Back at the hotel, Ran spoke to the rest of the team and gave them the evening off. Then he and Eve went downstairs to the hotel dining room for supper.

Ran was only a little surprised when Detective Inspector Daniel Balfour walked into the restaurant in search of them.

"Ah, there you are. The front desk said I could find you in here." The dark-haired detective was wearing what appeared to be his usual attire, a brown tweed sport coat and slacks. His gaze went to Eve, swept over the pretty white silk blouse she was wearing, lingered a moment on the hint of cleavage the blouse exposed, and irritated the hell out of Ran.

"What can we do for you, Detective?" He didn't invite the man to take a seat, a slight that didn't seem to bother Balfour, who pulled out a chair and sat down to join them.

"I wanted to talk to you about the trouble last night at the old asylum," Balfour said.

"As I told your sergeant, when we went inside to inspect the property, we noticed someone had been using the room off the kitchen for what we believed might be criminal activity. Zane Tanner, the man in charge of my security, went over last night to see if he could figure out what was going on."

"And?"

Ran considered how much more to say. "Tanner saw four men take a young woman into the room by force. She was bound and gagged. Tanner's former military. He managed to get the girl away from them. No one was hurt."

"What happened to the young woman?"

"She disappeared while Zane was dealing with the men."

"Can Tanner give me a description of the assailants? License plate numbers? Anything that might help us look into the matter?"

"You can ask him." But Zane would say as little as possible.

Balfour eyed Ran shrewdly. "So you know all about it, but you weren't involved."

"As I said, Zane's my employee. In that sense, I was involved."

Balfour's gaze went briefly to Eve, moved over her with appreciation before returning to Ran. "One last question. Any guess what the men intended to do with the young woman? Was this a gang rape situation or something else?"

Ran wanted the criminals who'd taken Anya dealt with. He just didn't want to involve the girl or her mother.

"Zane mentioned overhearing some of their conversation. From what he could tell, they planned to sell her, perhaps to someone who'd made contact with them over the Internet. Of course, that's mostly speculation."

Balfour's mouth thinned. "Of course." Clearly, he realized there was more to the story than Ran was telling him.

The detective rose from his chair and pushed it back under the table. "Enjoy the rest of your meal." He turned to Eve and a smile softened his features. "Good night, Dr. St. Clair."

Eve returned the smile. "Good night, Detective."

Ran tamped down another surge of jealousy. Balfour was smart and damned good-looking, and he was more than a little interested in Eve. Would she return that interest after Ran was gone? The notion did not sit well.

"I hope the police find the men who took Anya," Eve said.

"So do I." He didn't say that earlier that morning, he had begun making phone calls to people who could help him find the silver-haired man in the black Mercedes who had bought the girl.

Eve already had enough to worry about.

As the meal of fresh seafood progressed, accompanied by a nice bottle of Latour Puligny-Montrachet, Eve began to relax. Unfortunately for Ran, every time she smiled at him or laughed at something he said, desire shot straight to his groin.

He was a man used to getting what he wanted. The heated glances that passed between them said it was what Eve wanted, too. But after such an emotional day, her defenses were down and she was vulnerable. He didn't want to take advantage.

"You ready to go upstairs?" he asked as he signed the dinner check and the waiter cleared the table. "Or would you rather go to the bar and have an after-dinner drink?"

Her long-lashed eyes found his, her gaze direct and unmistakable. "I'd rather go up to my room."

Ran's body tightened. "All right."

The elevator let them off and he walked her down the corridor to her suite. Eve used her key card to unlock the door. Ran told himself he should just say good night, let her go in and get some rest.

But when he bent his head for a brief, end-of-evening kiss, Eve's arms slid around his neck and she pulled his mouth down to hers for a very thorough tasting.

Ran groaned. The heat that burned in his blood scorched through every good intention he'd had. He took the kiss deeper, hotter, wetter, claiming her mouth as he hungered to claim her body.

As he backed her through the door and closed it behind him, his hands slid down to cup her bottom, and he pulled her into the vee between his legs. There was no stopping the freight train of desire that felt unlike anything he had ever known.

Eve moaned as he wedged his knee between her legs and lifted her a little, nudging her slim skirt up as he pressed her shoulders against the wall and his mouth against the side of her neck. Ran knew all too well how short life could be. Tonight he intended to take what he wanted. What Eve wanted.

His fingers fumbled with the buttons on the front of her white silk blouse as he parted the fabric to reveal the sweet swell of her breasts in a lacy white bra.

When Eve's head fell back, encouraging him to take more, his uncertainty disappeared and his control returned. Though he had no right, tonight she was his. He would take her, pleasure them both, and face the consequences tomorrow.

"I need you," he said, nipping the side of her neck. He used his tongue to soothe the tiny bite marks and trailed kisses down to her shoulder. "I want you here. Now. Say you want that, too."

"Yes . . ." Eve said. "Right here. Right now."

A growl came from his throat. Ran slid Eve's slim skirt up around her waist and allowed his hands to roam over her thighs, her bottom, cupping the firm globes, sliding down her white lace panties. Eve stepped out of them, and he found her feminine heat.

Eve moaned as he kissed her again and his arousal strengthened. She was wet and ready, her soft pleas urging him on.

Ran unzipped his fly and freed himself, wrapped her long legs around his waist. She was open to him, making little pleading sounds as he slid himself inside. Sensation washed through him, sweet and erotic. Need bore down on him with such urgency he nearly lost control.

The sex was hot and consuming, a fierce ride from arousal to burning pleasure. Careful of his cuts and scratches, Eve clung to his neck while Ran took her, desperately and without restraint, pounding into her, bringing her to a shattering climax.

It wasn't enough.

Driving her up again, Ran sent her over the edge once more before joining her in a fierce release.

For several seconds he just stood there, his forehead tipped against hers, Eve's shapely legs wrapped around his waist, his body still flushed with heat.

It was too much.

It wasn't nearly enough.

"I'm sorry," he heard himself say as he let her go and she slid down along his body. He fastened the button on his waistband and closed the zipper. "You deserved better than that."

Eve just smiled. "You can make it up to me next time."

Ran's gaze locked with hers. There was no regret, just the remnants of a still-burning fire he could easily rekindle.

Lifting her into his arms, Ran carried her into the bedroom. *Tomorrow,* he told himself. *Tomorrow he would figure all of this out.*

Tonight there was only Eve.

Eve awoke later than usual the following morning. The moment her eyes cracked open, she remembered the night she had shared with Ran. Her hand shot to the other side of the bed, but Ran was already gone. A rush of disappointment filled her, though she wasn't surprised. While she was dealing with her own set of demons, Ran was dealing with his.

She pulled on her bathrobe and walked into the living room, jolted to a halt when she saw him sitting on the sofa, his cell phone pressed against his ear.

The smile he gave her was sweet and endearing, completely unexpected. He motioned toward the linen-draped table laden with an array of juices, croissants, and cinnamon rolls, a selection of cheeses and fruits. A silver pot of coffee sat next to a porcelain cup and saucer.

Trying not to read too much into his thoughtfulness, Eve poured coffee into the cup and added a dash of cream. She cast Ran a glance. Since he appeared to be involved in a business call, she headed for the shower.

Dressed in a pair of black slacks and a pink blouse over a white silk tank top, her hair swept up in a loose bun on top of her head, she returned to the living room just as Ran ended his call.

He rose from the sofa, his eyes running over her possessively. "Sleep all right?" She couldn't miss the trace of male smugness in his voice.

Her lips twitched. "Very well, thank you." Limp and thoroughly sated, she had slept the sleep of the innocent, which after last night she most certainly was not.

Her face heated. The man was insatiable.

"What's our schedule for today?" She started filling a plate, then freshened her coffee.

"Lucas Deveraux will be arriving this afternoon. With your approval, I'm planning to take the team back to your house tonight. I'd like you to reach out to Wally. If you make contact, I want Luke to be there. I'd like his opinion on what's going on and the best way to handle it."

"What about the orphanage? We have to help the other children."

"We won't abandon them, I promise you. But we need to take things one step at a time. I've got Zane digging into the past again. He's searching Warrington family genealogy, hoping to come up with something that mentions Wally and the cause of his death."

"I think whatever it was happened to all of them."

Ran frowned. "A single event? You think the other children died at the same time?"

Now that she had said it, the thought felt right. "It's possible."

"Like a plague, maybe? A measles or flu epidemic, something like that?"

"I don't know. I just . . . I feel like whatever it was, their death formed a bond between them. That's why the others are still here."

"I'll speak to Zane. Maybe he can find the old asylum birth and death records. That could give us some answers."

"That's a great idea," Eve said. She felt Ran's presence as he walked up behind her, bent and kissed the nape of her neck.

"About last night . . ."

Eve laughed as she turned to face him. "If there was ever a cliché, that's it. If you regret it, that's up to you. For me, last night was wonderful. A memory I'll cherish. I don't expect any sort of commitment."

His beautiful blue eyes looked stormy. "Damn it, Eve, I don't regret it. I want you again right now." He leaned down and softly kissed her. "No matter what happens, this feeling between us . . . it's not like anything I've ever felt before."

But all Eve heard was *no matter what happens*.

After this was over, Ran would go his way and she would go hers. Their parting was inevitable. Deep down, she had already accepted it. It didn't make her feel any better.

She released a slow breath and checked her watch. "I've got to get to my office. I have an appointment with Donny Beck this morning."

"I figured you'd be ready to get back to work. I'll drive you over."

"That isn't necessary. I'm sure you have work of your own to do, and your friend Lucas will be arriving. There are bound to be things you need to discuss."

His black brows pulled together. "Are you sure?"

"I've never had any problems in my office. It's outside the house, attached to the garage and built at a much later date. No connection to ghosts of the past. I'll grab a taxi, meet with Donny, and be back this afternoon."

"You don't need a taxi. I'll send for the Bentley. Willard can drive you home. You can call him when you're ready to come back to the hotel."

She nodded. She wasn't prepared to stay in the house. Not yet. She didn't want to think about what might happen when they went over there tonight.

Eve sighed. At the moment, she had real-life problems to contend with. Donny Beck was first on her list.

CHAPTER TWENTY-FIVE

THE BENTLEY DROPPED EVE OFF AND SHE WENT STRAIGHT TO HER office. She wanted to review Donny's file before their meeting.

As she stepped inside, the office felt musty and cold. She opened a window to let in fresh air, then closed it a few minutes later and turned up the thermostat. She needed to get to work, needed to set up an appointment with Bethany and Mrs. Michaels, if the older woman was back from her visit with her son, and work on her website to attract a few more patients.

She didn't want too many. She would rather focus on a small number and be able to spend more time with each one. Money had never been a priority. She needed only enough to pay her bills and live comfortably.

A concept her ex-husband would never understand. Phillip had been all about building his financial portfolio. That, and his reputation as one of the country's top psychiatrists, meant everything. A wife was merely an accessory, a necessary part of the equation.

Unfortunately, he also believed it was his right and duty to service every desirable female he chanced to meet.

Eve hadn't sensed that need in Ran. He was as virile as any man she had ever met, and yet his entire attention seemed focused on her.

At least for the time being. From personal experience, Eve knew how fast that could change.

Ransom King was one of the smartest, most attractive men she had ever met. He was wealthy, but considerate of the people around him, and a skillful and generous lover. A man like that could have his pick of women.

Eve told herself it didn't matter. They would soon be heading in different directions, returning to the lives they'd lived before. She was prepared, she told herself, yet her heart squeezed at the thought.

A solid knock announced Donny's arrival. Eve closed his file and came out from behind her desk to open the door. Donny sauntered toward her in his usual cocky manner, blond hair a little too long and slightly mussed, his thumbs hooked in the front pockets of his jeans.

Eve smiled. "Hello, Donny, how are you doing today?"

Donny shrugged. "Fine, I guess."

"Why don't you sit down?" Eve returned to the chair behind her desk, while Donny sprawled on the padded leather lounge where patients could sit or lie down.

"So what's been happening since the last time I saw you?"

Donny scratched beneath his chin where a skimpy blond beard was trying to take root. "Me mum's been raggin' me. Says she's frustrated seein' me hanging round the house all the time. Keeps talking about me takin' that job at Iceland Foods."

"That's not a bad idea. It would give you something positive to do."

"I'm thinkin' about it."

"That's great." And a big step for Donny.

"I'm going in to talk to the manager first of next week."

Eve smiled. *Progress,* she thought. It was subtle, but she could hear it in Donny's voice. "What else is going on?"

"I been seein' that girl, Amber, I told you about."

The former addict. It was risky, but there was always a chance it could work. Perhaps that was the reason for the change.

"How's the relationship going so far?" she asked.

Donny smiled, his surliness evaporating as if it had never been there. It lit up his sky-blue eyes. "I quite like her, you know? Real easy to talk to, not like me mum."

Eve listened to Donny tout Amber's virtues and thought that maybe the girl was good for him. "You could bring her to a session sometime," she suggested. "I'd like to meet her."

"Maybe," Donny said with a casual lift of his shoulders. Eve thought the gesture wasn't really casual at all. Donny liked this girl very much. He needed a positive influence in his life and Amber might be it.

The hour slid by faster than usual. It was a joy when a patient began to move ahead. She hoped that was happening with Donny.

It was almost time for him to leave when Eve heard an odd sort of humming. She turned, trying to locate the source, and the noise increased. The sound seemed to vibrate through her body, and a strange tension settled at the base of her neck. A sudden thickness filled the air and the vibrations increased.

Fear gripped her.

Eve looked over at Donny, whose eyes were huge, his face eerily pale. Panic shot through her. Blood pounded in her ears and thundered in her temples. Her head throbbed as Donny rose slowly rose to his feet.

His gaze fixed on a spot on the wall. "What . . . what is that?"

Eve's legs trembled as she rose behind her desk, her gaze following Donny's to the dark shadow beginning to form in the corner, taking the hazy shape of a man. The figure slid toward Donny, who stood frozen, his eyes wide and staring, slowly glazing over as if he were in a trance.

Eve rushed around her desk. "Get out of the office, Donny! Hurry!"

But Donny just stood there, staring at the shadowy form that continued to grow and slide like a spreading grease stain toward him. The two figures merged into one and the shadow disappeared. The next thing Eve knew, Donny was leaping toward her, his hands reaching out, fingers curled into claws.

Eve screamed as he grabbed her, shoved her backward onto her desk, and his hands fastened around her throat.

"Don-ny . . ." The word came out as a croak, her fingers digging into his, trying to tear them away so she could breathe. She sucked in air, fighting to get enough into her lungs. "Let . . . me . . . go, Don-ny . . ."

But he seemed unable to hear her. His eyes had turned a shade of blue so dark they looked black.

"Donny . . ." She clawed at the hands around her throat, but they felt like steel bands, growing tighter and tighter. "Donny . . . please . . ."

She barely heard the squeak of the door swinging open. Then Ran was yanking Donny off her, whirling him around and slamming him into the wall next to her desk. His muscular arm went back to deliver a powerful blow.

"Don't hurt him!" Eve screamed, latching on to his biceps, holding on as hard as she could. "It isn't him—it's the ghost! It's not his fault!"

Ran pulled his punch at the last moment, his body shaking with the effort to bring himself under control. He released his grip on the front of Donny's plaid shirt and the young man slid down the wall to the floor.

Ran strode toward her, pulled her into his arms, and held her trembling body tightly against him. "What the hell's going on?"

Eve was shaking, grateful for Ran's solid presence when the whole world seemed to have gone mad. She swallowed past the tightness in her throat. "Something . . . something came into the room. Whatever it was, it . . . it went after Donny." Eve broke away and hurried over to her patient. "What happened wasn't his fault."

Eve crouched down beside him, checked Donny's pulse and his breathing. As Ran crouched next to her, Donny groaned and his eyelids fluttered.

"Looks like he's going to be all right," Ran said. "Let's get him out of this room."

Eve just nodded, desperate to escape whatever might still be lurking in the office. Ran hoisted Donny's limp figure over his shoulder and carried him out to the small garden behind the house, set him down in one of the white mesh lawn chairs around the garden table.

Donny groaned as he roused himself, blinked, and opened his eyes. He looked from Ran to Eve. "What happened?"

Dear God, what could she say? "You don't remember?"

Donny shook his head. "I guess I passed out."

Ran answered the question for her. "Looks like the room got too hot and you became overheated. I think you're okay now."

"Who are *you?*"

"I'm Dr. St. Clair's friend, Ransom King."

Eve looked at Donny, felt a twinge of guilt at the bruise forming on his cheek where Ran had crashed him into the wall. Her attention swung to Ran. "Do you think we should take him to the hospital?"

"Hospital?" Donny repeated, still half dazed. He sat up straighter in the chair. "Hell no. I don't need no bleedin' 'ospital."

"How are you feeling?" Eve asked.

Donny rubbed a hand over his face. "Kind of foggy, but I'm okay. You should get something done about that heating problem in your office."

"Yes . . . yes, I will." Eve turned back to Ran, who was watching Donny closely.

"How did you get to your appointment today?" he asked the boy.

"I walked," Donny said.

"How would you like to ride home in a Bentley limo?"

Donny's eyes widened. His focus had returned, for which Eve was grateful. And the color was back in his cheeks.

"You serious?"

Ran nodded. "It's waiting right out front."

Donny grinned. "Wicked! Thanks, Mr. King." Donny turned to Eve. "See ya next week, Dr. St. Clair."

Eve managed a half-hearted smile. "Think about that job, Donny."

Donny made no reply, his mind already on his upcoming ride in the Bentley. Ran slid an arm around Eve's waist, urging her to join them as he walked Donny to the vehicle out front.

She watched the young man settle inside the limo. Ran gave instructions to the driver and the car rolled away.

Eve thought of Donny and the way he had attacked her, thought how much worse it could have been. A shudder ran through her as Ran's long strides carried him back to her.

"Thank God you showed up when you did," she said. "But why did you come?"

"The more I thought about you being so close to the house by yourself, the more I didn't like it."

Eve shook her head. "Nothing's ever happened in my office before."

"Since the day we arrived, everything's changed. Evil doesn't like that. Whatever we're dealing with, it's determined to stop us. We aren't going to let that happen."

After the limo had given Donny a brief ride around the neighborhood and dropped him off at his house, Willard returned to drive Ran and Eve back to the hotel.

Lucas Deveraux would be there by now, checked in and probably sleeping. Ran was eager to talk to him, even more so after the attack in Eve's office. As he sat in the deep red leather seat of the Bentley, Eve's voice pulled him out of his thoughts.

"What happened to Donny . . . have you ever seen anything like that before?"

Ran shook his head. "No, but Lucas has. I saw him cleanse a house where a murderer once lived, the spirit of a man who was preying on the female owner. I'll give him a few hours to adjust to the time change. He probably slept on the plane, but the difference is still tough to handle."

"So you think Donny was . . . possessed?"

"It's the only answer I can come up with. I've read about a person being possessed, but I've never actually been there when it occurred."

"Until today."

"Maybe. Or maybe Donny had some other problem."

Eve shook her head. "I was there, Ran. You should have seen it. This dark shadow formed in the corner. It shaped itself into something that vaguely resembled a man, then moved across the room toward Donny. I tried to get Donny to run, but there wasn't enough time. The shadow merged with Donny; then Donny went crazy and attacked me."

"Attacked and tried to kill you."

When she trembled, Ran eased her closer to him in the back seat and settled an arm around her shoulders. "From now on, you don't go near that house alone."

"I can't stay in the hotel forever."

"You won't have to. We're going to figure this out—we won't stop until we do. But it's going to take all of us working together. I can't tell you how relieved I am that Lucas is here."

"I look forward to meeting him."

"We'll fill him in on everything before we go back to the house tonight." Ran didn't miss the tremor that passed through Eve's body. She was worried. So was he. Anything could happen, and both of them knew it. So far no one had been seriously injured—or killed—but after today, he knew it was possible.

It wasn't a comforting thought.

CHAPTER TWENTY-SIX

Zane waved down one of the taxis parked in front of the hotel. He was on his way back to the General Registrar's Office to look for any records pertaining to the asylum he might have missed, in particular, orphanage death records.

Catching his wave, the driver cranked the engine of a white sedan with red markings that read STATION TAXIS and included a phone number. The vehicle rolled away from the curb and pulled up in front of the hotel.

Just as Zane opened the door, he saw Kate walking toward him. She was wearing a short white skirt and a lightweight yellow sweater that displayed the perfect amount of cleavage. To say Kate Collins was a blond bombshell would be understating the obvious.

She smiled as she walked up to him. "Want some company? I hear you're doing more research on the asylum. I thought it might go faster with both of us working on it."

"I wouldn't turn down the help." Though up until now he had done his best not to spend time with her. Zane liked his job, and he made it a rule not to get involved with people he worked with. Still, she was a valuable member of the team.

She smiled. "Okay, great. Let's go." As she stepped past him and slid neatly into the back seat, strands of long blond hair slid against his cheek. Damn, an attraction to Kate was the last thing he wanted.

The taxi pulled away as Zane settled himself in the seat beside her. "You didn't have anything more exciting to do than examine musty old records?"

"I've done all the sightseeing I can stand, and I feel sorry for Eve. I can see how difficult this is for her. I want to help any way I can."

Zane understood the sentiment. He had missed a lot of the ghostly happenings in the house and asylum—assuming what the video and audio equipment showed was true—but the stress level for the team members was palpable.

And Eve was carrying the brunt of it.

The taxi wove its way through the streets, then made a sharp turn. Katie leaned forward at the change in direction. "Where are we going?"

"Register office is in Tyne and Wear. It's about twenty miles away. Take us half an hour or so to get there. Jesse borrowed the Beamer to run some errands, which was fine by me since I'm not that comfortable driving on the left-hand side of the road."

"So what's in Tyne and Wear?"

"In 1974, the historical records for Sunderland were transferred there from Durham. We're looking for information on deaths that occurred in the orphanage, particularly in the 1880s."

"Got it." She relaxed back in the seat. "Jesse says you're from Arizona."

"Northern Arizona. My family owns a ranch in a place called Skull Valley."

Her dark blond eyebrows arched up. "Seriously?"

He chuckled. "Seriously. I never gave it much thought, but considering the job I'm working now, I guess it is kind of an odd coincidence."

"I'd say. How long since you were a cowboy?"

"Not for a long time. I went into the army after college, ended up in Special Forces. I pretty much left ranching behind. Now that I'm out of the service, I go back every Christmas. That's about it."

"I'm from L.A.," Kate said. "I moved to Seattle for a job after I got out of Cal State. Then Ran King offered me more money and a job I couldn't resist, so here I am. That's about all there is to my story."

Zane doubted it. A woman as gorgeous as Kate had to have plenty of stories to tell.

The ride was surprisingly companionable. Neither of them felt they had to speak. Enjoying the scenery was enough. The taxi pulled up in front of an old, historical brick building that had been added onto. Zane got out and so did Kate.

"I hope we find something," she said.

"So do I." *And soon.* The less time he spent with her, the better off he'd be. He'd been attracted to Kate Collins from the moment he'd met her. He had no idea what Kate thought of him, and he didn't want to find out.

He just wanted to do his job and get back to Seattle before his willpower ran out.

Eve was back in her suite at the hotel. Ran had insisted she nap for a while, and though it had crossed her mind to ask him to join her—and the look in his eyes said he was hoping she would—she had decided against it.

They would be returning to the house this evening. An afternoon in bed with Ran would leave her deliciously satisfied but drained of the energy she needed to face what might be waiting for them tonight.

Determined to be practical, she slept instead and dreamed of him, woke up in the middle of an erotic fantasy that left her body flushed and unfulfilled—and Eve was sorry she hadn't asked him to stay.

She checked the time, saw it was nearly five p.m., and went in to shower and dress for what could be a very long, disturbing evening.

She was tying the laces on her sneakers when her cell phone rang. At the sight of Ran's name on the caller ID, her stomach contracted. Lord, she had it bad, and it seemed that wasn't going to change.

"Lucas Devereaux is here," Ran said. "I'd like you to meet him. Can you come over?"

"I just finished dressing. I'll be right there." She checked her makeup, no longer deluding herself that she hadn't made a special effort for Ran, fluffed her dark hair, which she'd left loose around her shoulders, grabbed her purse, and headed out into the hallway.

A few steps down the corridor, she knocked on Ran's door and he immediately pulled it open. She could feel those hot blue eyes assessing her and a curl of heat slipped through her as she walked past him into the entry.

Another pair of eyes, these a warm brown rimmed with gold, moved over her as she made her way into the living room. The man's dark gaze was less intense than Ran's, but somehow equally compelling.

Ran led her farther into the room. "Dr. Eve St. Clair, this is my good friend Lucas Devereaux."

"Mr. Devereaux." She extended a hand he captured between both of his. He was well over six feet, extremely handsome with his dark brown hair, solid jaw, and the faint cleft in his chin. And younger than she had expected, about Ran's age, no more than midthirties.

"It's Luke or Lucas," he said, smiling. "It's a pleasure to meet you, Eve."

Ran settled a proprietary hand at her waist that caught Lucas's attention. Whatever he was thinking, he didn't seem surprised by the gesture. Maybe Ran was that way with all of the women he dated. The thought made her sad.

"Would you like something to drink?" Ran asked her. "Cola Light?"

"Yes, please."

"Why don't we sit down?" Lucas suggested as Ran fetched the soft drink. Eve settled on the sofa, Lucas in one of the matching chairs. "Ran has filled me in on much of what's been going on. He told me what happened in your office this morning."

Unconsciously, she reached up to the base of her throat. There were bruises where Donny's fingers had dug into her neck. It was slightly painful to swallow.

"It was terrifying, if you want the truth."

"I'm sure it was. I understand all of this is new to you."

She managed to nod. "Yes. I have no idea why the spirits—or whatever they are—have chosen to communicate with me, but that seems to be what's going on."

Ran walked up and handed her the glass of cola, then sat down beside her on the sofa.

"What happened in your office is extremely unusual," Lucas said. "Ghosts are basically placid entities, most of them behave like a recording that plays the same image over and over."

"You mean like walking up and down a staircase," she said. "Or floating through a garden. That sort of thing." The usual way people described ghostly encounters.

"That's right. The kind of violent behavior you witnessed doesn't happen often. Of course, there are a number of well-documented cases, but as I said, it's not common."

"According to Ran, this isn't new to you."

Lucas nodded. "Demon possession has been happening for thousands of years."

A chill washed over her. Eve glanced toward the window, but it was solidly closed. "A demon? That's . . . that's what you think it was?"

"What do you think it was? From your own description, the body of a young man you've been treating for weeks was invaded by a shadowy figure who then tried to kill you. Is that about right?"

She swallowed. She couldn't deny it. "Yes . . ." The word came out as a whisper. She felt Ran's hand reach for hers, lacing their fingers together.

"Zane is digging for more information," Ran said. "This should be a lot easier once we have all the facts. Or at least as many as we can come up with."

Her gaze returned to the former priest. "Ran told you about Wally and the other boys in the orphanage?"

"He mentioned it. I know about Wally, your imaginary childhood friend. We haven't had a lot of time to discuss the rest, not after what took place in your office this morning. That matter took precedence."

Ran sat forward. "Eve thinks whatever caused Wally's death happened to other children in the orphanage at the same time, or that their deaths were somehow linked."

One of Lucas's dark eyebrows winged up.

"That's the feeling I get," Eve said. "That something terrible happened and a number of children were killed."

"Perhaps a sickness swept through the orphanage," Ran suggested. "Could have been typhoid or measles, a flu of some sort."

Lucas fell silent. As Eve tried to imagine what thoughts might be running through the former priest's head, she steadied herself with a drink of soda.

"Something isn't adding up," Lucas finally said. "Maybe we'll know more after tonight." His expression turned kindly and she glimpsed the caring sort of priest he must have been. "Eve, are you sure you're up to this?"

"To tell you the truth, Father—" Her face flushed at the error, though she was beginning to understood why people called him that behind his back. There was just something about him. . . . "I'm sorry. I know you left the priesthood sometime back."

"That's right. I couldn't live within the rules. The truth is, I fell in love with a woman. Centuries back, priests were allowed to marry, but that was long ago."

"I'm sorry."

"Don't be. Turned out Maria was the wrong woman for me, and I was the wrong man for her. In a way, as it always seems to, God's plan worked out for the best."

She liked this man, Eve realized, liked his straightforward honesty, his sincerity, and the trace of humility he wore like a cloak.

She returned to their earlier conversation. "You asked if I was up to returning to the house tonight. The way I see it, Lucas, I don't have any choice. Whatever this is, its attention is fixed on me. After today, I have no doubt of that. I'm willing to do whatever it takes to make this all go away."

Lucas just nodded.

Ran gave her hand a gentle squeeze. "All right, let's leave this for now." He rose from the sofa and pulled her up with him. "The food in the hotel is surprisingly good. Let's go down to supper. I'll call the team, let them know what's going on. We'll meet in the lobby at eight for the trip over to the house."

"What about the asylum?" she asked.

"One problem at a time," Lucas replied. "Maybe we'll learn something new that will help us."

"There's always a chance Eve won't be able to make contact," Ran said. "So far that hasn't been a problem. I'm feeling a strong sense of urgency about all of this. I think something bad is going to happen. We need to stop it before it does."

CHAPTER TWENTY-SEVEN

*R*AN STOOD IN FRONT OF THE HOTEL. AFTER A BRIEF MEETING IN his suite, the team had headed downstairs for the trip to Eve's house. Dusk had fallen, the sun out of sight beyond the edge of the sea. Clouds had pushed ashore to settle over the town.

The valet brought up the BMW. The limo was already there, loaded with their audio/video equipment and miscellaneous gear. Jesse stood next to Ran and Luke, Violet stood talking to Eve.

Ran checked his waterproof wristwatch. "Zane and Katie should have been back by now."

Jesse checked the Apple watch wrapped around his thick wrist. "Zane went to Tyne and Wear to see if he could find the death records for the asylum. Katie went with him. They probably stopped for supper on the way back."

Ran nodded. "Zane texted earlier. Said he was waiting for the registrar to finish going back through the digital archives to see if she could find the records we're looking for. I hope he's got something."

Ran rechecked his messages. Still nothing new from Zane. "I'll text him again. Tell them to meet us at the house. We'll get as much of the equipment set up as we can."

"I can set up Katie's gear," Jesse offered. "I'll have everything dialed out by the time they get there."

"All right, that sounds good. Let's go." Ran turned. "Eve, you can ride with me."

Luke flashed him a knowing look, but made no comment. They hadn't had much time to talk, not enough to get into personal matters, which was fine with Ran. His friend knew him far too well. He didn't need advice on his love life, especially not now.

He settled Eve in the passenger seat while Jesse, Violet, and Luke climbed into the limo. Rounding the hood of the Beamer, Ran slid behind the wheel and fired the engine.

"What do you think is keeping Zane and Katie?" Eve asked as the car pulled out of the hotel driveway.

He thought about the looks Katie had been sending in Zane's direction. She was interested. She'd made that more than clear. So far, Zane had resisted temptation. Ran hoped that would continue. A casual affair meant little to Katie. Ran had a feeling Zane wasn't built that way.

Neither was Ran, a fact that at the moment did not serve him well. He was in too deep with Eve. He needed to pull back, get his head on straight. Sex was one thing. These feelings that seemed to keep growing between them were an entirely different matter.

His instincts had been warning him since the first time he had met her, maybe even before that, during the conversations that had taken place between them from halfway around the world.

"Maybe Zane's turned up something that's worth the wait," Ran said.

"I hope so," said Eve.

"So do I." Ran's feeling of urgency had only kept growing. He felt as if they were all riding the razor's edge, waiting just out of reach for the flash of the blade.

He parked in front of the white-trimmed redbrick house and the limo pulled up behind him, disgorging its occupants, who all went around to the trunk to help unload the gear.

He ushered Eve inside, where silence greeted them. A few dust motes swirled in the air, leftover from the recent construction. The newly installed basement door was closed, and yet he felt an odd pull in that direction.

"I'll be right back." Giving in to the urge, he left Eve in the foyer and headed down the hall, opened the door, and descended the stairs. Crossing to the camel-backed trunk, he knelt and began to carefully sift through the contents. Beneath Priscilla's gowns, he found Wally's little blue sailor suit, lifted out his tam-style hat, and reclosed the lid. The others were in the hall when he returned.

"We setting up downstairs?" Jesse asked.

Ran nodded. "Our best chance, I think."

Jesse took off with an armload of gear. Luke carried a load downstairs behind him. Violet walked up beside Eve, who spotted the object in Ran's hand.

"Is that . . . ? That's Wally's hat."

"That's right. We'll use it as a trigger object. It's often a way to bridge the time/space distance between us and them."

Her hand trembled as her fingers closed around the little blue hat.

Violet moved closer. "What are you feeling, dear?"

Emotion swamped her. She didn't know where the feelings came from, but she knew in her heart they were real. Eve swallowed and her eyes filled. "The hat belonged to Wally, but I can feel his mother's emotions." She looked into Violet's worried eyes. "After . . . after he died, Priscilla didn't want to live."

"Zane said she died of pneumonia a year later," Ran said.

A fact Eve hadn't known.

"More likely a broken heart," Violet said. "It's obvious how much she loved her son."

Eve's fingers smoothed over the tattered blue wool. "Priscilla isn't here. I'm sure I'd be able to feel her. She gave in to her illness because she wanted to join her little boy." She looked up, into Ran's face. "Instead, Priscilla's gone and Wally's trapped here."

Ran gently settled his hands on her shoulders and turned her to face him. "We're going to change that. We're going to change a lot of things." He wasn't surprised when the chandelier over their heads started swinging. He glanced at Luke, whose features looked grim.

At the sound of footsteps coming from outside, Ran walked over to the front door, checked the peephole to be sure who was there, then pulled open the door. A white and red taxi pulled away from the curb as Zane and Katie walked into the foyer.

"We found it," Zane said, holding up a copy of a printed page. "It was right there in the asylum archives."

Eve's face went pale. Ran took hold of her hand.

"Go on," he said.

Zane cast a sympathetic glance at Eve. "Twelve orphan boys, ages four to thirteen, died on June 16, 1883. Wally's name wasn't among them, but there was a Herbert Jones listed."

"Herbie," Ran said.

"Wally wouldn't have been in the orphanage at that time," Zane continued. "He would have been living with the Warringtons." Zane looked over at Eve. "I found a Walter Augustus Warrington listed in the death register that same day."

Eve made a sound in her throat.

"Easy." Ran led her into the dining room and urged her down in one of the high-backed dining chairs. "So not an epidemic or something like that."

He turned back to Zane. "Wally and twelve of his friends died the same day. What was the cause of death?"

Zane looked at Eve, whose eyes had filled with tears. Katie moved protectively closer, rested a hand gently on Eve's shoulder.

"They varied," Zane said. "Wally died of suffocation. Apparently there was an accident."

Eve bit back a sob.

"What about the others?" Ran asked, determined to get the truth.

"There were numerous causes of death. Most of them died of compressed asphyxia, but others died of heart failure, punctured vital organs due to broken bones, crushed ribs that led to collapsed lungs, fatal lacerations—"

"Stop it!" Eve leaped up from her chair. "Stop it right now! Please . . . I can't stand anymore." Covering her eyes, she started crying, great sobs tearing free as if her heart were breaking.

Ran pulled her into his arms. Holding her close, he kissed the top of her head. "It's all right, sweetheart. It's over. It happened more than a hundred years ago. It's all in the past."

She looked up at him, tears streaming down her face. "It isn't over, Ran. The children . . ." She swallowed. "The boys are still there, trapped in the asylum. That . . . *thing* . . . in my office. It's keeping them there. Oh, God, Ran, I can't stand it."

He just held her as she cried against his shoulder, and he wished there was a way he could take away her pain. Katie and Zane had both left the dining room, Zane to stand guard outside the house, Katie to allow them some privacy. Violet and Lucas remained.

"Give us a minute," Luke said.

Violet nodded and headed for the door. She had worked with Luke before. Ran reluctantly let Eve go, easing her back down in the chair.

"Lucas wants to speak to you."

She gripped his hand. "No, please don't go."

He bent and brushed a soft kiss over her lips. "I'll be right outside."

It took every ounce of his will to leave her, to walk out of the dining room and close the door behind him.

Eve looked into Luke's warm brown eyes. There was something in them, something that compelled her to trust. Her mind went back to the little orphan boys who had died, and fresh tears welled in her eyes.

Dressed in dark blue jeans and a white dress shirt, the top button undone and the sleeves rolled up, Lucas pulled out a chair and sat down across from her. A small gold medallion gleamed a few inches below the hollow at the base of his throat.

Eve accepted the white cotton handkerchief Lucas handed her. "Thank you." She wiped her eyes. "The pendant you're wearing . . . what is it?"

"St. Michael's medallion. Archangel Michael is the defender of humankind against evil." He pulled the circle of gold out so she could see. "This one is from Italy. I was there for a while before I left the church."

A warrior with huge wings wielded a massive sword against a demon-like creature who appeared to be Satan.

She looked up at Lucas. "Considering what you do, I can understand why you wear it."

Lucas smiled faintly. "I know you're worried about the orphans. We're going to help them."

"It breaks my heart to think of the pain they must have suffered. And it seems to have no end."

"Those children belong to God. They're God's children, and He wants them with Him. He's going to help us free them."

A surge of anger brought her head up. "If God loves them, why did he leave them here all these years, leave them at the mercy of those . . . *things*, whatever they are?"

"Sometimes it's hard to understand God's will. Keep in mind that time and space aren't the same for Him as they are for us. Years are merely instants in His domain. It's the same for the children."

Eve said nothing.

"Perhaps God was waiting for you, Eve. Waiting, perhaps, for all of us in order to do what's necessary for the children to reach the light."

Eve said nothing, just looked into those kindly brown eyes that had a way of reaching deep inside her. Her throat ached. "They all died at once. The records confirm that. What could have happened to them?"

"I don't know. Tomorrow we'll have Zane start looking through old newspaper accounts. With an accident like that, there should be something. I think it's only a matter of time until we find out."

Eve drew in a shaky breath. "You really believe God's going to help them?"

"I think He's going to help *us* help them."

Something loosened inside her. According to Lucas, God needed her. He wouldn't want her to quit. It strengthened her resolve. She wasn't quitting. Nothing was going to stop her from helping those children.

"Ran said you've seen this kind of thing before," she said.

"Yes, malevolent entities holding less powerful spirits captive."

"And you were able to help?"

"Yes."

"How?"

"It's complicated."

The look on his face said that for now it was all the answer she would get. She glanced toward the door. "You were a priest. Were you able to help Ran after his wife and child were killed?"

"He never asked for my help." He flicked a glance at the door; then his gaze returned to her. "Watching him with you, I think perhaps you're the one meant to help him."

Eve just shook her head. "He won't let me. I don't think he's punished himself enough."

"Maybe you can change that." Lucas rose from his chair, indicating the conversation was over. "Will you be able to handle what might happen tonight?"

Her chin inched up as she rose to join him. "I'll handle it. God wants those children to be with Him and so do I."

Lucas crossed the living room to the entry. "Then let's make it happen." He pulled open the door.

CHAPTER TWENTY-EIGHT

*E*VE AND LUKE RETURNED TO THE HALL TO FIND RAN WAITING. THE rest of the team had already gone down to the cellar. Ran walked over and eased Eve into his arms. He gave her a supportive hug, then moved away. They both had important things to do.

"The equipment will be set up by now," Ran said. "I know Zane's news wasn't something you wanted to hear. We have no idea what might happen next. Are you sure you're prepared to go through with this?"

"As I told Lucas, I'll handle it. I'm not letting evil win."

Ran smiled. "That's my girl."

They headed down the hall. Lucas opened the door and preceded Eve downstairs. Ran followed. She had a feeling that unconsciously they were protecting her. Eve figured she could use all the protection she could get.

Jesse had set up the folding chairs to face the direction of the once-more bricked-up tunnel.

"Maybe they won't be able to get through now that the tunnel is closed," Eve said.

"Walls aren't a problem for ghosts. If they want to get in, they'll be here."

"I don't suppose you have any idea how that works," Eve said, and caught Ran's faint smile.

"Actually, I do. Or at least it's a current theory. It started with Albert Einstein back in 1905. Einstein theorized that particles can behave like light, which can pass through barriers. Think of a screen or a window. In the 1990s, Sir Roger Penrose, a mathematical physicist and Nobel laureate, carried the theory further. He believed consciousness originates at a quantum level, that quantum information can't be destroyed—even by death. He also believed quantum information can exist outside of the body, in the form known as consciousness, soul, or spirit. It's a lot more complicated than that, but you get the general idea."

Her eyes remained on his face. He had lost his wife and child. Clearly, he had researched the possibility of life after death.

"So, like light, quantum particles can pass through objects," Eve said. "That must be what happened to Donny in my office."

"Sir Roger would probably agree. Most scientists don't buy it because the testing can't be controlled in a lab. But astronomy, anthropology, and geology don't rely on controlled lab testing, either."

Eve mulled over his words. She had seen the evidence herself. She had seen Wally, who must have crossed through solid objects to be with her. That was all the proof she needed.

Ran turned to the others. "You guys ready to get started?"

"All set, boss," Jesse said. "Let's kick some demon ass."

Laugher broke some of the tension in the damp, chilly cellar. Ran looked at Eve, his gaze intense. "I'll be right here with you every second."

She knew he wouldn't leave her. She thought of the entity that had invaded Donny's body, but somehow she didn't believe it would risk tangling with a man as strong as Ran.

"I'm ready." She sat down in the single metal folding chair in front. Ran sat behind her next to Violet and Lucas. A few feet away, Katie manned the FLIR imaging cameras, while Jesse handled the EVP voice recorder, the temperature measurement gauge, a meter called an EMF recorder that measured electromagnetic fields, and whatever else he and Katie had brought. She'd learned some of the names, but not all.

Eve fiddled with the little blue woolen hat in her hand. She looked over her shoulder at Ran, who gave a faint nod of encouragement. For an instant, her gaze went to Lucas. His solid jaw looked carved in stone. At least this was something he had seen before. Eve took comfort in that.

The lighting changed as Katie turned on the eerie, infrared camera that filled the room with a thick, dull red. Eve fixed her gaze on the boarded-up tunnel and took a deep breath.

"Wally? Wally . . . it's Evie. Are you here?"

Nothing. Not the slightest stirring in the air.

Tension tightened the muscles in her neck. "Wally, can we talk? I've missed you."

Nothing.

She tried a few more times, turning the little hat in her hands. Still nothing.

"I learned something today, something about you and your friends in the orphanage." She let the words hang, hoping to tempt him. "I know something bad happened to all of you. I want to help you and the other boys. Can you hear me, Wally?"

From the corner of her eye, she caught movement. Then the stillness returned.

"Wally, please. I really need to talk to you. You can bring Herbie if you want."

A wisp of something set the air stirring around her. She kept her gaze fixed on the boarded-up wall that closed off the tunnel. It occurred to her it might have been better to use her upstairs bedroom, where she had seen Wally before. Too late for that now.

"Wally . . . ?"

Evie . . . is that you? The words were indistinct, more a murmur than a sound.

"It's me, Wally. I'm right here. Remember how we used to play together out in the garden?"

She saw a thin trickle of something that looked like fog seeping into the room, and her heart began to pound. The fog thickened to a pale-white mist that began to have substance and take shape. She prayed it was Wally and not the vicious creature that had come into her office.

"Do you remember the garden, Wally?"

I . . . remember. A little boy's voice. She wondered if anyone else could hear it and glanced over at Jesse, who gave her a thumbs-up. He was getting something. The pounding in her heart went up another notch.

"Heaven is like that, Wally. As pretty as the garden, only a thousand times better. It's the place you were supposed to go after the accident."

He made a noise and she realized he was crying. She could hear his little-boy sobs and her heart just broke in two.

Eve steeled herself. She couldn't afford the luxury of tears. "Your mother is up there waiting for you. She's missing you, Wally. She's waiting for you and the other children."

I miss her, too.

"I know you do. All you have to do is look for the light and it will take you to her."

What about Herbie and the others?

"I'll help them, I promise."

Wally seemed uncertain. His image floated a few feet off the cellar floor.

I don't see the light. I can't find it.

Eve glanced frantically back at Lucas, who had risen from his chair. He was repeating something in Latin, saying it over and over. She looked back at Wally, saw his wavering image.

Then the red light on the camera went off and everything turned black. She could hear Katie and Jesse both moving around, trying to get their equipment working again.

Lucas kept speaking in Latin, praying, she thought.

Her heart nearly stopped when a shaft of light cut through the darkness, a yellow circle that glowed like pure gold. It went right up through the ceiling and gave off a warmth that beckoned in the chilly air.

I see it!

Her heart was beating so hard she could feel it in her temples. "Just move toward the light, Wally. Just keep going no matter what happens."

Wally's hazy image was the only thing she could see in the darkness. He was wearing his little blue sailor suit, floating toward the light.

A fierce voice cracked through the silence. *You! Will! Not! Leave!* The angry voice she'd heard before. The demonic thing that held the children captive. *I command you to stay!*

Wally's small figure wavered.

Eve leapt to her feet, her heart in her throat. "Don't stop, Wally! Your mother is waiting!"

The small figure began to move again, moving closer and closer to the light.

Katie gasped as her camera and tripod sailed into the air and crashed against the wall. Some of Jesse's equipment tore apart, flew up in the air, then shattered on the floor.

"Let's go!" Ran reached over and gripped her arm, hauling her up from the chair.

"I'm not leaving!" She jerked free and turned back to the hazy figure of the little boy. "Hurry, Wally! Don't stop! Just keep moving toward the light!"

A rushing began, swelling like the roar of a tornado, and then a furious thunderclap shook the walls. Eve's gaze never left the small figure floating toward the light. She could hear Lucas's desperate incantations.

Wally's wavy image stepped into the glowing circle, and it bathed him in its warmth and golden light. Wally started rising upward. Then, in a brilliant white flash, he was gone.

I! Will! Kill! You! The terrifying words vibrated through the air.

"Let's go, damn it!" Ran jerked her roughly toward him, dragging her across the room toward the stairs. She should have been angry, but she found herself smiling, filled with joy instead. Wally was safe. He was with his mother now. Nothing could change that. Not even a demon.

By the time they reached the bottom of the stairs, the other team members were halfway to the top. Lucas looked over his shoulder to be sure she and Ran were on their way, then continued climbing again.

Behind her, Eve could hear the crash of equipment being torn apart, hear the vicious howl of the wind. No one paused in the hallway. They bolted out the front door into the night.

Eve's throat tightened and fresh tears welled. Tears of happiness this time.

It was dark as pitch outside, clouds blocking the stars, the air crisp and cold. Eve inhaled a deep breath. Jesse was cursing, his equipment destroyed. But Katie was crying, moved by what she had witnessed. In the porchlight, Violet looked stunned. Lucas's face was pale. He looked completely drained.

Zane appeared out of the darkness just in time to witness the tears she'd held back sliding down Eve's cheeks. Then she heard Ran's voice and it centered her.

"I'm sorry, honey." He pulled her against him, wrapped her in his arms. "I didn't mean to be so rough. I was just so afraid you'd be hurt."

Eve pulled back to look at him. She wiped the wetness from her cheeks. And she smiled. "We beat him, Ran. Wally's with his mother now. He's safe."

Ran returned her smile. "You did it. Wally's safe."

Then his smile slowly faded and he glanced away. But Eve had seen the faraway look in his eyes. He was thinking of his wife and child, wondering, perhaps silently praying, that they were safe as well.

She took his hand and tugged him forward, out of the dark place he had slipped into. "Call the limo. Tell the driver we're ready to go back to the hotel."

He nodded, his powerful shoulders straightening as he went to work setting things in motion.

He led her over to the BMW and held the door while she settled inside and clicked her seat belt in place, then closed the passenger door. All the way back to the hotel, Eve thought of what had happened in the house. There was so much to say, so many questions that needed to be answered.

Most important of all, Herbie and eleven more orphans remained trapped between this world and the next.

The euphoria she was feeling slowly drained away, replaced by worry and fear.

CHAPTER TWENTY-NINE

*R*AN SPENT THE NIGHT IN EVE'S BED. AFTER WHAT HAD HAP-pened, she needed him, she'd said. Ran hadn't admitted that he needed her, too. He couldn't get thoughts of Sabrina and Chrissy out of his head. Had they traveled together through the tunnel of light into the safety of the world beyond? He could only pray it was so.

Sleeping with Eve wasn't fair. Not when his dark thoughts had plummeted him into the past, when they kept him engulfed in guilt and despair.

And yet when he was with her, those dark thoughts disap-peared. He'd made love to her like a madman, taking and taking, desperate to cleanse his mind and heart. Eve had met his every demand and tossed out a few of her own.

Ran almost smiled. Eve was his match in every way, and yet . . .

He let the thought trail off, unwilling to go there. The timing wasn't right. Eve deserved someone who could give her a future, not a man who was trapped in the past.

Still, he was selfish enough to take what she offered for as long as it lasted. He only hoped he was giving her something in return.

He did smile then. Something more than incredible sex.

"What are you smiling about?" Eve asked as she walked out of her bedroom, freshly showered, dressed in tan slacks and a silky blouse beneath a navy wool blazer.

His gaze ran over her conservative clothes. "You have a patient today?" he asked, wisely dodging the question.

"I was supposed to meet with Bethany Parsons this afternoon. She sounded good, so I put the appointment off until next week. I have an appointment this morning with an older woman named Margaret Michaels who lost her husband two months ago. She's doing her best to cope, but it isn't easy."

"After everything that's happened, you should be a great help to her in that regard."

She shoved her fingers through her thick dark hair, lifting it away from her face, making the ruby highlights shimmer. "I still can't believe what I saw last night was real."

"But you do."

Her spine subtly straightened. "Yes, I do."

He nodded. "So what about Mrs. Michaels?"

"Since I couldn't chance meeting her at the office, I told her some problems had come up with the sewer line. I said there was a crew working on my home and office. I suggested we meet in a coffee shop near where she lives."

"Good idea."

"I hate lying, but—"

"It's only a white lie and partly true. You are having problems with the house and office, and you do have a crew working to fix them."

"I hadn't thought of it that way, but I guess you're right."

"What about your housekeeper? What was her name?"

"Mrs. Pennyworth. Thanks for reminding me. I'll put her off for another week."

Ran nodded. "I need to go back to my own room to shower and change." He glanced at the door, though he didn't really want to leave.

Eve walked over and slid her arms around his neck. "You should have joined me in the shower when you had the chance."

He thought of soaping his hands and sliding them over her delectably slender body, the tempting curves and valleys, her body flushing beneath his touch. Ran blocked the image when he started getting hard.

Leaning down, he lightly kissed her. "At the moment, I'm very sorry I didn't."

Eve laughed. She seemed brighter today, some of the weight lifted off her shoulders. Her little friend Wally was safe. Whatever happened next, she could be proud that she had helped him.

"You think Zane will be able to find out what kind of accident killed the children?"

"He and Katie are going down to the newspaper office, the *Sunderland Echo,* to look into the archives. When an accident like that happens in a town the size of Sunderland, I have a feeling it's not going to be hard to find."

"After what Zane told us yesterday, I'm not sure I want to know."

"But you want to help the orphans, and the more you find out, the better your chances of succeeding."

Eve made no reply.

"I won't be long," Ran said. "Why don't you order us some breakfast? Afterward we'll take that drive I promised."

She perked up. "Really?"

"Really."

"I can't do breakfast. I have to meet Mrs. Michaels at the coffee shop, but once our appointment is over, I'm free for the rest of the day."

Since he couldn't resist the eager look in her pretty hazel eyes, he walked back to her, hauled her into his arms, and kissed her the very thorough way he'd been wanting to.

"The Bentley will be waiting to take you to your appointment," he said a little gruffly. Before temptation could get a firmer grip, he turned and walked out of her suite.

The white and red taxi pulled up in front of an ornate five-story building in Blandford Square, Newcastle on Tyne. In 2019, the *Sunderland Echo* archives, Zane had discovered, had been moved into the building that housed the Tyne and Wear Archives and Museum.

Zane got out and paid the driver while Kate got out to join him. After what she'd witnessed in Eve's house last night, she'd insisted . on coming along.

"I wish you could have been there, Zane," she said as the taxi rolled away. "I could only hear Eve's side of the conversation, but I could see this small, hazy figure floating across the room. I caught hints of blue—his sailor suit, I guess. Eve's mentioned it several times. She was using his hat to make contact."

"What about the tunnel of light?" Zane asked. Everyone was talking about it. He wanted to hear Kate's firsthand account.

"It was amazing—I can tell you that. This golden shaft cut right down through the ceiling." She gripped his hand. "It was . . . I can't describe the feeling, Zane. Like joy spilling through me. I'll never forget it."

She seemed so happy as she told the story. Zane looked down at their intertwined fingers and felt her warmth sinking into him. He eased his hand away.

"Jesse said some kind of paranormal force destroyed all your equipment."

Kate shivered and rubbed her arms as if she were cold. "Lucas was saying all this stuff in Latin. The room was shaking. It sounded like a hurricane was going to tear the cellar apart. Then I heard this violent shouting. 'I will kill you!' " Kate shook her head, shifting her long, honey-blond hair. Zane forced himself to concentrate.

"It was terrifying, Zane. Each word was filled with so much hatred. We couldn't get out of there fast enough. We all ran up the stairs and didn't stop until we were out of the house."

"That's where I found you."

She nodded.

"Ran told me you're going back to the orphanage, either tonight or tomorrow night. He says the spirits of the other dead boys are still trapped inside."

"Ran says Jesse and I don't have to go, since our equipment was destroyed and he can't get new stuff here in time, but . . ."

"But you're going anyway." Somehow he didn't doubt it. Kate was a firebrand. Zane was beginning to know her a little too well.

She looked up at him with a hint of defiance. "You weren't there. You can't imagine what it felt like. If there are children trapped between earth and heaven, then I'm going to do what I can to help them."

Zane still wasn't sure how he felt about ghosts and spirits and whatever the hell was happening in Eve's house, but he couldn't deny a feeling of admiration for Kate. Facing a demon was far more frightening than taking on gang members and kidnappers.

Zane squeezed Kate's hand. "You want to help? Let's go see what we can find out."

The interior of the building had mostly been modernized. A helpful clerk stood behind the counter, sporting frizzy, gray-blond hair and a friendly smile. Mrs. Burbage listened as Zane laid out what he was looking for—*Sunderland Echo* newspaper archives for June of 1883.

The woman smiled. "Some of them are in digital format now, but not all of them."

"I'd like to see the originals, if that's possible."

Mrs. Burbage nodded her approval. "Always better to get the entire story. Follow me."

She led them down modern white corridors, into an area that looked like an old-fashioned library, with narrow rows of big leatherbound volumes on metal shelves stacked eight feet high. In another area, he could see rows of yellowed, tattered, rolled-up papers that appeared to be maps.

"This way, please."

They followed the woman down one of the aisles, where she shoved on a pair of reading glasses that had been dangling from a chain around her neck and began to skim the dates.

"There are four volumes for that year. I'd suggest going through May, June, and July, just to be safe."

Those months consisted of two different volumes. Mrs. Burbage pulled both of them out.

"Let me carry those for you," Zane offered.

The woman smiled and handed them over. "Well, thank you."

Zane carried the heavy volumes over to a big, rectangular, claw-foot oak table and set them down on top. "We can take it from here."

"Just leave them there when you're finished and I'll see they're filed back where they belong."

"Thank you, Mrs. Burbage," Kate said. She turned to Zane. "I'll take this one, you take the other."

Zane just nodded and opened the second heavy leather-bound book. It was filled with day after day's worth of yellowed *Sunderland Echo* newspapers, back then called the *Sunderland Daily Echo and Shipping Gazette*.

He thumbed through pages until he reached the end of May.

"Zane . . . ?"

Kate's voice held a tremor that had him glancing in her direction. "I think . . . I think I've found it." When her eyes met his, he saw that her face had gone pale. "Oh, God, Zane. Oh, God."

His chest tightened at the sight of the tears that welled and began to stream down her cheeks.

Zane moved quickly to her side. "You found the date of the accident? What happened?" But remembering the causes of deaths of the twelve children in the orphanage and seeing the devastation on Kate's beautiful face, he almost didn't want to know.

Kate swallowed. "I found out what happened. Oh, God, Zane, it's going to destroy Eve." Kate scrubbed at the wetness, but more tears washed down. "Oh, God."

Zane's gaze caught on the yellowed page. The date read June 16, 1883. There were drawings, black-and-white pencil sketches etched into the paper. His stomach knotted. For an instant, his own eyes burned and he quickly glanced away. He took a moment to steady himself.

Kate touched his arm and looked into his face. "How could Eve live right here in Sunderland and not have known?"

He wasn't ready to look back at the paper. He kept his eyes on Kate. "She never really lived in England, remember? She just came to visit her uncle. She's only been back in the house a few months. This happened nearly a hundred and forty years ago. In the States, a lot of people don't even know who fought in the Civil War."

Kate dabbed at a last stray tear. "You're right." She gazed up at him with those big blue eyes, and he was touched by the pain he saw. He didn't want to like Kate Collins, but he did. She was a party girl, just looking to have some fun. A fling would be meaningless for her, but for him? Zane wasn't so sure.

Though he had to admit, he was tempted.

He returned to the moment, began turning the heavy yellow pages from one date to the next. "There's a lot of information here. We need to have them make copies for us so we can take them to Ran. He's going to have to tell Eve." He turned to Kate, whose eyes were still moist, her face still a little too pale. "Eve is going to need him more than ever."

CHAPTER THIRTY

*E*ve was back in her suite. Her meeting with Margaret Michaels had gone better than any of their earlier appointments. They had talked about death, this time in a far less general manner. Eve had asked questions about Margaret's husband, asked if John had visited her at any time after he'd died.

Mrs. Michaels, a tiny, prim, silver-haired woman, looked astonished by the question but clearly intrigued.

"It's something that's commonly reported by widows," Eve continued, having done some research after their last meeting. Though she hadn't intended to mention it to Margaret, after last night, her attitude had changed.

Margaret's fair complexion colored to a soft shade of rose. "If you want the truth, there I times I can feel him. It's like my John is lying right there in our bed, curled by my side the way he did for nearly fifty years. I know it's only my imagination, but it feels so real, and it comforts me."

Eve reached across the table and took Margaret's hand. "Other women have reported the same kinds of things. I think when the time is right and John knows you're going to be okay, he'll go on to where he's meant to be."

Margaret gave her a watery smile. "I knew when I picked you, I picked the right person. Thank you so much for saying that."

Eve just nodded and smiled, but a feeling of rightness settled over her. The rest of the hour was relaxed, the conversation light and hopeful. Margaret's shoulders seemed straighter when she left the café, and Eve felt as if she had done her job.

Back in her suite, she changed into more casual clothes: stretch jeans, a long-sleeve jade-green velour, and flat-heeled boots. Weather at the beach was still chilly. More storms were predicted, but no rain was expected today. Ran had mentioned a drive along the shore, and she was excited to escape her worries for a while.

At the sound of a firm knock, she hurried across the room. But instead of Ran, when she pulled open the door, Detective Inspector Daniel Balfour stood in the hallway.

"I have some news I thought you'd want to hear." His British accent matched the tweed jacket he usually wore, today with a pair of jeans instead of slacks. She wondered if he was off duty.

"Of course, please come in."

He stepped into the suite, a handsome man with his thick brown hair and dark brown eyes.

"I have soft drinks in the fridge. Would you like something?"

"I wish I could, but I don't have time. I just wanted you to know they identified the man whose body was found in the tunnel."

Since he seemed to be in a hurry, she didn't invite him to sit down. "Tell me about him."

"His name was Asif Rahim. He was an immigrant, twenty-three at the time of his death. He was arrested three years ago on a burglary charge but was released. That's why we have his DNA. Rahim was known to run with a group of young men called the East End Boys. Most of them have been arrested. Charges ranged from burglary to assault, even attempted murder. They may be the men your security guard saw at the old asylum. Of course, there's no way to know for sure."

"Do you think they killed Asif Rahim?"

"These men are violent. If Rahim did something the rest of the gang didn't like, there's a very good possibility."

"What will you do now?"

"We'll continue our investigation. And we're following up on the incident at the orphanage. Unfortunately, we don't have much to go on. If Tanner remembers anything else, be sure to have him contact us. That goes for King as well."

Eve just nodded. "I appreciate you coming here to tell me."

The detective shrugged a set of wide shoulders. "Rahim was found in the tunnel under your house—or near enough. I figured you deserved to know."

Eve walked him to the door.

Detective Balfour turned to her as she pulled it open. "So you and King . . . you're together?"

Were they? Not really. "We're friends. He lives in Seattle. I live in England. That isn't going to change."

A smile broke over his face. "Then I hope you'll call me Daniel. With luck, maybe our paths will cross again."

Eve managed to return the smile. "If it happens, I hope it isn't official police business."

His smile widened. He was a very attractive man. "So do I." Walking past her, he headed out into the hall.

Eve had just started to close the door when she spotted Ran striding down the corridor, passing the detective on his way. Neither man paused to say hello. Ran was frowning when he walked into her suite. Even with the dark look on his face, her breath caught, her mind flashing back to the morning they had spent together in bed.

She forced the embarrassing thought away. "You don't have to look like that. Detective Balfour only stopped by to let me know they've identified the man we found in the tunnel." She went on to tell him about Asif Rahim and the East End Boys, surmising that they were the gang involved in killing the man, perhaps the same group who had kidnapped Anya.

"Sounds like the police are making progress."

"Detective Balfour said if you or Zane thought of anything that might be useful to please give him a call."

"I'll give it some thought."

She knew Ran's first concern was for Anya and her mother. Their safety had to come first.

Ran's cell phone rang just then, putting an end to the conversation. He pulled the phone out of his jeans pocket and looked down at the screen.

"It's Zane." He listened for a moment, then turned and walked a few feet away. He returned when the call was over. "Zane wants to talk to me." She could read the turbulence that had turned his eyes a darker shade of blue. "He asked if we could speak privately. We're meeting in my suite. I'll be back as soon as we've finished."

Eve didn't ask what the meeting was about. There was something grim in his features that said he wouldn't tell her if she asked.

As Ran walked out the door, a sliver of ice slid down her spine.

Ran was pacing the living room when the knock came at the door. It had been only minutes since Zane's phone call. He had found the information they were looking for, Zane said. He needed to speak to Ran in person and requested Eve not be included.

The grim note in Zane's voice put Ran on alert. He walked over and opened the door to find Katie, Jesse, and Zane all standing in the hallway. He had never seen darker looks on three people's faces.

His worry kicked up a notch. "Come on in."

They walked inside and Ran closed the door. No one said a word.

"That bad?" he asked.

"Worse," Zane said. He was carrying a folder tucked under his arm. It was thick with sheets of copy paper. Apparently, there was a lot of information. Ran's stomach knotted.

"We figured you'd want to be the one to tell Eve. We haven't told Violet yet. We thought the women would take it the hardest, especially Eve."

"Sweet God, what is it?"

Zanc passed the file to Ran. "This is what we've found so far. There's a lot more out there. When it happened, the story was in newspapers all over the country."

"But that was a hundred and forty years ago," Katie added. "At the time it was considered the greatest tragedy in the history of Britain."

Ran frowned. "So it happened right here in the area."

Zane nodded. "I think the people who lived around here were consumed by it for decades afterward. All of their lives were affected. They just wanted to forget it. Make it go away."

"I guess that's why they don't talk about it anymore," Jesse said. "Even now, it's still too painful."

Ran carried the file over to the sofa, sat down, and opened it in his lap. His stomach churned as he read the headlines.

> Victoria Hall Disaster
> On June 16, 1883, at the Victoria Hall in Sunderland, England, a massive stampede for free toys caused 183 children to be crushed to death.

The last words rang in his head. *183 children. Crushed to death.* Ran closed his eyes. The file trembled in his hands.

No words broke the silence. None of them moved. Ran reopened the file and forced himself to keep reading.

> On a summer afternoon in June, laughter turned to screams in a tragedy that broke the hearts of people across the nation.

The paper went on to describe Victoria Hall, a large Gothic brick structure seating 2,500 people, in three tiers of seating. Located on Toward and Laurel Street, it was used for public meetings and entertainment.

> On that Saturday, the Hall was offering a pair of entertainers called The Fays in a special children's matinee performance. There was a chance for presents, too.

Ran could feel every beat of his heart.

> Alexander Fay was a magician and illusionist. Annie Fay gave what was called Spiritual Entertainment, which in-

cluded demonstrations of clairvoyance, seances, and strange manifestations. One of their most popular acts was the Great Ghost Illusion.

Toward the end of the performance, the children began to rush down a narrow staircase to collect the toys they had been promised, but the door at the end had been bolted. They began to fall, one of top of the other . . .

Ran closed the folder, nausea roiling in his stomach. He took a deep breath to collect himself.

"The date of the newspaper is June 30th," Zane said. "I put that one on top. The articles written in the days right after it happened . . ." He shook his head. "They give firsthand accounts by the children who survived. There are drawings, etchings of what it looked like inside the stairwell where it occurred. The pictures are horrifying, Ran, the articles are too awful to describe. I wanted to give you a chance to understand what happened before . . . before you had to deal with the details."

"It's bad, Ran," Jesse added. "Little kids, ages from three to thirteen. What they suffered, it's one of the worst tragedies I've ever heard of."

Ran took another breath and let it out slowly. "I'll read the file. Violet needs to know. I'll have to find a way to tell Eve."

He didn't want to imagine what it would do to Eve to find out the terrible way Wally and the other children had died. And not just 13 of them, but 183.

Ran scrubbed a hand over his face. His chest felt like a bulldozer sat on top of it. He thought of the death of his own wife and child, and fresh grief rolled through him. He closed his eyes, trying to block the memory. At least their deaths had been mercifully quick.

"I can talk to Violet," Katie offered softly.

He glanced over to where she stood, her fingers curled into her palms. "You sure?"

"Violet understands this stuff better than the rest of us. Except, I guess, for Father Luke."

Ran's gaze drifted over the three of them. "I'll speak to Eve. I think it might be good to have Luke there."

Katie's features darkened with concern. She knew him, knew what had happened to his family, perhaps understood how strongly this affected him.

"That's a good idea," she said. "Luke always seems to know what to say."

Zane shifted. "There's so much information in those newspapers. There was an inquest to find out who was responsible. Two inquests, in fact. It's all in there."

Ran nodded. "I'll need some time to go over it."

Jesse rubbed a hand over his dark face. "After what we saw last night at Eve's place, there's one thing about this that stands out."

Ran rose to his feet, the folder gripped firmly in his hand. "What's that?"

"The Fays. They were dabbling in the occult. Seances, magic, the Great Ghost Illusion. Now, some kind of evil spirit has the souls of those poor dead kids trapped in the orphanage."

"Fay," Ran repeated. "One of the voices Eve heard in the hall that first night said a word that sounded like Kay or Hay. It could have been Fay."

"I bet you're right," Jesse said. "Another word was *accident*. Fact is, he was one of the people responsible. Maybe he's still here, too."

Ran mentally logged the information. "What proof do we have that the orphans were actually in Victoria Hall?"

"Aside from their injuries?" Zane said. "What else could have happened to them on that same day?"

"Good point."

"I'm still digging," Zane said. "I may find something more tangible."

Ran nodded. "We'll go over all of it later. I'm going to postpone the trip to the asylum. Eve's going to need some time to deal with this."

"The three of us talked about it," Katie said. "Whenever you decide to go, we're going with you."

"We're all in this together," Jesse put in.

"You'll need someone on the outside," Zane added.

"Jesse and I both have a few extra pieces of handheld equipment," Katie said. "We might be able to document something."

"Even if we don't, it doesn't matter," Jesse finished. "As long as we help those kids."

Something warm filtered through him. They were a team. Team members stuck together. Ran was proud of them. "All right, we'll tackle the problem together. I'll keep you posted as things move along."

Zane, Jesse, and Katie turned and walked out of the suite. File still gripped in his hand, dreading to read the articles, Ran returned to the sofa.

CHAPTER THIRTY-ONE

*E*VE SAT ON THE COUCH IN THE LIVING ROOM OF HER SUITE, LUCAS seated next to her. Her palms were moist, her hands gripped together in her lap. Her heart hurt, her face was wet with tears. She felt numb all over.

She looked up at Ran. He'd been alternately pacing and hovering over her, his face lined with worry, ever since he'd told her the news. Lucas's presence exuded quiet strength.

Eve swallowed past the knot in her throat. "How could I not . . . not have known?"

"It happened a long time ago," Ran said. "They closed the building afterward. Victoria Hall didn't reopen for twenty-three years. Even then, it was never successful. Too tainted by what had happened. A bomb destroyed it in World War II. They tore it down, and the whole incident faded from people's memories. All that's left is the statue of a woman and her fallen child in a memorial in a quiet part of Mowbray Park."

Eve wiped a tear from her cheek. "You said Toward and Laurel Street. Victoria Hall was only a little over half a mile from the house." Only a little farther from the asylum, close enough for the boys to walk to the performance. Her throat ached. She couldn't bear to think of it.

"Maybe I did hear something about it way back and I just didn't remember," she said. "I was a teenager. I was too busy with my own problems at the time." She looked up at Ran, read something evasive in his face.

"Oh, no, there's more, isn't there? Oh, God, how could there be more?"

Ran took a deep breath. She could see he was affected as deeply as she. Perhaps more so after the loss of his family.

"The tragedy wasn't just an accident. It wouldn't have happened if someone hadn't purposely closed the door at the bottom of the stairwell."

A sound escaped Eve's throat. She doubled over, clutching her middle. Several seconds slipped past before she sat up and leaned back against the sofa.

"I can't . . . can't believe it. Surely, no one would do something so heinous on purpose."

"Perhaps whoever it was didn't understand what would happen," Lucas said. "I'd like to believe that."

"There was an inquisition to find out who was responsible," Ran continued. "Apparently the door was partially closed to keep people from coming in from outside without paying. But there was a bolt on the floor that could close the door, and once it was put in place, they couldn't get it out in time to save the children."

Eve felt like throwing up. She reached down to the coffee table and picked up the glass of water Ran had brought. Her hand shook as she took several long swallows and set the glass back down on the table.

"Did they . . . did they find the man responsible?"

"The caretaker, a man named Graham, was accused. Some of the children testified they had seen him close the bolt with his foot. Some said a fair-haired man had done it, others said it was a dark, curly-haired man. Alexander Fay's personal assistant, Charles Hesseltine, was questioned extensively."

"They thought Fay's assistant might be responsible?"

"All of them were under suspicion. The owner of the building was investigated, the architects who had designed the structure, and, of course, the Fays. But there was never enough evidence to charge anyone."

Eve closed her eyes, wishing she could block the terrible images from her heart and mind. She glanced at Ran and a distressing thought occurred.

"Dear God, we know there are orphan boys still trapped in the asylum. What about the other children who died that day? How many are still caught somewhere between heaven and earth?"

"The children who died came from all over Sunderland," Ran explained. "Burleigh Street, Thompson Street, Broughton, Gilsland, Chelsea Terrace. All sorts of different locations. They had relatives, families. People who cared about them. The boys in the orphanage had no one. That made them easy targets for the evil that has them trapped."

Eve fell silent, her mind spinning. She rose shakily to her feet. "What about you, Lucas? Do you believe the other children were able to find peace?"

Luke rose in front of her. "There's no way to know for sure what happened to each one of them. But these were innocent children. They would have been welcomed into God's kingdom."

Eve's chin went up. "Then it's time for Herbie and the orphan boys to join them."

In the end, Ran stuck with his decision. Tonight was too soon to tackle the malevolent presence in the asylum. Eve would be the children's main contact. She would need all of her strength to reach them. It would be Luke's job to call down the tunnel of light, and Eve's job to guide the children toward it.

At Ran's insistence, Eve had gone into the bedroom for a badly needed nap. As he had expected, learning about the tragedy had broken her heart. She was exhausted. He felt battered and bruised himself.

"I think you made a wise decision," Luke said from his seat on the sofa, while Ran sat in one of the matching chairs. After Eve had left the room, Luke had gone over to the minibar, found two small bottles of Courvoisier, and poured them each a drink.

Luke raised his heavy rocks glass and took a sip. "Eve is new to all of this. I'm amazed by her courage." His golden-brown eyes remained on Ran's face. "Besides being beautiful, she's intelligent and determined. Whether you're ready to admit it or not, Eve's good for you."

Ran took a sip of brandy, grateful for the burn. "If things were different—"

"You're sleeping together. It's clear you have feelings for her. It's not like you to get in this deep. Since the accident, you've always been able to cubbyhole your emotions where women were concerned."

Ran sipped his brandy. "I've never met anyone like her. She senses what people are feeling—including spirits. She's an empath, Luke. Eve doesn't even realize what that means."

"It means she understands you on a level no other woman ever has. Not even Sabrina."

At the sound of his wife's name, a tremor shook his hand. "We had a good marriage. We made a family together."

"That's right, you did. But an accident happened and things changed. It doesn't mean you have to punish yourself forever."

Ran took another drink, the warmth of the liquor settling him a little. "The timing isn't right. Eve knows that."

"Does she? Because when I see the way she looks at you, I see the same feelings you have for her reflected in her eyes."

Ran upended the glass and drained the contents, stood up from his chair. "If you're finished analyzing my love life, I think I'll go for a walk. Or better yet, I'm going down to the hotel gym and burn off some of this excess energy."

"You look more like you need about eight hours of sleep."

Ran thought of Eve and the heat that burned between them whenever they were together. He smiled. "Every minute of sleep I've missed has been worth it."

Luke's lips curved. "I'm sure it has." He drained his glass. "Think about what I said, Ran. Eve's special and we both know it."

Ran said nothing. Eve was special. She deserved more than he would ever be able to give her.

With the extra key to Eve's room in his pocket, he went back to his own suite and changed into a pair of sweats and a T-shirt. A long, hard workout would be good for him. Take his mind off evil and demons and what lay ahead. Take his mind off desire and yearning.

Take his mind off Eve.

Eve sank deeper into an exhausted slumber. Just a moment's rest, she'd told herself, and then she would rejoin the others.

But her mind was crowded, cluttered with images that dragged her down. She shifted on the mattress, determined not to see them, fighting the pictures forming in her head.

The hall was huge, the stage wide, draped with heavy velvet curtains. A magician wearing an old-fashioned black frock coat and top hat stood in the center, conjuring pigeons, snatching them up and tossing them into the air, the pigeons flying away.

The scene changed and the man began throwing prizes into the audience, a tin whistle, a small wooden horse, a tiny stuffed dog. A sea of children in their Sunday best, seated in three different tiers of the theater, jumped up to catch the toys. But the magician couldn't throw them far enough to reach the upper balconies.

One of his assistants shouted, "First ones downstairs will get the best toys!"

Eve began to toss back and forth. She didn't want to see the narrow staircase packed with children, all of them rushing down, trying to reach the bottom to claim one of the promised prizes.

She could hear the thunder of small feet and remembered the pounding footsteps racing down the hall in her house. Ahead, she spotted a big wooden door, watched a man sliding a heavy bolt in place, partially closing the exit at the bottom of the staircase.

A few children were able to slip through the narrow opening, but others began to fall, one on top of another. The tiny bodies began to stack up, weighing down the children below, pushing the air out of their lungs.

Eve began to thrash on the bed, her head tossing from side to side as she tried to escape the nightmare. She couldn't breathe, began to gasp, fought to suck in air. Wheezing and struggling, darkness pulled at her, tried to drag her under. She was dying, her soul slipping away to join the others.

A scream tore loose, jerking her awake, her heart viciously pounding as memories of the dream rushed back full force. A sob tore free. She fought to block the images.

Then the door swung violently open and Ran was striding toward her, scooping her up from the bed, sitting down and cradling her in his arms. She rested her head against his shoulder as he rocked her, whispered soothing words.

"It's all right, love." He smoothed a hand over her hair. "It was only a dream. Everything's all right."

Eve looked up at him, saw him as only a dark shape through the haze of her tears. "I could see everything, Ran." She shook her head, sending the wetness down her cheeks. "All those children. It was too horrible to imagine. How could God let something like that happen?"

Ran brushed damp strands of dark hair away from her cheek. "God didn't do it, sweetheart. Man did."

Eve clung to him, catching the scent of soap and aftershave that told her he had freshly showered. Eve took a shaky breath and eased away from him.

"I'm all right," she said, wiping her eyes. Steeling herself, she rose from the bed. "I don't know if it was a dream or perhaps something more."

Ran sighed. "I was hoping you'd be able to distance yourself. I should have realized what this would do to you. From the start, you've felt all of it. I wish I could have saved you from that."

Eve paced over to the window and stared out at the view of the sea. She turned back to Ran. "None of this is your fault. From the moment I moved into the house, Fate has played a part in my life. It's too late to go backward. All I can do now is go forward."

Ran walked over to join her. "I'm afraid you're right. Going forward is your only option. But sooner or later all of this will be over. With luck, you'll be able to find the peace you deserve."

"Will I?"

Ran said nothing. There was no way he could know what was

in store for her in the future. No one knew. Eve was beginning to understand it was better that way.

"Get dressed," Ran said. "You and I are going for that drive I've been promising. When we get back, we'll have dinner and turn in early."

"What about the asylum?"

"Not tonight," he said. "Tonight, we clear our minds and hearts. Tomorrow night, we have a meeting with the devil."

CHAPTER THIRTY-TWO

*E*ARLY THE FOLLOWING MORNING, RAN SIPPED COFFEE AS HE LOOKED out the balcony doors at the ocean, a calmer sea than it had been for the past few days. Eve was still asleep in his bed. Though he'd wanted her as he always did, last night he'd just held her. He'd been surprised to find his own comfort in that.

Today, he had a plan to lighten some of the darkness around them. So far, the weather seemed to be cooperating. A few white clouds floated past a warm spring sun, the breeze brisk but not unruly.

Ran had phoned a friend in London who'd arranged for the use of a sleek little Bristol 30, floating in a slip at the Seaham Harbour Marina, less than ten miles away. Eager to be back on the water, Ran smiled. When you owned a string of hotels around the world, there was always someone, somewhere, willing to solve a problem.

He heard the bathroom door open and close, heard the shower go on. His body tightened at the thought of joining Eve beneath the warm spray; then his cell phone rang, putting an end to the notion.

Ran pulled the phone out of the pocket of the jeans he was wearing with the white deck shoes he never traveled without. Holding the phone between his neck and shoulder, he finished rolling up the sleeves of his blue denim shirt.

"Ransom King."

"Mr. King, it's Alec Summersby." Alec had worked for King En-

terprises for the last six years. Before his retirement, he'd been a
senior intel agent for Interpol, working out of the office in Manchester, where he still lived.

Alec had proved to be invaluable in digging up information on
potential investors and business associates, running deep background checks on just about anyone interacting with the company.

"I hope this call means you've found something." Ran had
phoned the investigator after Anya's kidnapping, hoping the former agent could turn up a lead on the abduction ring and the
wealthy man who had tried to purchase an innocent girl.

"Looks like there's a gang working in that area," Alec said.
"Call themselves the East End Boys, and it wasn't the first time
they've abducted a young woman off the street. I believe the police have lately become aware of their activities, which should
help put a stop to them."

"I was recently made aware of that information, myself. Anything on the buyer?"

"Actually, finding him wasn't as difficult as I imagined. His
name is Carlton Fieldhurst. His sexual preference for underage
girls is an open secret. From what I gather, a man named Evan Jeffers acts as his procurer. A girl fitting Anya Petrova's description
was purchased by Jeffers through an Internet site on the Dark
Web just a few days after she disappeared from her home in Newcastle."

Ran clenched his jaw.

"The trouble is Fieldhurst is a shirttail aristocrat, third cousin
of Viscount Melford, a powerful man in Britain. Bringing him
down won't be easy."

Depends on how it's done, Ran thought. "I want everything you've
got on him. You have my private email."

"I'll send the file as soon as we're finished."

"Nice work. Thanks, Alec." Ran ended the call.

A few minutes later, as promised, he found the file attached to
an email. Ran started to open the file, heard footsteps coming out
of the bedroom, turned to see Eve walking into the living room.
Ran closed his laptop, leaving the file for tomorrow.

Today he was doing something for Eve and for himself. Tonight, they would return to the asylum, refreshed in mind and heart.

Or at least Ran hoped so. The forces of evil were powerful. To defeat them, they would need all their strength.

The shore was a long, low slash of color on the horizon. A crisp wind blew Eve's dark hair into her face. She laughed as she pulled it back into a ponytail and held it in place with a scrunchie.

Eve had been sailing before, at a boating party with her husband, Phillip, on a hundred-foot yacht reportedly once owned by J.P. Morgan. She'd been tense, determined to be on her best behavior for Phillip's sake. She hadn't relaxed until the yacht sailed back into Boston Harbor and its elite group of passengers disembarked.

This was different, utterly liberating instead of intimidating. The thirty-foot sailboat was as sleek and agile as a seal, cutting through the waves, the sails popping in the wind, following the skillful commands of Ransom King.

She had never seen Ran this way before, completely free, his burdens left behind, at least for today. She loved just looking at him.

As he worked the sails, he grinned like a schoolboy, making Eve laugh again. He was happy out here on the water. She was, too, she realized, inhaling the scent of the sea, feeling the warmth of the sun on her face.

When the boat began to lean into the wind, she settled herself next to Ran and just allowed herself to enjoy.

They sailed for several hours, soaking up the sensation of freedom, the sight of the white foam breaking against the bow, the feel of the fresh, stimulating breeze. Then Ran headed for a place called Nose's Point, where he anchored in a quiet cove out of the wind at the bottom of the cliffs along the shore.

"Time for the snack I promised," he said, and they ducked into the cabin, the low ceiling and light wood interior giving it a cozy feel. Bright blue canvas cushions brightened the galley nook and the bed in the bow of the boat.

Ran pulled a tray of gourmet cheeses, olives, pickles, nuts, and dried fruit out of the galley fridge, added an array of crackers, then opened a bottle of Pinot Grigio to enjoy with the food.

Thinking of what they could be facing that night, Eve looked hesitantly at her half-full glass.

"A little wine won't hurt," Ran said. "We'll have time for a nap before we—" He broke off. By unspoken agreement, they were not discussing what they could be facing that night.

Eve relaxed and raised her glass. "To this beautiful moment on the sea."

"The moment," Ran repeated. Glasses clinked and they sipped. They nibbled and tasted the various cheeses, sampled the olives, pickles, and other delicious treats the hotel had assembled; then Ran took the glass from her hand and set it next to his on the galley table.

He drew her into his arms. "It seems like forever since I've touched you."

Eve linked her hands behind his neck. The Band-Aids were gone, his cuts mostly healed. "You looked so sexy when you were sailing. I've been fantasizing all afternoon about getting you down here."

Ran laughed and kissed her. What started as light and fun quickly morphed into deeper, wetter, hotter. His big hands cupped her breasts through her sweater, a promise of things to come. Desire washed through her, the kind of need she had never felt with another man.

It occurred to her that if the night went as planned, Ran would have finished what he had come for, and his time here would be over. He would be leaving England, returning to Seattle. Returning to the life he'd had before, a life that didn't include her.

She managed to push the thought away as he led her to the V-shaped bed in the bow, kissed her, and began to strip off her clothes. Eager to feel the hard body she had been fantasizing about, Eve slid her hands inside his denim shirt, ran her palms over the muscles she had been admiring, and felt them bunch at her touch.

Ran was a big man, with wide shoulders, long powerful legs,

and a flat stomach. Eve loved to touch him, to run her fingers over his pecs, his washboard abs, lower. When both of them were naked, he pulled her down on the bed, then surprised her by lifting her and setting her astride him.

Her breathing went faster. She could feel his arousal and hunger burned through her, the same desire that darkened Ran's eyes and made his nostrils flare.

He caressed her breasts, rubbed her sensitive nipples, making them harden, making her moan.

"I can't get enough of you," he said, touching her exactly where she wanted him to, reading her mind as he managed to do far too often. She tried not to think about how much she would miss him, miss being with him this way.

She tried to tell herself she hadn't fallen in love with him. It was just an infatuation. But a lie had no place on this beautiful day. She had fallen hard for Ransom King and because she was in love with him, she forced thoughts of a future without him aside and leaned over him, her dark hair falling forward, cocooning them as her breasts pressed into his chest.

Eve kissed him with all the feelings she had kept hidden in her heart until now, and Ran kissed her back. As she straightened, her eyes met his and she wondered if he were reading her thoughts as he had before.

Determined to make the most of the time they had left, Eve sat up, lifted her hips, and took him deep inside. Her body tightened around him, and Ran hissed out a breath.

"Sweetheart, if you had any idea what you do to me . . ." Resting his hands on her hips, he held her in place, giving himself time to adjust to the feel of her damp heat and bring his body back under control.

Eve inwardly smiled, enjoying the power she held. He felt amazing. So big and male. The fire burning in his blue eyes told her how much he wanted her. Eve wanted him, too, and this time she was in charge.

Slowly she began to move, rocking against him, taking what she wanted. She increased the rhythm, moving faster, her head falling back, her dark hair sliding around her shoulders. For long moments, the pleasure built. Eve took and took and demanded more, until Ran's iron control snapped.

"My turn," he said. Gripping her hips to hold her in place, he drove into her again and again, pushing her toward the brink, taking what she was more than willing to give.

"Eve . . ." he whispered, saying her name like a vow. Her climax neared and her body tightened. Bright lights flashed behind her eyes as sweet joy filled her. Ran's jaw clenched as he followed her to a pounding release.

Long seconds passed as Eve slumped over his chest. He held her as if he didn't want this moment to end, running his hand gently up and down her back.

Her eyes burned. If only things could be different. She swallowed, blinked away tears before he could see them. Whatever happened, she would never regret the time she had spent with him. She would never regret loving Ran.

After nestling her beside him, he rose and left the bed. They had work to do. Tonight she would return to the asylum. Lucas would be there. Violet would be there to give her support, along with Jesse, Kate, and Zane. Ran would be by her side every moment. She knew she could count on him, knew he wouldn't let her down.

It was just another reason she loved him.

"I suppose we had better be getting back," Ran said, returning from the tiny bathroom sailors called a head.

"I suppose." She eased off the cushions, took her turn in the bathroom, then began pulling on her clothes.

Ran was already up on deck, making preparations for the journey back to the Seaham marina. From there they would return to the hotel to prepare for the night ahead.

Eve told herself she was ready to face whatever dark forces lay in wait for her. But every time she thought of it, her heart began to pound, and she felt lightheaded.

It was not a good sign.

CHAPTER THIRTY-THREE

*R*AN HAD SENT WORD TO THE MEMBERS OF THE TEAM. THEY planned to gather for dinner in a private salon off the main dining room, where they could discuss what might happen at the asylum and address any concerns.

Afterward, Jesse and Katie would collect whatever audio/video equipment they could piecemeal together. Each still had several handheld devices that hadn't been destroyed. Jesse could probably jury-rig something that could be useful.

At this point, Ran didn't really care what they were able to document. He simply wanted to send the ghosts of the orphan boys on to the Other Side.

Violet planned to go along to counsel Eve and give her support. So far, Violet had been unable to interact with the spirit world, either in the house or orphanage. It was Eve's show all the way.

Lucas was coming to supper. He was preparing himself for another spiritual encounter with whatever hellish creature had threatened to kill them the night they had all been together in Eve's house.

Grabbing his black wool jacket off the back of a chair, Ran left the suite, headed down the hall, and knocked on Eve's door. He had left her alone since their return to the hotel, but memories of the glorious afternoon they had spent together would not leave him.

Whatever happened, he would cherish the hours he had shared with the woman who had stolen a piece of his heart.

If things were different . . .

But nothing had changed, and there was nothing either of them could do. Ran buried his unpleasant thoughts as Eve pulled open the door and joined him in the hallway.

Ran smiled. "Hungry? That snack on the boat wasn't nearly enough." *No truer words,* he thought as a memory surfaced of the two of them in the bow of the boat. The brief interlude had hardly satisfied the hunger he felt every time he looked at her.

Eve smiled, but her eyes held the same underlying sadness that had been there all day. Both of them knew the end of their time together was near.

"I'm starving," Eve said, sliding her arm through his. "Are we eating here in the hotel?"

Ran caught her hand to keep her close. "We're meeting the others," he said. "With luck, it'll be a farewell supper. The orphans will finally be where they belong, and our work here will be over."

Eve smiled sadly. "I'm sure you'll all be glad to leave behind the cold and damp and be back in Seattle."

He had been telling himself that for days. He only wished he believed it. "Just as cold and damp in Seattle this time of year." Before either of them had to deal with where the conversation was headed, Ran urged her down the corridor to the elevator.

The rest of the team, all but Zane, was waiting for them in the private dining room, sitting around a table set for six. Ran took the chair saved for him at the head of the table. Eve sat on one side, Lucas on the other.

"Anybody seen Zane?" Ran asked as the server appeared to take their orders.

"He had an errand to run," Katie said. "He should be here any minute." The look in her eyes said she and Zane had been together at least part of the day. Ran hoped Zane was prepared to deal with Katie's capricious approach to romance.

"How was the sailing?" Luke asked as a server took their orders. "The bit of sun you two got looks good on your faces. I'm glad you decided to take a break."

"It was wonderful," Eve said. "Ran's an amazing sailor."

Ran's mouth curved. "I think she means she's grateful I managed to get us back to the marina alive."

Luke laughed.

Eve smiled. "Not at all. I went out on a yacht once, but until today, I'd never really been sailing before. It was incredible."

"I'm glad you enjoyed yourself," Ran said, with just enough huskiness in his voice to make Eve blush.

Their orders arrived just as Zane appeared, bomber jacket slung over his shoulder. "Sorry I'm late, but I was following a lead I picked up yesterday." He draped the jacket over the back of a chair and sat down, and a server quickly approached. Zane pointed at the fresh cod in lemon butter on Ran's plate, the special of the day. "I'll have what he's having."

The server hurried away and Zane took a drink from the glass of water in front of him. "We've been looking for something that would connect the orphanage with the events of that day at Victoria Hall."

Ran glanced at Eve, already beginning to worry about her. "That's right." He dragged his gaze away and swallowed a bite of succulent fish.

"Turns out the owner of the hall, Frederick Taylor, was a noted philanthropist. He often gave out free tickets to the poor kids in the community. Since this was a performance especially designed for children, it's logical and more than possible that Mr. Taylor would have given free tickets to at least some of the boys in the orphanage."

Eve stopped eating.

Ran noticed and silently cursed.

"Sorry," Zane said as his supper arrived. "I thought you'd want to know."

Ran nodded. "That's what this meeting is for. We need as much information as possible before we go over to the asylum." He saw Violet reach for Eve's hand and give it a gentle squeeze.

"Why don't we enjoy our dinner and resume this conversation after we're finished?" Ran looked at Zane. "Good work, Zane."

Zane made no reply. Ran had a feeling the research he had done was every bit as hard on Zane as it was on the rest of them.

It was almost nine p.m. by the time they had talked things over, collected their gear, and were ready to make the trek to the abandoned asylum.

They had all dressed warmly. Being together for dinner seemed to have bolstered everyone's mood and determination.

Jesse was loading their gear into the limo when Ran walked up with Eve. Lucas joined them. Ran noticed that tonight Luke carried a Bible.

Considering what had happened the last time, Ran figured they needed all the help they could get.

As the BMW approached the asylum, Eve sat forward in the seat. Blue lights flashed behind the derelict building.

"What the hell?" Ran's hands tightened on the steering wheel.

"Police," Luke said from the rear passenger seat.

Eve saw the parking lot behind the asylum was filled with yellow and blue Sunderland police vehicles, the lights on top flashing blue neon into the night.

"What is it?" Eve asked.

"No idea," Ran said, and Eve was afraid to guess.

Ran braked to a stop some distance away, turned off the engine, and all three of them got out of the car. The Bentley pulled up behind them, and Violet, Zane, and the others got out.

Across the way, police officers were filing in and out of the door to the room off the kitchen.

"What's going on?" Katie asked as she walked up.

"Stay here while I find out." Ran started walking, his long legs carrying him swiftly across the unmanicured grass. Eve spotted Detective Inspector Balfour walking toward her and started in his direction. He intercepted her halfway.

"Dr. St. Clair. What are you and the others doing here at this time of night?"

Since she had no answer, she went on the offense. "We saw the blue lights, Detective. What's going on?"

"All I can tell you is that this is a crime scene. You and your friends will have to leave."

Eve spotted Ran striding back to them. Balfour turned his attention to Ran. "This is a crime scene, Mr. King. You need to leave."

"I understand there's been a murder."

Eve wondered how Ran had wrangled the information, but nothing he accomplished surprised her.

"That's right." Balfour's gaze returned to Eve. He hesitated, as if making a decision. "You remember the East End Boys we talked about?"

"You said the man we found in the tunnel was Asif Rashid, a member of the gang. You said it was possible one of the East End Boys could have been responsible for his murder."

"That's right. Tonight, an anonymous call came in claiming there was at least one person dead in the old asylum. Turned out there were two victims."

Eve's stomach tightened.

"Can you tell us what happened?" Ran asked.

The detective shrugged. "Since you have a history with the East End Boys and you showed up here tonight, you're going to be questioned. Which means you'll find out most of it anyway."

None of them spoke, just waited for the detective to continue.

"Both victims are gang members. We figure there was a fight, one of them stabbed the other. The second victim—that's where this gets interesting. Let's just say the coroner hasn't figured out exactly how he died."

Eve caught the brief glance Ran sent her.

"Any guesses?" he asked.

"I heard Ozzie say it looks as if a projectile of some kind was hurled through the air with enough force to cave in the back of the guy's skull."

Oswell Townsend. Eve remembered meeting the Sunderland coroner when he came to her house.

"You think a third gang member committed the murder?" Ran said.

"Maybe. But that isn't the impression I'm getting. The angle's wrong or something. The projectile was thrown from somewhere up near the ceiling. They're still searching for the murder weapon. We'll have to wait for the coroner's report before we know exactly what occurred."

But Eve remembered the vicious assault by whatever soulless entity inhabited the asylum. Projectiles flying with deadly force. The power and rage were beyond anything she could have imagined. They had been lucky to get out without anyone being seriously hurt. Or killed.

"I need to get back," the detective said. "You might as well get comfortable. You won't be leaving anytime soon."

"The others aren't involved," Ran said. "Is it all right if they go back to the hotel?"

"Sorry. You showed up at exactly the wrong time. Detective Inspector Charlene Leighton is also working the case. I can have her interview the others while I talk to you and Dr. St. Clair."

Ran wasn't pleased but clearly understood the police had a job to do. "All right. Give me a minute to let the others know what's going on."

"I'll find Detective Leighton. That'll give you a couple of minutes." Balfour flashed a look at Eve. *That'll give you time to get your stories straight,* his look said.

Balfour was giving them a break. He didn't like criminals any better than she did. And he was probably fairly sure they weren't involved in the murder.

Fairly sure.

"I'll be back in a minute," Ran said as Balfour walked away. Ran took off at a jog, hurrying over to the limo, where Lucas stood next to the other members of the team. Ran spoke quickly to all of them, then returned to Eve's side.

"When they ask why we're here, tell them we came over on a lark. Lucas was in from out of town and we had been telling him how scary this place was. We figured we'd be safe now that the police are patrolling the area."

If two people weren't dead, Eve might have smiled. *A lark.* As if they actually wanted to be in a place as terrifying as the abandoned asylum.

"I guess it's as good a story as any," she said.

"Makes me sound like a fool, but it's the best I could come up with on such short notice."

Eve surprised herself by laughing. It eased the tension she was feeling. Amusement touched Ran's lips and she realized he had done it on purpose.

Eve's smile slowly faded. "I just hope stirring all of this up didn't cause these deaths."

"If Balfour is right, the guy who got hit in the head had already stabbed the other man. He was a murderer. Hard to feel sorry for a killer."

She looked back at the towering shadow of the dilapidated asylum. "I still don't like it."

"I don't like the idea this thing could kill someone else, someone far less deserving."

Eve looked up at him. "Oh, God, you're right. What are we going to do?"

"Balfour says the police should be out of here day after tomorrow. If that's the case, we can go in that night."

More time waiting, Eve thought. More time worrying. She steeled herself, resigned to the fact that there was nothing they could do.

Half an hour passed before she spotted Balfour walking toward them. She liked him, she realized. Perhaps once Ran had gone back to Seattle—

Eve glanced away. She liked him, but she wasn't ready for another romantic entanglement.

She thought of Ran and how much she loved him and wondered if she ever would be.

CHAPTER THIRTY-FOUR

*B*ALFOUR ESCORTED RAN SOME DISTANCE AWAY FROM THE OTHERS.
"So let me get this straight. According to you and your friends,
you drove over here to . . . what? Scare yourselves? That's what
I'm supposed to believe?"

Ran shrugged. "You've been in the asylum at night." Balfour
had showed up the night of the abduction. "You have to admit,
the place is pretty much terrifying. I thought they'd get a kick out
of it."

"Bollocks. You really think anyone's going to believe that?"

"Maybe not. The alternative is we saw the blue lights flashing
and stopped to see what the police were doing. Either way, it's not
a crime."

"I looked you up, King. One of your hobbies is hunting for
ghosts. Paranormal Investigations, right? If there was ever a place
to look for spirits, this has to be it. Admit it. That's why you came.
You think this place is haunted."

Ran just shrugged. "Close enough, I guess. Still not a crime."

"I assume you have the owner's permission."

He nodded. "I do."

The detective blew out a breath. "As you say, being in this location isn't a crime. And beyond wanting revenge for the abduction
of a young woman—which has yet to be proved and whose identity remains a mystery—you had no motive to kill these men."

"None whatsoever," Ran said.

"Since Detective Inspector Leighton has finished her questioning and come to the same conclusion, you and your friends can go."

"Thank you."

"We may have more questions. Be better if you didn't leave town."

Ran felt an unexpected sweep of relief knowing he couldn't go back to Seattle—at least not yet.

He delivered the news to the others. They climbed into the cars and all returned to the hotel. Willard had done them a favor, telling the police he knew nothing, just drove people wherever they wanted to go.

Back at the Grand Hotel Sunderland, the team members went up to their rooms, all but Eve and Lucas.

"I need to speak to both of you," Luke said.

Reading the exhaustion on Eve's face, Ran drew her a little closer. "I had room service deliver a bottle of brandy to my suite. After tonight I thought we might need a drink. As it turns out, I was right, though not for the reason I thought."

"I could use a brandy," Luke said.

"I was praying this would all be over tonight." Eve gave him a weary smile. "Since that isn't the case, a glass of brandy sounds good."

They settled themselves in the living room, Ran next to Eve on the sofa, Luke in a matching chair. Each held a crystal rocks glass filled with amber liquid.

Ran took a drink, appreciating the warmth that eased some of the tension still thrumming through him. "Luke? You had something you wanted to say."

"Yes. As Eve said, I was hoping we'd make a good deal of progress this evening. Unfortunately, the deaths at the orphanage tonight change the dynamics. They also change our timeline. Two men are dead. From what the detective told us, I'm guessing there's more than a good chance the second man's death didn't happen at human hands."

Ran had been thinking the same thing. "Whatever is in the orphanage, the power it wields is incredible."

"It's a miracle we escaped without injury the night we were there," Eve said.

"Someone else could wind up getting killed," Luke said. "We need to do the exorcism now, not later."

Eve leaned toward Lucas. "What about the children?"

"If things go our way," he said, "we can make all of it happen at once."

Eve settled back on the sofa and Ran rested an arm around her shoulders. "I promise you we won't abandon them."

"No," Lucas agreed. "With God's help, we'll defeat Satan's henchmen, release the boys, and show them the way to the Other Side, where they belong."

The sound of his cell phone ringing awoke Ran for the second time the following morning. At first light, he had found Eve nestled against him, her fingers stroking over his chest, moving lower. He was already aroused. Eve urged him into her welcoming heat, and afterward, they had drifted off again.

Ran wiped the sleep from his eyes and reached for the phone, disturbing Eve, who made an unhappy sound in her throat.

Ran smiled. Easing her gently away, he sat up on the edge of the bed and pressed the phone against his ear. "King."

"Alec Summersby here, Mr. King. Sorry to bother you, but this news involves Carlton Fieldhurst. You said I should let you know if anything new came up."

"I did. What is it, Alec?"

"Fieldhurst has left London for a weeklong visit to his country house in East Gilling. It's only a bit more than an hour's drive from where you are now. I thought you would want to know."

"Interesting news, Alec. I'm glad you called."

"The thing is, sir, Fieldhurst is having a very exclusive party at the estate tonight. A charity ball, formal affair, over a hundred guests."

Ran sorted through the possibilities. "Any chance you could get me an invitation?"

"Already done, sir. An invitation for you and a guest. I'll have it messengered to you at the hotel today."

"Nicely done. Text me any other pertinent information, will you?"

"Certainly, sir. I shall do so immediately."

The call ended and Ran looked up to see Eve standing next to him in a silky robe and a pair of fuzzy slippers. She looked delectable.

"I was hoping we'd have a little more time this morning before we had to leave. But life interferes."

Eve smiled. "Yes, it does. What was that about?"

So far he'd been able to keep her out of this, but he wasn't willing to lie to her, either. "I've had a private investigator, a man who works for me named Summersby, looking into the matter of Anya's abduction. Summersby has discovered the identity of the man who purchased Anya through a site on the Dark Web."

Eve dropped down on the bed beside him. "What's the man's name?"

"Carlton Fieldhurst. Apparently, he has some powerful relatives, including his cousin, Viscount Melford."

She eyed him with the certain knowledge he was far from done with Fieldhurst. "You're going after him?"

"One way or another Fieldhurst is finished. I'm not sure of the details yet. But according to Alec, the man is spending the week in East Gilling. He's having a charity ball at his country estate tonight. I thought I would attend."

"Are you sure that's a good idea?"

"No, but meeting him could give me a little more insight. It's always best to know your adversary."

"Whatever you're planning, I want to go with you."

"That isn't going to happen."

"You can't attend an event like that without a date—and I might be able to help."

Ran thought of the lovely distraction Eve would pose. It could give him a chance to look around. Inwardly, he was relieved that she was far too old for Fieldhurst's warped tastes. Perfect for Ran, but not for a man who preyed on young virgins.

"All right, you can come. It's a little over an hour's drive." He looked at her in the silky robe that outlined her slender curves, and wished he had more time. "It's a formal affair. You're going to need something to wear."

"I have several things at my house. My ex-husband was very socially active."

"I don't want you going back there until we're finished at the asylum. We passed some lovely boutiques downtown. Why don't we go shopping?" He smiled. "My treat."

Eve started to object.

"You're doing this for me," Ran argued. "It's only fair I pick up the tab. Besides, we'll make it fun."

"What about you? Surely you didn't pack a tuxedo?"

"No, but I can have one sent from my apartment in London. It'll be here by this afternoon."

"You have an apartment in London?"

"I rented it when I was flying back and forth, negotiating a hotel merger. It took several months to close the deal. I ended up liking London, so I kept it."

Eve just shook her head. "Of course. A great place to store your clothes. A man can't spend time in London without a Savile Row tuxedo."

As far as he was concerned that was true, so he just smiled.

"Fine. We'll go shopping," Eve said. "I hope I can find something that meets your approval." With that she sashayed out of the bedroom into the bathroom and turned on the shower.

Since he liked her best in nothing at all, Ran joined her.

CHAPTER THIRTY-FIVE

*E*VE CHECKED HER APPEARANCE IN THE MIRROR IN THE ENTRY. THE gown she wore was a full-length sapphire-blue sheath that hugged her curves and had a split up one side to her knee. It was expensive, in perfect taste, and stunningly beautiful.

She felt guilty letting Ran pay for it, but he had insisted, and she couldn't really afford a dress that cost so much.

She turned to study her reflection and approved of the way she had swept her dark hair into a loose chignon at the back of her head and left soft tendrils beside each ear. She reached up to touch the magnificent dangling diamond earrings that had arrived with Ran's tux, borrowed from a Bond Street jewelry store apparently well acquainted with Ran's sophisticated tastes.

A knock came at the door. With a calming breath, she walked over and pulled it open. The man in the designer tuxedo and snowy-white shirt was so handsome her breath caught. And he was hers for the evening.

"You look even more beautiful than I imagined." Ran's gaze swept over her, the heat in his incredible blue eyes making her wish they were already back from the party.

"So do you," Eve said without thinking because it was true.

Ran just smiled. "Thank you. Are you ready?"

"Let me get my bag." Rhinestones glittered on the designer purse Ran had chosen at a boutique shop on Fawcett Street. Eve grabbed the bag and they headed down the hall.

The Bentley limo waited in front of the hotel for the hour-plus ride to Fieldhurst's country estate. They sipped from a chilled bottle of Christal along the way, making the time pass quickly. Eve glanced out the window as the limo turned onto a road that wound through vast green parkland sprinkled with leafy trees.

"I wonder how many acres Fieldhurst owns," she said.

"According to the information Alec sent, the house sits on a hundred acres. It was originally built in the late fourteenth century, completely remodeled and added onto late in the fifteen hundreds, and, of course, remodeled and updated many times after that. Fieldhurst inherited the property about ten years ago."

The limo continued its journey and eventually pulled up behind a Rolls-Royce and a Mercedes-Benz limousine rolling toward the front of a U-shaped, three-story mansion built of buff-colored stone.

"We should be among the last to arrive," Ran said. "I prefer to blend in, give ourselves some time to look around before I speak to Fieldhurst."

Eve made no reply. Her nerves were suddenly thrumming. The historic home was lovely, profoundly beautiful in its ancient way. It occurred to her the upkeep and taxes must be tens of thousands of pounds per year.

"Fieldhurst must have more money than he can count."

"I'm sure he does," Ran said. "These days, virgins don't come cheap."

The words sparked a fire inside her. Eve's nerves settled beneath her determination to see this man got what he deserved. They made their way up the stone steps, through ornately carved wooden doors, into a grand entrance hall, which, with its black and white marble floors, towering ceilings, and heavy glass chandeliers, was spectacular.

There were only two people left in the receiving line. A weak-chinned man in his forties with thinning blond hair and a beautiful auburn-haired woman a few years younger, both of their smiles reflecting how much they wished the affair was over.

"Good evening," the man said. "I'm Gideon Fieldhurst and this is my wife, Barbara. Welcome to East Gilling Hall."

Ran made a brief nod of his head. "Ransom King and Dr. Eve St. Clair. A pleasure to meet you."

"You as well," Gideon said. "Unfortunately, my mother wasn't feeling well enough to attend this evening. My father has already gone into the ballroom to join the other guests. If you'll just take the staircase to your right, you'll find it on the second floor."

Ran had mentioned that Claudia Fieldhurst rarely attended events with her husband. Eve wondered if the woman was aware of her husband's infidelities and figured she probably was.

Eve took Ran's arm as they climbed the wide marble staircase to the second floor. The house was huge and spectacularly lovely, the ballroom filled with guests decked out in their finest, wandering and chatting beneath a high molded ceiling and heavy chandeliers.

Knowing a little of the history of the ancient property, Eve couldn't help wondering if there were any notorious ghosts in residence. In truth, she sensed only the lingering echo of souls who had once filled the halls and chambers of the house.

Ran led her toward a bar at the end of the ballroom. Another bar served guests at the opposite end. Waiters streamed past with glasses of champagne and hors d'oeuvres on gleaming silver trays. Potted palms and colorful orchids set an elegant tone throughout the opulent chamber.

"Do you know what Fieldhurst looks like?" Eve asked.

"Oh, yes. I know." The crowd parted as Ran guided her across the ballroom to the bar, ordered himself a scotch, and plucked a glass of champagne off a passing waiter's tray.

Handing Eve the glass, he leaned down to whisper in her ear. "I believe that's Fieldhurst in the circle of people off to your right." He gave her a devious smile. "Why don't I introduce you?"

Eve managed to nod. She was going to meet a man guilty of heinous crimes. Pasting on a smile, she followed Ran into the circle of guests surrounding their host. Since Ransom King had a presence few people could ignore, he immediately drew the older man's attention.

Carlton Fieldhurst was midsixties, silver-haired, with the cold blue eyes of a predator and the same weak chin as his son. Eve pitied the innocent young women Fieldhurst had forced into his bed.

"I don't believe we've met," their host said, smiling. "Carlton Fieldhurst."

"Ransom King."

"Ah, yes. King Enterprises."

Fieldhurst's gaze went to Eve, and though she was far older than the young girls that appealed to him, she could feel his gaze sliding over her like day-old grease.

"And your lovely companion?" he asked Ran.

"Dr. Eve St. Clair," she answered for him.

Fieldhurst took her hand and pressed the back against his lips. "A pleasure, Dr. St. Clair."

Ran's jaw tightened. Eve drew her hand away and took a sip of champagne, hoping to diffuse the tension. "Lovely party."

"Thank you," Fieldhurst said, still smiling.

"I wonder if we might chat in private?" Ran suggested.

One of Fieldhurst's silver eyebrows winged up. "I have other guests, of course, but since I'm hoping you'll make a generous donation to the Fieldhurst Family Charity Fund, I can certainly spare a few moments. If you'll follow me."

Ran leaned down to whisper in her ear. "Stay out of trouble. I'll be right back." He kissed her cheek in a show of possession and followed Carlton Fieldhurst out of the ballroom.

Eve felt a trickle of annoyance. She wanted to see Fieldhurst get what he deserved as much as Ran did. On the other hand, Ran seemed to have the situation under control. While he was gone, perhaps she could learn something useful. Eve took a sip of her champagne and began to wander around the ballroom.

Ran followed Carlton Fieldhurst into an anteroom with heavy square beams overhead and ornate gilded sconces on the walls. A dark green velvet sofa and chairs surrounded an ornately carved coffee table on a thick Persian carpet.

Fieldhurst walked over to an ancient oak sideboard against the wall and lifted the stopper off a crystal decanter. "Freshen your drink?"

"It's fine."

Fieldhurst poured an inch of amber liquor into his glass and the stopper went back in the bottle with a crystal ring. "What can I do for you, Mr. King?"

Ran took a sip of his scotch. "I'd like to purchase a virgin. I hear you're quite good at locating them. Since I'm new to this kind of thing, I was hoping you would assist in my endeavor."

Fieldhurst's silver eyebrows looked glued to his forehead. "I haven't the slightest idea what you're talking about."

"Perhaps an introduction to Mr. Jeffers would solve my problem."

Fieldhurst went pale. He must have realized Ran was the man who had confronted him at the asylum. He set his glass down on the oak sideboard, walked over, and pulled open the door. The sound of classical music drifted in from the ballroom. "I think you had better leave."

Ran took a drink of scotch. "I'll be more than happy to do that. But first let's clear the air. To begin with, I'm not the only one aware of your highly illegal proclivities."

The door closed with the solid thump of heavy wood. "What do you want?"

"I want your days of debauchery to end. I'm determined to make that happen at any cost. You're a wealthy man, Fieldhurst, but so am I. I hear a word about you and another young woman, you won't be able to hold your head up in London society or anywhere else. Do you understand?"

"Who the hell do you think you are?"

"I'm the man who's holding you by the balls, the man who was there the night you showed up at the asylum to claim your prize. I know the young woman you tried to debauch. For now, she isn't interested in pursuing the matter, but that could change. At this very moment, the police are interviewing the thugs who abducted the girl and sold her to you. They may not know your name, but they could certainly contribute useful information. All of it taken together—you could be in very serious trouble."

"You're insane."

Ran ignored him. "If you want your fancy lifestyle to continue, if you want your wife and family kept in the dark, you'll keep your fly zipped and get rid of your procurer. You and Jeffers are finished with your disgusting games."

"Get out!" Fieldhurst shouted, but he was shaking.

Ran had built a career out of reading people. Fieldhurst was done. He wouldn't risk humiliating himself or his family. Ran left his drink on the table and returned to the ballroom. He found Eve talking to a woman and her husband not far from where he'd left her.

"Something's come up," Ran said. "I'm afraid we'll have to leave."

She turned to the couple in front of her. "I enjoyed meeting you. Have a pleasant evening."

"You as well," the woman said.

The couple wandered away and began chatting with someone else. Ran took Eve's arm and in minutes they were downstairs waiting for the limo. The Bentley pulled up just seconds after their arrival.

Ran opened the rear door before the driver had time to get out, and both of them slid into the back seat. "Take us home, Willard."

"Yes, sir."

The chauffer had been invaluable during Ran's tenure in England. He planned to give Willard a very sizable tip. The limo pulled away and Ran leaned back in his seat. He wished he had the glass of scotch he had left in the anteroom.

"What happened?" Eve asked.

"Fieldhurst has decided to reform his lecherous ways."

"He has?"

"Not exactly. But I have a hunch, now that his sexual perversions have been exposed, he'll think twice before engaging in them again."

"So that's it? Fieldhurst promises to be a good little boy and he gets off scot-free?"

Ran took her hand and brought it to his lips. "Bloodthirsty little creature, aren't you?"

Eve pulled her hand away. "He deserves to be in prison."

"That may happen yet. Even if it doesn't, I can pretty much guarantee, he's going to experience a great deal of financial trouble in the near future."

Eve relaxed back in her seat. "Now who's the bloodthirsty creature?"

"As you say, Fieldhurst deserves to pay and so he shall."

Eve smiled, apparently willing to leave retribution up to him. Ran wasn't going to let her down.

"I met an interesting couple while you were gone," Eve said.

"Did you now?"

"Mr. and Mrs. Turner-Wilcox. They live in the area. We talked about the history of Gilling Hall, and Martin Turner-Wilcox told me a story about a ghost in the residence who liked to leave flowers on the pillow next to someone sleeping in one of the guest rooms."

"A romantic ghost."

She smiled. "People reported all sorts of sightings: floating white specters, a long-haired maiden carrying a bridal bouquet. Turned out it wasn't a ghost at all. It was a hedgehog. A household pet named Hedgie. He roamed through the old servants' passages that had mostly been sealed up."

Ran laughed. It dissipated some of the adrenaline still pumping through him. Looking at Eve, he knew exactly how to relieve the rest. "So the hedgehog stole flowers from around the house and left them as gifts."

"Exactly."

It was good to hear a funny ghost story and see the smile on Eve's face. Ran leaned over and kissed her. She looked so beautiful he wanted to take her there in the back seat. Since neither of them were teens anymore and he didn't want to shock Willard into wrecking the car, he would have to wait.

"I'll be glad when we get back to the hotel," he said.

Eve's gaze, warm, inviting, and tinged with the same desire he was feeling, met his. "Me too," she said, and then she kissed him.

CHAPTER THIRTY-SIX

*E*VE DRESSED IN BROWN PANTS AND A LIGHTWEIGHT TURQUOISE sweater before joining Ran in his suite. Both of them had been working all morning: Ran on King Enterprises business; Eve making calls, one to her housekeeper to postpone this week's cleaning, another to her CPA, then doing some online banking. She had checked on Donny, then called Bethany to see how she was feeling and confirm their upcoming appointments.

By that time, she told herself, all of this would be over.

Zane had told Ran the police had released the crime scene this morning. They were planning to go over to the asylum tonight.

The team had the day to themselves before meeting in his suite. From there they would drive over to the orphanage. In the meantime, Ran was taking her to a late lunch at a country inn called the Wayside Farm. Eve was grateful. Anything to keep her mind off the evening ahead.

Eve made her way down the hall, and Ran opened his door before she had time to knock. Cell phone against his ear, he motioned her into his suite, holding up a finger to tell her he'd be finished in a minute.

Eve wandered over to the windows that looked out on the sea. In the distance, ominous clouds hovered above the ocean. Rain and wind were predicted for tonight.

It figured, Eve thought. Everything about the task they faced had become more and more difficult.

She felt Ran's big hands on her shoulders, gently turning her to face him. He bent and pressed a soft kiss on her lips.

"Sorry for that," he said. "That was Amsterdam. A situation arose that needed to be resolved. Fortunately, we're in the same time zone."

Eve smiled. "It's all right, I was enjoying the view." They both turned to look out the window, stood for a moment just watching the swell of the waves. "Unfortunately, with a storm coming in, I don't think tonight is going to be pleasant."

"No, especially not with all the leaks in the roof and the broken windows in the asylum."

"To say nothing of a demon who can turn a windstorm into a hurricane."

Ran's jaw tightened. "For now, let's enjoy the day and worry about all of that later."

He escorted Eve out of the suite and they took the stairs to the lobby. The limo waited out front. "You aren't driving the Beamer today?" Eve asked.

Ran smiled. "Willard knows how to get to the restaurant, and this way I get to cuddle with you in the back seat."

Eve laughed.

They had just settled themselves inside the Bentley when Ran's cell phone rang. He took it out and looked down at the screen.

"It's Tom Mason, the estate agent." As the limo pulled away from the curb, he put the phone on speaker.

"Mr. King. Tom Mason here. Afraid I'll be needin' that key back today. Mr. Stanhope sold the old asylum."

Ran frowned. "Do you know who bought it?"

"Somebody local. They're gonna do a big remodel, use it for an ol' folks' home."

Eve's gaze locked with Ran's.

"I was about to make an offer," he said, "but to do that, I'll need a few more days."

"Sorry, deal's done, Mr. King. The seller wants the key back right away. I'll be over in just a few minutes to pick it up."

"I'm on my way to lunch, Tom. I'll bring the key by in the morning."

"Beggin' yer pardon, sir, but I stuck me neck out on this already. The buyer is comin' over to get the key in an hour. Just tell me where ye are and I'll come right there an' pick it up."

Ran sighed. "The key is in my suite at the hotel. I'll meet you there."

"All right, then. I'll be seein' ye soon." The line went dead.

Ran turned to the limo driver. "Willard, you need to turn around and take us back to the hotel."

"Yes, sir."

"We don't have time to make a copy of the key?" Eve asked.

"Even if we had time, as old as the lock is on that front door, it might not be easy to make one."

"So what are we going to do?"

Ran flashed her a roguish grin. "We're going to trespass. We did it once. In that place, another broken window won't even be noticed."

Ran returned the key to Tom Mason as promised; then Willard drove them out to the Wayside Farm, a lovely old country inn with dark wood paneling, quiet booths, and the incredible food of a two-star Michelin restaurant.

Afterward they strolled the open green fields surrounding the inn and enjoyed the brisk spring weather.

Back in Ran's suite, they spent the rest of the afternoon in bed. Time for them was running out. They both knew it. There was a quiet desperation in their lovemaking, yet afterward, Ran felt a kind of peace he had never felt before.

He ignored a trickle of guilt. He didn't want to think about Sabrina. What they'd had together was different. They'd been happy. They'd had a child they both worshipped. But Sabrina had built her set of friends and Ran had his own. They spent time together, but his work often kept him away from home.

With Eve, he felt a closeness, a bond that he and Sabrina had never shared. He was going to miss Eve badly when they parted.

Which sent his mind in a direction he had never allowed it to go. What if their relationship didn't have to end? What if he asked Eve to consider a future with him? Was there a chance her feelings for him were as strong as his for her?

Ran had never believed in long-distance romances. Eve deserved more than that and so did he. There would be sacrifices involved. He couldn't move to Sunderland. He lived in Seattle, had built a giant corporation, a business that affected the lives of hundreds of employees and their families.

He would have to ask Eve to give up the life she was building in England and make a home with him in the States.

The notion stirred a deep longing inside him. Was he actually thinking of marriage? They hadn't known each other that long, and yet Ran felt as if he knew Eve better than any woman he had ever met.

You have time, he told himself. *You don't have to make a decision right now.* At the moment, they had a huge problem to solve, and he was consumed by worry over putting his people in danger.

He looked up to see Eve walking out of his bedroom. Her dark hair was mussed, her makeup mostly gone. She looked pretty and sexy. Like a woman who had been deliciously tumbled. He wanted her all over again.

"I've got to go back to my suite to shower and dress," she said. "What time are we going to the orphanage?"

"I need to talk to the others, bring them up to speed. Since we no longer have a key or the owner's permission, we'll be going in late, well after dark. No use risking a run-in with the police. I'm thinking we should all have dinner together at the pub down the block before we head over."

"That's a good idea. If tonight goes the way we hope, we won't be together much longer."

Ran's chest tightened. "No," was all he said.

Eve glanced away, as if their parting was equally upsetting for her. Ran could only hope.

"What time's the meeting?" Eve asked.

"We'll meet in my suite at eight p.m. We can talk things through, then go over to the pub. I'll let the others know."

Eve just nodded. "In the meantime, I have some things I need to do."

Ran watched her leave, and the longing he'd felt before re-turned. Then a memory surfaced of his wife and daughter lying on the icy ground, a white sheet draped over their lifeless bodies, Chrissy just a tiny bundle next to her mother. He remembered the tears that had frozen on his cheeks, remembered wiping the blood off his forehead as the EMTs insisted he get into the ambulance. He didn't remember anything after that. Not until he awoke. Not until he was forced to deal with the deaths of the two people he loved most in the world.

Ran swallowed and shoved the memory away, but his heart was pounding.

He raked a hand through his hair, settling himself, pulled out his cell and began texting Luke and the members of the team.

CHAPTER THIRTY-SEVEN

DARKNESS ENVELOPED THE SHADOWY, DILAPIDATED BRICK STRUC-
ture. Low clouds hung over the landscape, heightening the eerie
feel, and a thin, wet drizzle had begun. The limo dropped them
off on an unlit street on the side of the asylum, everyone but
Lucas, who had left supper early and gone back to his room to
make last-minute preparations for the ordeal ahead.

Ran and Zane had come over while it was still light to find the
best way in. Zane had pulled some boards off a broken window,
gone in and come out through an old arched doorway mostly
hidden by overgrown shrubs.

Now they were back. Eve walked next to Ran as Zane silently
led the group to the hidden door.

"Stay in the shadows," Zane said. "I'll be right back."

Eve watched him disappear around the corner out of sight. No
one spoke until the old wooden door inwardly creaked open and
Zane motioned them inside. Both Jesse and Katie carried canvas
bags slung over their shoulders. Jesse used his flashlight to lead
the way. Katie followed with a light, then Violet, Eve, and Ran with
his own flashlight.

Zane went back outside to wait for Lucas. The limo had gone
back to the hotel to pick him up, and Eve prayed he would be
there soon.

Flashlights burned through the darkness as Eve walked inside
the asylum and the group picked their way through the filth and

debris into the main salon. One of the large paned windows was broken, letting in the wind and drizzle that continued to build.

Ignoring the smell, the scummy water on the floor, and the graffiti on the walls, they continued to the little chapel off to one side of the main structure. Ran had told Lucas about the asylum chapel, and he had insisted that was the spot the exorcism should take place.

Shining a light over the walls and the altar at the front, Jesse went in ahead of them. Eve followed, holding on to Ran's hand. The place was as grim as Eve remembered, the destruction and bloodred Satanic symbols filling her with dread.

The pew in the front row was splintered and unusable. While Katie held the light, Jesse righted the second pew and one on the other side of the aisle near the back of the room. Pulling a towel from his gear bag, he wiped down the wooden seats as best he could; then he and Katie positioned themselves on a pew near the back, hoping to get something with their handheld equipment— what little remained after most of it had been destroyed in Eve's cellar.

Ran guided Eve to the front of the chapel. "We're waiting for Lucas?" she asked.

"He just texted. The limo's outside. Zane's bringing him in. Let's take a seat."

Both of them were dressed in jeans, sweatshirts, and warm jackets. Ran wore his low-topped leather boots, and Eve wore the hiking boots she'd been wearing in the tunnel. All of the team members were dressed warmly. There was no way to know how long they would be there. It could be minutes or hours, or maybe nothing would happen at all.

Eve heard a noise at the back of the room, and Jesse shined his flashlight in that direction. Lucas stood in the doorway wearing a long white robe with a wide gold band that slanted in a vee from his shoulders to a line down the front. A heavy crucifix dangled from a long chain around his neck, and Eve could just make out the thin gold chain that held his St. Michael's medallion, which he'd tucked inside the robe.

Lucas held a Bible in one hand. A string of rosary beads was draped over the palm of his other hand as he walked down the aisle in her direction.

Lucas bent, brushed a kiss on each of Eve's cheeks, and took a compact Bible out of his pocket. He handed her the Bible. "God be with you, Eve. God be with all of us tonight."

Lucas walked back up the aisle toward the doorway, his robes floating out as he turned to face the front of the church.

As per the plan, Jesse took a portable light out of his gear bag that could be angled in any direction, set it on the floor in the middle of the aisle at Lucas's feet, and powered it up. A soft yellow circle illuminated the former priest, a man who had special dispensation from the church to do God's work. All the other lights went off.

In the glow of the yellow circle, Luke made the sign of the cross. Eve sat on the second pew facing the altar, Violet on one side, Ran on the other. The faint cooing of pigeons came from the rafters near the broken stained-glass window. There was a jagged hole in the roof above the altar, letting in the wind and misty rain.

"I'm right beside you, dear," Violet said, squeezing her hand.

"Whatever happens, Violet, I'm glad you're here."

Ran shifted toward Eve on the bench. "Go ahead, honey. See if you can reach Herbie."

Eve clenched her hands together in her lap and said a silent prayer. She wished she had brought Wally's little sailor hat, though it might not have worked to attract the ghost of the older boy.

She took a steadying breath. "Herbie . . . ?" Her voice echoed across the empty chamber. "Herbie, it's Evie. You remember me, don't you? I'm Wally's friend."

Nothing.

"Wally's gone to a place where it's warm and bright, and there are people there who love him. It's the place where all of you were supposed to go. He's waiting for you and the others to join him."

Nothing.

In the background, Eve could hear Lucas repeating the rosary over and over, first in Latin, then in English. She recognized the conclusion of the Lord's Prayer.

"'. . . forgive us our trespasses as we forgive those who trespass against us; and lead us not into temptation, but deliver us from evil. Amen.'"

She listened as he started speaking in Latin again.

"'*Ave Maria, gratia plena Dominus tecum benedicta tu in mulieribus, et benedictus fructus ventris tui, Jesus. Sancta Maria mater Dei, ora pro nobis peccatoribus, nunc et in hora mortis nostrae. Amen.*'"

Eve concentrated on reaching Herbie. "Can you hear me, Herbie? I came here to help you and the other boys. You can be with Wally. You don't have to stay here anymore."

Lucas continued the exorcism, each of his words heightening the tension gripping her insides.

"'Hail Mary, full of grace, the Lord is with you; blessed are you among women, and blessed is the fruit of your womb, Jesus. Holy Mary, Mother of God, pray for us sinners, now and at the hour of our death.'" More Latin followed. "'*Gloria ria Patri, et Filio, et Spiritui Sancto, sicut erat in principio, et nunc, et semper, et in saecula saeculorum. Amen.*'

Eve concentrated on Herbie, forming a mental picture of the bone-thin boy who had lived in the orphanage.

Evie . . . ? The word was so faint and distorted she almost didn't recognize the sound of her name.

Her heart rate kicked up. "I'm right here, Herbie. Let me help you."

Something was happening in the asylum. The grating noise of wood scraping across the floor sent chills creeping over her skin. One of the broken wooden pews was moving. The sound of the wind outside intensified, rustling the branches against the windowpanes.

Eve's heart rate speeded. "Herbie? I'm right here, Herbie."

The soft strains of an old-fashioned music box began to play. In her mind, she could see a tiny carousel with miniature horses spinning around. Her breathing quickened. "Herbie, are you here?"

I'm here, Evie. I wanna be with Wally.

A piece of wood crashed down from the ceiling, smashed into the once-ornate altar, and slammed to the floor. The music suddenly stopped.

Eve's pounding heart accelerated. Behind her, she recognized part of the Latin incantation Lucas had chanted that night in the cellar, and the shaft of golden light appeared as it had before.

It was beautiful. Mesmerizing. Eve took a shaky breath and focused on Herbie. "Are the others here, Herbie?"

Long seconds passed. The wind increased and the rain picked up, heavy drops knocking against the slate roof.

Eve's breath caught as thin drifts of eerie white fog began to glide into the chapel, emerging through the walls and ceiling. As the fog began to take shape, little by little, she could make out what appeared to be a group of hazy figures.

Dear God, the boys from the orphanage. The translucent shapes were of various sizes. Children ages three to thirteen had died in the disaster at Victoria Hall.

With a flutter of wings overhead, the pigeons swooped down from the rafters, then shot out through the hole in the roof. A gust of wind rushed in, followed by a bright bolt of lightning outside that lit the stained-glass window.

Eve heard the roar of the evil voice she had heard before.

Leave this place! Now!

Lucas's tone subtly shifted, grew deeper, more intense. "In the name of the Father, the Son, and the Holy Spirit, I command you, demon, to depart this place. St. Michael, the mighty archangel, defend us in this battle. Be our protection against the wickedness and snares of the devil. May God rebuke him, we humbly pray; and, you, O Prince of the Heavenly Host, by the power of God, cast into hell Satan and all the evil spirits who prowl the world seeking the ruin of souls. Amen."

Eve was shaking. "Can you see the light, Herbie? Take the other boys and move toward the light."

Lucas was repeating the intonation in Latin, calling for St. Michael to help them.

Eve steeled herself. "Herbie, move the boys toward the light. You'll all be free. You'll be with people who love you. You'll be with God, Herbie."

The thin white wisps began floating toward the light, the tallest in front, Herbie, she thought, leading the way, inching closer and closer to the golden shaft that would lead to their salvation.

"Keep going, Herbie." The shapes continued to move, floating closer and closer to the warm golden circle. Then another figure began to take form. It was a cold grayish black, dense and obscure, with round, glowing red eyes.

It shot into the air and hovered above the children. *You will not leave! You belong to me!*

The small ghostly figures stopped moving. *We're afraid.*

Eve's heart clenched. She didn't think anyone else could hear them; the thought had just come into her head.

"Keep going," Eve said. "God will protect you." Eve prayed it was true. "Just keep moving toward the light."

The small apparitions started drifting again, floating above the floor.

Stop! Now!

The figures paused, their hazy images shaking with fear.

"Don't be afraid. Don't let the evil monster stop you!"

Something moved through the air, something dark and deadly. Eve kept talking.

"You can save them Herbie!" Tears rolled down her cheeks.

Herbie began to move, leading the other children. He was the first to reach the light. In a sudden flash of brilliant white, he was gone. Two more shapes stepped into the circle. Brilliant light flashed, and they disappeared. Each pair disappeared into the light until only the smallest figure remained.

"Keep going!" Eve shouted above the roar of the wind.

No! He is mine! Lightning cracked and thunder rumbled.

A second voice argued, *Let him go!*

Eve recognized the other man she had heard in her hallway.

Mama? The smallest figure began crying for a mother lost long ago.

Eve swallowed. "Don't be afraid!" Fresh tears streamed down her cheeks. "The others are waiting for you!"

I will kill you! The broken stained-glass window began to crack, spidering out in a jagged pattern, and pieces of colored glass started flying across the room.

"Get down!" Ran shouted.

Violet ducked behind the broken front pew, and Ran pulled Eve down just as the stained glass exploded into a thousand pieces, slicing like knives across the room. Shards of colored glass flew over the heads of everyone crouched on the floor. Then the wind tore at the hole in the roof, and a deadly barrage of slate roof tiles shot through the opening.

"Run!" Ran shouted as soon as the barrage had passed overhead. "Hurry!" He urged Eve and Violet up the aisle and they raced toward Lucas, who stood like a statue, repeating, over and over, the incantations he had spoken before.

Zane rushed into the chapel and ran toward Katie, who had stumbled on her way up the aisle. Violet made it out the door, but Eve pulled away from Ran and turned back toward the small gauzy figure still floating near the light. "Keep going, sweetheart—you're almost there!"

The child-size ghost drifted a few feet farther. The small figure floated, inching closer and closer to the golden light.

"Go!" Eve shouted.

In a single quick flash, the small ghostly figure was gone.

The children were safe. A sweet burst of joy swelled inside her as more tears poured down her cheeks. Eve was smiling when Ran scooped her into his arms and carried her out of the chapel. Lucas strode out of the chapel behind them.

"Don't stop!" Ran shouted to the others, all of them scrambling through the main salon toward the arched wooden door where they had come in. As they raced outside, every window in the asylum imploded, vicious shards of glass slicing through the freezing air inside.

They were out of the building, racing for the limo, when Eve realized Zane carried Katie draped lifelessly over his arms.

CHAPTER THIRTY-EIGHT

*R*AN STOOD IN THE STERILE CORRIDOR OUTSIDE THE WAITING ROOM of the Sunderland Royal Hospital in Kayll Road, a compound of tan-and-white brick buildings three to four stories high. Doctors in white lab coats and nurses in pale blue scrubs hurried impatiently past him, too busy to notice another worried face.

While Eve, Jesse, Violet, and Zane sat in the waiting room behind glass windows, Ran paced the hallway, too tense to stay in one spot for long. Sharing the same restless energy, Luke had removed his robe, leaving him in his jeans and white dress shirt, and walked over to St. Gabriel's Catholic Church, just a short distance away.

Luke had gone to pray for Katie, who lay in the Neuroscience ICU with a traumatic brain injury. Ran wished with everything inside him that he was the one lying in the room instead of Katie.

He blew out a slow breath. This was all his fault. He was the one responsible for the members of the team. He had known going in tonight could be dangerous. He never should have let the others come along.

Ran thought of Eve and why he had gone to Sunderland in the first place. He and the team had flown all the way from Seattle to help Eve, but as things progressed, he should have realized he was in way over his head.

Ran was no expert on the paranormal. He was well read and open-minded, but he had never experienced anything like the madness he had witnessed in the asylum tonight. Even Luke seemed unable to handle the level of Satanic evil they had encountered.

"Ran . . . ? Are you okay?"

He looked up at the sound of Eve's voice. Was he okay? Definitely not.

"I'm worried. The doctor says the swelling on the brain hasn't lessened. They're waiting to see how things progress, but there's a chance she'll need surgery to release the pressure."

"I know," Eve said softly.

Katie had been racing up the aisle toward the door when one of the heavy slate roof tiles had hit her in the back of the head. Thank God Zane had seen what happened, braved the vicious onslaught to reach her, and carried her to safety. But by then it was too late.

Willard had driven the limo like a madman, rushing to the emergency room at Sunderland Royal. In minutes, Katie had been swept off to one of the curtained enclosures.

Ran felt Eve's hand settle gently on his arm. "Katie's going to be okay. You have to believe that."

He rubbed a hand over his jaw, felt the roughness of his late-night beard. They'd been at the hospital all night. It was still dark outside, but dawn wasn't far away.

"I've got a call in to one of the best brain surgeons in England," Ran said. "If Katie needs an operation, I'll have him flown directly here."

"It hasn't come to that yet," Eve said. "Katie's young and strong. We have to wait and pray she'll be okay."

But Ran wasn't good at waiting. Or praying for that matter.

"I'll leave the praying to Luke. If anyone can convince God to intervene, it's Lucas Devereaux. I just wish there was something I could do."

"You did do something," Eve said. "Because of you, we got the children safely away from that monster in the orphanage."

Ran made no reply. It all seemed surreal. If it weren't for the woman lying in the ICU, he might be able to convince himself none of it had actually happened.

"Violet and I are going to the cafeteria for a cup of coffee," Eve said. "Can I bring you back something?"

"I'm fine."

Eve went up on her toes and kissed his cheek, left to join Violet, and the women headed down the hall.

A few minutes later, Zane walked up. "Any news?"

Ran noticed the worry that drew Zane's dark eyebrows together, the stiffness in his shoulders that betrayed the tension he was feeling.

"Nothing you haven't heard already." His gaze met Zane's. "If it hadn't been for you, Katie could have been hurt even worse." Perhaps even killed. "You've been a real asset to the team, Zane. I'm glad to have you with us."

"I shouldn't have waited outside. As soon as I heard the commotion, I should have gone into the chapel. Maybe I could have gotten Kate out before she was hurt."

"What happened wasn't your fault. If anyone's to blame, it's me."

Zane shook his head. "I don't think so. I didn't see everything that happened, but I saw enough. I'm not a religious person, but after what happened to the kids at Victoria Hall, and what went on in that chapel, I'm pretty sure there's a battle going on here between good and evil. I think good mostly won tonight."

Ran said nothing.

Zane looked up hopefully as a door opened down the hall. "That's the doctor. Maybe he's got news."

Good news, I hope, Ran thought as Zane took off and Ran fell in behind him. It was becoming more and more apparent that Zane had feelings for his teammate. Ran wondered if Katie's feelings ran in the same direction. Since they worked together, it wasn't a good idea, but there was no rule against it.

At the moment, Ran just wanted Katie to get well.

As the doctor approached, he and Zane both increased their stride. Eve and Violet walked up to join them just as the doctor arrived. Dr. Rishi Patel was Indian, a dark, slender, smoothed-faced man with course black hair.

"I have news," the doctor said. "I know how anxious you all are."

"No question of that," Ran said. "What can you tell us, Doctor?"

"The best news is, unlike many traumatic brain injuries, such as those caused by a car accident, a fall down the stairs, or an assault, in this case, only one area of the brain has been affected. Ms. Collins has been sedated, though she can be awakened quite easily to check her mental status."

"What else?" Ran pressed.

"We're using hypertonic saline to control the pressure in the brain. The drug draws out the extra water and allows the kidneys to filter it out of the blood. We are hoping to avoid surgery, but we won't know if that is possible for at least another day."

"As soon as she's released from the ICU, I want her moved to a private room," Ran said.

"I understand. Your very generous donation to the hospital revitalization fund should certainly make that possible."

Patel turned to the rest of the group. "Visitors' hours are long over. Even if that were not the case, there is nothing more any of you can do for Ms. Collins at this time. I would advise you to return to your hotel, get some rest, and come back later in the day. Perhaps we will know more by then."

Tucking his clipboard beneath his arm, the doctor turned and walked off down the hall.

"He's giving us good advice," Ran said.

"I'm staying," Zane said.

"So am I," said Eve.

"Me too," said Jesse and Violet at the same time.

Ran just shook his head. "Fine, we'll take turns. I'm going back to the hotel to shower and change. I'm taking Violet with me. None of us got any sleep last night. We'll nap, get something to eat, and come back in a couple of hours. Then Jesse, Zane, and Eve can do the same."

"I'm not leaving," Zane said stubbornly.

"We'll see," Ran said, hoping the man's common sense would kick in by the time he returned. "Violet, you ready?"

Obviously exhausted, the older woman made no protest. Ran walked over to Eve. "Sure you don't want to come with us?"

"Not this time, but I'll be ready for a break when you get back."

Ran leaned down and kissed her cheek. "I'll see you in a couple of hours."

As he walked away, anxious to leave the hospital smells and sadness behind, Ran thought about the woman in the ICU. What if that woman were Eve? What if she had been injured, or even killed?

Losing his wife and child had nearly destroyed him. The thought of losing Eve, another woman he loved, was simply unbearable. As he strode down the corridor, his stomach pulled into a hard, tight knot.

Another woman he loved. The words rang in his head. Ran told himself he was too jaded to fall in love again, too far beyond those youthful dreams.

And yet he loved Eve.

His jaw clenched. True or not, it didn't really matter. The attack on Katie had shown him he'd been right from the start. He wasn't prepared for a long-term relationship with Eve. He couldn't handle the thought of losing her.

Ran simply couldn't survive it.

Lucas sat in a pew at the back of St. Gabriel's Church, his rosary beads in his hand. The old stone church, built in the '20s, had high arched ceilings and beautiful paned windows. It was quiet inside. At this early hour of the morning, the huge nave was empty except for a heavyset man in the front row and an old woman lighting candles near the altar.

Luke took a weary breath. After last night, he was tired clear to the bone. Drained of every ounce of strength.

Over the years, he had done a number of exorcisms. He knew the tremendous mental strength it took to engage a powerful entity. Relying on the forces God could provide, he had mostly been successful.

Luke had never encountered evil as strong as he'd faced in the chapel last night. The demon had already killed one man. Criminal or not, the man was dead. Kate Collins lay in a coma in the hospital in critical condition.

Luke had been praying for Katie's recovery since his arrival at St. Gabriel's. He'd had no word of her condition, but he believed his prayers would help.

Luke had also prayed for guidance, a prayer that had been answered. He was prepared to undertake the task God had set for him.

Luke couldn't leave Sunderland without destroying the evil in the asylum. An abandoned building was dangerous. Most people steered clear. But the orphanage had recently been purchased. The new owner would be refurbishing the place to use as a rest home. The elderly occupants would be vulnerable to any sort of attack.

Luke had no choice but to face the Satanic menace in the asylum and purge it.

He rubbed a hand over his face. He needed rest, needed to regain his strength. There were at least two entities in the orphanage, one far more powerful than the other. The dominant entity was the face of evil itself. It would take every ounce of Luke's strength, along with all the help God gave him, to deal with it.

Once the more powerful entity was eliminated, the other spirit would go to whatever place God ordained.

Luke looked up at the sound of the heavy door swinging open and the echo of footsteps coming down the aisle. Ransom King strode toward him, his clothes wrinkled, the shadow of a beard along his jaw, looking nearly as exhausted as Luke.

He rose from the pew. "You have news?"

"Not much. Katie's still in a coma, but it looks like the doctors think that's a good thing at the moment. Helps her deal with the pain and gives her body time to heal. She's had all the necessary tests, CAT scan, MRI, whatever else they needed. We have a surgeon lined up if it comes to that, but the decision hasn't been made yet. For now, it's a waiting game."

Sometimes no news was good news. "Let's talk outside." Luke led the way up the aisle out of the church into the anteroom.

"I appreciate the update," Luke said.

"I had the limo take Violet on to the hotel. The driver is coming back for us."

Luke's head came up.

"Don't bother to argue. You look even worse than I do. You need to get something to eat and some rest. Then we can figure out what to do."

"From here on out, there's no *we* involved. I'll deal with the problem at the asylum. That's why I came here."

"Fine, but I'm the one who brought you. That means I'm responsible for what happens to you."

Luke shook his head. "You aren't responsible for any of this. Evil is responsible."

"I'll concede that much. We're facing pure malevolence, and together we'll figure out how to defeat it. In the meantime, we both need to recover our strength. The car should be back by now. Let's go."

Luke had been friends with Ran King long enough to know he wouldn't back down. Besides, Ran was right. Luke had to collect his strength. They settled into the back of the limo, and the driver headed for the hotel.

"What about Eve?" Luke asked.

"She's with Zane and Jesse at the hospital. We're taking turns. I'm hoping they'll have more news by the time I get back."

"So . . . you and Eve? How are the two of you faring?"

Ran's features darkened. Luke could almost see his friend shutting down. "Our work here is almost finished. As soon as it is, I'll be returning to Seattle."

"And Eve is staying here? Are you sure that's what you want?" Luke couldn't miss the turbulence in his friend's blue eyes.

"It's the very last thing I want. The truth is, after what happened to Sabrina and Chrissy, I'm not willing to risk getting in too deep. If the two of us were together and something happened to Eve, I couldn't . . . I couldn't handle it, Luke. I just can't take the risk."

"Some things are worth the risk. You're still young. The two of you could make a family. You could both live long, happy lives. Accidents happen, yes. But there is no reason to believe God will take Eve from you."

Ran just shook his head.

"Think about it, at least."

Ran made no reply.

Worried about his friend, Luke leaned back in the seat of the Bentley and closed his eyes. The weariness he was feeling swept over him. He was sound asleep by the time the limo drove the few blocks back to the hotel.

CHAPTER THIRTY-NINE

Zane blinked awake, the kink in his neck rousing him from a fitful sleep. He straightened in the chair next to Kate's bedside. Dawn light seeped through the curtains. Early last evening, Kate had been transferred to a private room. Ran had pressured the hospital staff into allowing someone to spend the night with her. Zane had volunteered.

He felt responsible for what had happened. If he had gone into the dilapidated chapel earlier, maybe he could have gotten Kate out without injury. Or at least that's what he told himself.

Deep down he knew nothing that had occurred in the chapel was his fault. That was merely an excuse. He was there because he couldn't stand the thought of Kate waking up alone. Likely she wouldn't recall what had happened and she would be frightened.

Zane didn't know much about Kate, but he sensed she had lived a mostly solitary life. The incident in the chapel had left her seriously injured. She needed someone. Zane wanted to be that person.

Wide awake now, he tuned into the beep of machines being used to monitor her heart rate and blood pressure. Saline solution dripped from a clear bag of fluids on a wheeled stand and ran down a tube into her arm.

Beneath the white bandage wrapped around her head, Kate's golden hair curled onto her shoulders. She lay deathly still on the mattress, looking ghostly pale and incredibly beautiful. As Zane watched her, Kate's big blue eyes slowly cracked open and came to rest on his face.

"Zane . . ." she said softly, and she smiled.

His chest tightened. Relief—and something more powerful—rushed through him with tidal wave force. His brain kicked in. Zane jumped up and ran out into the hall.

"She's awake! Come quick!" As one of the nurses at the station, wide-hipped with iron-gray hair, leaped up and hurried around the desk, Zane ran back into the room.

He sat down in the chair and gently took hold of Kate's hand. "It's all right, darlin'. Everything's going to be fine."

"Zane . . ." she repeated. "You're . . . here."

His chest ached. Kate was still watching him, still smiling, as her eyes slowly closed and she drifted back to sleep.

"The doctor's on his way," the nurse said. "I'm afraid you'll have to leave."

Zane squeezed Kate's hand as he rose from the chair and turned toward the nurse. "This is good, right? She's awake. That means she'll be okay."

"I'm afraid you'll have to ask the doctor about that." She shooed him out the door into the hall. Zane pulled out his cell phone and hit Ran King's number. It was early, but he knew his boss would want to know.

"Kate's awake," Zane said when Ran answered. "I think that's good news, but I'm not sure."

"I'm on my way." Ran hung up the phone, and Zane sat down on a bench outside Kate's door. Ransom King was on his way. Zane almost smiled. As soon as his boss arrived, the wheels would start to turn.

Knowing Kate Collins was in the best possible hands, Zane relaxed for the first time in days.

It was late afternoon two days later. After the phone call he had received from the police department, Ran knew who stood in the hallway outside his suite.

He walked over and answered the door. "Come on in." Ran

stepped back, inviting Detective Inspector Daniel Balfour into the living room. "I understand you have news."

"Very good news," the detective said.

"Something to drink? A beer? Something nonalcoholic?"

"Thanks, I'm fine. I just came by to let you know we've made an arrest in the kidnap case. Bloke named Carlton Fieldhurst has been arrested on sex trafficking charges. The encounter at the old asylum with the East End Boys set off a departmental investigation. That combined with a robbery assault committed by one of the gang members led to Fieldhurst's arrest."

"Great news. Exactly how did that play out?"

"Two days ago, one of the boys, name's Saad Fadel, was arrested on a burglary assault charge. Fadel had a long arrest record, which meant he was going away for a good long time. Instead, he traded a lesser sentence for information on an Internet sex trafficking ring. He gave us the name of one of the victims."

"Go on."

"We located the young woman. According to her, she had been kidnapped and sold to a wealthy man who purchased her off the Internet. She'd been a virgin when the man assaulted her. Fortunately, she managed to escape. After we assured her we could protect her, she gave us the name of the fellow who bought her."

"Carlton Fieldhurst."

"That's right. After Fieldhurst's arrest, another young woman came forward, a fifteen-year-old prostitute."

"Not a particularly credible witness."

"Perhaps not under normal circumstances. In this case she was a twelve-year-old virgin when she was abducted and sold to Carlton Fieldhurst. Not much family. No one looking for her. After Fieldhurst was done with her, his procurer, a fellow named Evan Jeffers, shunted her off to a pimp in Manchester. That's how she wound up in the life."

"So you believe the two young women's testimonies will be enough?"

"Maybe not in themselves. But Jeffers is terrified of going to prison. He's about to cut a deal with us. With the addition of Jeffers's testimony, plus the circumstantial evidence we're amassing, Fieldhurst is going to prison. Even if the bastard manages to drag the case out long enough to win a not-guilty verdict, he'll be ruined."

He's already well on his way, Ran thought. He smiled. "Couldn't happen to a nicer guy."

The detective smiled back. "I figured you'd want to know."

Ran stuck out a hand. "Thanks for all your hard work on this."

"My pleasure." Balfour accepted the handshake, and Ran walked him to the door.

The detective paused and turned back. "You'll tell Dr. St. Clair?"

After I leave, you can tell her yourself, were the words on his tongue. Ran couldn't force himself to say them. "I'll tell her," he said.

Other than at the hospital, Eve hadn't seen Ran in the past three days. Katie had been released early this morning. The swelling in her brain had lessened. She would need rest and observation for at least a few more days, but it looked as if she was healing very well. Ran had set her up in a suite at the hotel and hired a nurse to stay with her. Eve had stopped by to see her, but Katie had been sleeping. The nurse seemed pleased with her continued improvement.

Though Katie wouldn't be attending, there was a team meeting tonight at eight. Eve had no idea what plans Ran had made. Whatever they were, they didn't seem to include her.

Her heart squeezed. She had known better than to get involved with a man who lived in the past. A man who still blamed himself for the death of his wife and child.

A man who still grieved for them.

She dressed carefully in a dark blue knit dress and heels. The meeting was simply a formality. The children in the orphanage were safe. Wally and Herbie were safe. The evil in the chapel no longer had a connection to her or anyone else. Now that the boys were gone, perhaps the malevolent entity had simply vanished.

Eve didn't care. She just wanted her life back.

To do that, she had come to a decision. She was going to sell the house and move back to Boston. She needed to get on with the task of living. Ran didn't love her. Eve had to accept that.

She also accepted there was nothing left for her in England. Too many things had happened. Too much water under the bridge. She still had friends in Boston. She was over Phillip entirely. Best of all, she would be three thousand miles from Ransom King.

Eve checked her reflection in the mirror, applied fresh lipstick, and fluffed her dark hair. At exactly eight p.m., she walked down the hall and knocked on the door next to hers. Ran pulled it open and her eyes went to his, the most incredible shade of blue she had ever seen.

Her heart took a leap.

"You look beautiful," he said, his gaze running over her with obvious approval.

"Thank you." Determined to ignore the flutter in her stomach, she started past him.

Ran caught her arm. "We need to talk. Not tonight. How about lunch tomorrow?"

"There isn't much left for us to say, Ran. We're both smart enough to know this is the end. I wish you the best and I hope you wish that for me."

"There are things I need to say," he insisted a little gruffly.

Whatever Ran had to say, Eve didn't want to hear it. Each word would only break her heart a little more.

"Let's worry about it tomorrow." She walked into the suite to find Violet seated on the sofa. Zane sat in one of the matching chairs. Jesse had pulled up the desk chair and sprawled in the black mesh seat. Lucas wasn't there.

Violet patted the seat beside her, and Eve walked over and sat down.

Ran stood in the center of the group. "As you all must have guessed by now, this will be our last meeting. The plane will be flying you back to Seattle at two p.m. tomorrow afternoon. That should get you there about eight o'clock in the morning. Take the day off, rest up, and check in with the office the following day. Connie's already looking at possible cases. She'll let you know if she's found something worth pursuing."

"What about Kate?" Zane asked.

"I'll be staying until she's ready to travel. We'll have a nurse on the plane with us. The doctor thinks it'll only be a few more days."

"What about Eve's house?" Jesse asked. "It still isn't safe for her to live there."

"The problem isn't the house, it's the asylum. Luke and I are taking care of it."

"What?" Eve leaned forward. "You aren't thinking of going back there?"

"Someone has to. Luke's the only person equipped to deal with that degree of evil. I'll be there if he needs help."

"Wait a minute." Jesse came to his feet. "You said we were all in this together. That hasn't changed."

"It changed when Katie wound up in critical condition in the hospital. I'm not risking any of the rest of you getting hurt."

"It's our decision," Jesse argued. "I'm choosing to go with you."

"It's *my* decision. You work for me, in case you've forgotten. If you want to keep your job, you'll do what I tell you."

It was the harshest Eve had ever heard Ran speak to his people. He was afraid for them. She hoped they understood.

"When is Luke going in?" Violet asked.

"Early tomorrow morning. He's preparing himself tonight. What he's planning to undertake won't be easy."

"So the two of you are going to handle this on your own?" Eve said.

"Mostly it'll be Luke. I'll just be there as an observer."

"In case Lucas gets in trouble," she added.

Ran's gaze found hers. "That's right."

Eve stood up from the sofa. "Well, it looks like this is good-bye, then." She made her way around the room, giving each team member a hug. She didn't hug Ran. "I'll never be able to thank you all enough for what you did."

"Just doing our job," Jesse said.

"Well, I'm extremely grateful." She turned to Ran. "Whatever happens, one way or another, I'm going back home tomorrow."

"No," he barked.

"This is one decision you have no authority to make." She

turned back to the others. "Good night, all of you. I will always consider you friends. Have a safe flight home."

Ran's jaw looked hard, but he made no move to stop her as she walked out of the suite. Eve wasn't surprised. It was over and both of them knew it.

Her eyes filled as she used her key card to get into the room. She would be checking out in the morning. She wiped her eyes. She didn't want to cry tonight. She would save her tears for the lonely days ahead.

But what about the monster in the asylum? Was she really going to sit back and do nothing while Ran and Lucas put themselves in danger?

She heard the door next to hers open and close as the meeting came to an end and the others returned to their rooms. With a sigh, Eve went into the bedroom to change. Kicking off her heels, she slipped out of the blue knit dress, pulled on a pair of sweatpants and a baggy sweatshirt, and curled up on the sofa.

For a while she watched TV, trying to tire herself out. But her nerves were still strung taut and she couldn't stop worrying about Ran and Lucas.

Ransom King was in England because of her. He was determined to deal with the entity he and Lucas believed still ruled the asylum. The job she and the others had begun together remained unfinished.

Eventually, her eyelids began to droop and she slipped into a restless sleep. She dreamed of Ran and ghosts and demons.

It was midnight when she awakened, her heart beating too fast, her stomach knotted. Something didn't feel right. Eve glanced out the window. It was pitch-black outside, no moon, no clouds.

Perfect, she thought. *Just what the demon ordered.* She raked a hand through her heavy dark hair and contemplated the decision she hadn't realized she'd made. She couldn't forgive herself if she just sat back and did nothing while Ran and Lucas faced such a powerful being.

At dawn, she would head over to the chapel.

She would be there to help in any way she could.

CHAPTER FORTY

*I*t was midnight. The witching hour. Luke stood in the moldy, crumbling foyer of the abandoned chapel, his flashlight the only illumination in the room. Dressed in the long white robe with the gold band down the front he had worn before, he carried the same Bible in one hand, same rosary beads in the other, wore the same large crucifix on a chain around his neck.

Beneath his robe, inside his white shirt, the St. Michael's medallion rode against his chest, the Archangel Michael, the protector of good against evil.

Luke drew in a deep breath. Soon he would cross the threshold into the dilapidated chapel itself and stand in the light he had set up in the middle of the aisle. In the confrontation ahead, he wanted his enemy to see him. To know he was unafraid, that God was standing with him as he fought against the Satanic evil oozing from the walls of the church.

Ran believed Luke would be coming to the asylum in the morning. Luke had considered waiting. Day versus night, light against dark, good against evil. But he was afraid the demon wouldn't show itself. It gathered strength from the darkness, spread its tenacles, grew in power.

The orphan boys had been freed from the demon's control. At the victory Ran's team had won, Luke had watched the entity's vicious anger swell into a blinding rage. Guided by the hand of God, Luke would be facing that rage tonight.

He hadn't told King his change of plans. Better to face the demon's wrath alone than to risk the lives of others.

Luke opened the heavy wooden door, stepped into the chapel, and turned on the battery-powered light in the middle of the aisle. Earlier in the afternoon, he had come to the chapel to make preparations. The sun had been out, shining in through the broken stained-glass window as he anointed the walls with holy oil in the shape of a cross. A total of sixteen crosses.

Luke had repeated the Epiphany Blessing of the Threshold, asking that peace and grace surround the doorways and all who passed through them. He had heard faint rumblings and what might have been hissing sounds but had seen no sign of the entity he hunted.

Now, as he stood in the light in the center of the aisle, it was time to begin. Luke made the sign of the cross. He had recovered his strength and the energy he needed to do spiritual battle. He would start as he always did, with the Litany of the Saints in Latin.

Luke began speaking, his voice resonant, echoing off the stone walls of the chapel. *"Kyrie, eleison. Christe, eleison. Kyrie, eleison. Christe, audi nos. Christe, exaudi nos. Pater de caelis, Deus. Miserere nobis. Fili, Remptor mundi, Deus. Miserere nobis. Spiritus sancte Deus. Miserere nobis. Sancta Trinitas, unus Deus. Miserere nobis. Sancta Maria. Oro pro nobis.'"*

Completing the litany took fifteen minutes. Luke repeated the words in English.

"'Lord, have mercy on us. Christ, have mercy on us. Lord, have mercy on us. Christ, hear us, Christ, graciously hear us. God the Father of heaven, Have mercy on us. God, the Son, Redeemer of the world, Have mercy on us. God, the Holy Spirit, Have mercy on us. Holy Trinity, One God, Have mercy on us. Holy Maria. Pray for us.'"

The litany was long and tiring, but Luke didn't hurry. He was prepared for the length of the full exorcism. It could take hours, even days.

He focused on the altar, the ornately carved wooden table tipped over and decaying. He began reading from the Gospel of

John, reminding the demon that he was a creature created by the Word of God, but he was not God, and he was not in charge.

"'In the beginning was the Word, and the Word was with God, and the Word was God. . . . All things were made by Him, and without Him nothing was made. In Him was life, and the life was the light of men. And the light shineth in the darkness.'" He continued reading, though the air in the chapel began to feel thick and heavy.

A roar began, the rush of the wind, though there was no wind inside or out. Luke kept on praying, reading from Scripture, repeating the Lord's Prayer over and over, in Latin and in English. Time spun out. Hours passed. It seemed there was no beginning and there was no end.

He started over, repeating the Litany of the Saints in Latin, then English. The growling and hissing continued to build. Luke didn't stop, his voice stronger now, more demanding.

"I command thee, unclean spirit, whoever thou art, along with all thy associates who have taken possession of this house of God, that by the mysteries of the Incarnation, of the Passion, Resurrection, and Ascension of our Lord Jesus Christ, thou shalt tell me thy name and prepare for the hour of your departure."

A bolt of lightning hit the altar, setting it aflame. The altar exploded into a thousand pieces, sending fragments of burning wood all over the chapel.

Get! Out! A voice, guttural and harsh. The voice of the devil, Luke thought, and kept going.

"In the name of God, I cast thee out, unclean spirit, along with the wicked enemy, Satan, and every phantom and diabolical legion. In the name of our Lord Jesus Christ, depart and vanish from this house of God and all of its surroundings."

The building shuddered. The howl of the wind was so fierce, a headache began to form behind his eyes. In front of him, black blobs oozed across the floor and crawled across the ceiling.

"Pay heed, Satan, you foe of the human race, you carrier of death, you robber of life. Thou are the root of all evil, the fomenter of vice, the seducer of men, the traitor of nations, the instigator of envy, the font of avarice, the source of discord, the exciter of sorrows. In the name of the Father and the Son and the Holy Ghost, I command you to leave this place!"

At the front of the chapel, a tornado of fire appeared and began to spin, flames licking outward like the branches of a tree. It whirled across the stone floor, then began slowly moving up the aisle in his direction. Luke could feel the heat of the fire intensifying as it came closer.

He took a deep breath and collected his strength. He had no idea how many hours had passed. Through the jagged hole in the stained-glass window, he could see the faint gray light of dawn.

"St. Michael the Archangel, defend us in this battle, be our protector against the wickedness and snares of the devil. Great Prince of the Heavenly Host, by the power of God, cast into hell Satan and all of the evil spirits who prowl this place."

From the corner of his eye, he saw Ran take a seat in the pew closest to where Luke stood. Luke closed his eyes, praying he would be able to keep both of them safe.

The whirling fire crept slowly toward them. Luke flicked a glance at Ran, a shadowy figure at the edge of the light. His jaw looked hard, his eyes a dark indigo blue. Luke could read his friend's resolve, the determination that matched Luke's own.

"Archangel Michael, Prince of the Heavenly Host, by the power of God, cast into hell Satan and all the evil spirits who prowl the world seeking the ruin of souls."

The fire had almost reached them, a single, sweltering spot of heat in the icy interior of the chapel.

An image appeared in Luke's mind. A huge, winged warrior surrounded by a pure-white aura, his face beautiful, his head wreathed in gleaming blond curls. Giant wings spread, he hovered in front of the stained-glass window, more than seven feet tall, wearing the armor of God, a massive broadsword in one big hand.

The spinning fire whirled toward him, morphed into a human-like creature with demonic features. A hideous scream rent the air, and a lightning bolt of fire flew toward the angel.

The angel's power seemed to swell. His great sword arched down, flashing, magnificent, cleanly severing the head of the demon, which flew into the air and disappeared. The Archangel became a flash of blinding light and disappeared as well. The only thing that remained was a vague white form in the outline of a man that also disappeared.

Luke stared at the place the Archangel had been. *The fires of hell versus the sword of God.* A beam of sunlight shone through the hole in the stained-glass window, illuminating the darkness inside the chapel.

Luke's knees gave way at the same instant he felt Ran's shoulder beneath his, propping him up. Another shoulder was wedged beneath his other arm. Luke looked over to see Jesse's smiling face.

They started up the aisle together. By the time the three of them had made it through the doors into the foyer of the chapel, Luke had regained some of his strength.

"I'm all right," he said, easing away from his friends, surprised to see Eve and Zane both standing in the foyer, where they had been watching.

"It's over," Luke said. "It's finished."

Eve rushed to Ran, who pulled her into his arms. The two of them clung to each other.

Jesse looked at Luke. "I don't understand what happened. One minute it looked like the fire was going to incinerate everything in its path—including you. The next minute the fire was moving away; then it was gone and the sun was shining into the chapel."

Luke frowned. "That's all you saw?"

"That's it," Jesse said.

He turned. "What about the rest of you? Ran?"

"I heard a terrible scream. Like something out of the depths of hell. Then the fire disappeared."

"I heard that, too," Jesse said.

"Me too," said Zane.

Luke turned to Eve, still in the circle of Ran's arms. "You have the gift, Eve. What did you see?"

"I don't know. It was all so confusing. Whatever happened, I don't feel the presence of either of the spirits who were in my house."

"The death of the evil one freed the other," Luke said. "God will deal with him."

No one made a comment.

"Let's get out of here," Luke said wearily.

"Good idea," Ran agreed. Together they walked back through the asylum, out the wooden door through which they had entered. A bright sun shone down from a cloudless sky.

"I drove over in the BMW," Ran said. "I'll drive us back to the hotel."

Ran said nothing to Eve on the way to the car. But Luke noticed he didn't let go of her hand.

CHAPTER FORTY-ONE

*T*HEY GATHERED IN RAN'S SUITE AT THE HOTEL. IT WAS STILL TOO early to check on Katie, but when Eve had spoken to Katie's nurse last night, she seemed to be doing very well.

Eve preceded Ran into his suite to join the others. Violet was still in her room asleep. Luke had gone to his bedroom to change. Zane sat down on the sofa next to Eve, all of them excited but unsure what to make of the happenings in the asylum.

Returning to stand in the middle of the room, Ran's gaze swept over them. "Let me start by saying I should fire both of you for disobeying my orders. The exorcism was even more dangerous than I imagined. Anything could have happened and almost did." The darkness lifted from his features. "That said, I'm not too stubborn to admit I admire your courage. And I'm proud to call you my friends."

Everyone smiled.

"That was really something," Zane said.

"So you believe in ghosts now?" Jesse teased.

"Well, something sure as hell happened. I was thinking . . . you remember the audio recording you made with the voice that said the name Hay or Kay or something like that?"

"I remember," Jesse said.

"At the time, you thought it might have been Alexander Fay, the magician."

"Yeah."

"If it was, maybe the malevolent spirit—the one who tried to kill Luke with the fire in the chapel tonight—was the guy who closed and bolted the door. It was an evil, twisted thing to do, and it wound up causing the deaths of all those kids. Fay was onstage, so he couldn't have done it, but maybe he felt responsible. Maybe that's the reason he was in the orphanage. Maybe he came back to try to help the children."

Ran nodded. "One thing I've learned, anything is possible."

A knock sounded at the door and Ran walked over to pull it open. All of them were eager to talk to Luke, who walked in wearing dark blue jeans, his standard white shirt, and a pair of sneakers. He looked nothing like the former priest who had rid the asylum of a demon.

"We've been discussing some possibilities. You got anything to add?"

"Maybe. You all heard my prayer to St. Michael the Archangel. I prayed for his help, and he came."

"You saw him?" Ran asked.

"I saw him in the eye of my mind."

"But there's no way to know for sure he was there," Zane said.

Lucas unbuttoned the top three buttons of his shirt and pulled it open. He was wearing the same gold medallion Eve had seen before. When he pulled the medal aside, there was a red mark on his chest. Everyone gathered around to look at it. The image of a winged angel brandishing a sword was burned into his skin.

"Any more questions?" Ran asked.

No one said a word.

It was midmorning by the time the others left Ran's suite. He'd had room service bring up a breakfast spread with enough food for all, and they ate their fill. Eve had stayed for a while, then returned to her suite. Ran still hadn't had a chance to talk to her.

The timing felt wrong. She'd been up since well before dawn. According to Jesse, Zane had called him last night to say he was going over to the asylum. He said security was his job, and he planned to be there before Ran and Luke arrived. Since Jesse had also planned to go, they decided to go together.

An hour before dawn, Zane had called a cab and gone down to

the lobby, where Jesse waited. They spotted Eve, dressed in the same warm gear they were wearing. Jesse asked if there was a chance she was going to the same place they were. Eve said that if it was the House of Mercy Orphan Asylum, the answer was yes.

"I warned her you were really gonna be pissed." Jesse smiled. "Eve didn't seem to care."

"I think she was glad she wouldn't be going alone," Zane said. "She told us the cab ride would be her treat."

After the strange events early that morning, Ran sat on the sofa, tired to the bone, but too restless to catch up on some badly needed sleep. He rubbed a hand over his unshaven jaw.

Why had Eve gone to the asylum after he had forbidden it? He almost smiled. Eve had never been good at taking orders. It was one of the things he loved most about her.

His stomach knotted. He knew she'd been worried about him. But was it more than that? Ran desperately needed to know.

He checked his watch. Eve deserved to get some rest. He waited, paced for a while, finally gave in to the urge to see her. Unfortunately, when he knocked on her door, he got no answer. Ran phoned downstairs to discover Eve had checked out of the hotel.

Worry settled in his chest. She had told him she was going back home. It was safe for her there now, he reminded himself, but he still didn't like it.

He drove the BMW over to her white-trimmed brick house and knocked on the door. No answer. She was probably in bed, trying to make up for lost sleep. He should come back later. Instead he rang the bell and knocked again. A few minutes later, Eve opened the door.

"Good . . . good morning," she said, but she didn't invite him in.

His heart was beating too hard, and his mouth felt dry. It wasn't like him. "Have you got a few minutes?"

Eve didn't move. Her dark hair was appealingly mussed, her hazel eyes more green than brown. "I was sleeping. I didn't get much rest last night."

"I know . . . it's just . . . I really need to talk to you."

Grudgingly, she pulled open the door, and Ran walked past her into the entry. He glanced around. There was still repair work to be done to finish the hallway. He would make sure the job was completed.

"How does it feel to be back in your own home?" he asked.

"I don't know. Different somehow. It doesn't matter anymore. I've decided to sell the house and move back to Boston."

He felt as if he'd been punched in the stomach. "Maybe we could sit down. I don't think we'll be interrupted by angry voices shouting at each other this time."

"No, I think that's over." Reluctantly, she led him into the living room, and they took seats, side by side, on the settee.

Eve sat stiffly. "You said before that you had something you wanted to say. I would appreciate if you said it and left. This is difficult for me, Ran."

He reached over and caught her hand. It felt icy cold as he brought it to his lips. "Why did you go to the asylum? It was dangerous. You knew that."

She eased her hand away and her chin inched up. "I was worried. I was afraid something bad would happen to you. Afraid you would be injured or worse, and I wouldn't be there."

Ran's chest clamped down. Something inside him had changed when he'd seen Eve in the chapel, braving unknown horrors.

She had been there for him, she said.

"I was afraid, too. I didn't want you to go because I was afraid something would happen to you and I would be the cause."

Eve's gaze held his. "Everything that occurs in life isn't your fault, Ran. You saw what went on in the asylum. Sometimes bad things happen, things completely out of your control."

"Yes." He picked up her hand again, linked her fingers with his. "In the chapel, for the first time, I accepted that." He looked down at their joined hands. "You went there because you were worried about me. Do you love me, Eve?"

Her beautiful hazel eyes welled with tears. "It's cruel of you to ask me that."

"Tell me."

A resigned sigh escaped. "I love you, Ran. Maybe from that first moment when you rushed into the hallway to save me from a ghost." She reached up and touched his face. "Every day I love you more."

His heart was beating too hard. Ran leaned over and pressed a soft kiss on her lips. "I don't want you to go to Boston. I want you to come to Seattle with me. I love you, Eve. So much. After what happened, I see things more clearly. I understand life as I never did before. I want the happiness I could find with you."

Eve started shaking her head.

"I want you with me," Ran said, refusing to give up. "I want you to marry me."

"What?"

"I'm asking you to marry me, Eve. Will you?"

Eve's pretty lips trembled. She brushed away a drop of wetness on her cheek. "Are you . . . are you sure, Ran?"

"Never more sure of anything. But if you think it's too soon . . . if you need some time to get to know me—"

She rested her palm against his cheek. "I know your heart, Ran. I know the man you are inside. That's the man I fell in love with."

Relief swept through him. "That's good because I feel like I've already waited years to find you. Say yes and put me out of my misery."

Eve's expression softened into a smile, and he felt as if the sun had finally broken through the darkness that had been his life for so long.

"I'd love to marry you."

Ran kissed her. "I love you, honey. So much." Since the house was no longer haunted, he took Eve's hand and led her upstairs to her feminine pink bedroom. He had a woman in his life again and what a woman she was.

Ghosts or spirits, the battle between good and evil, he would never really know why he had been brought here, at this time, to this place.

But as Eve leaned up and kissed him, Ran would be forever grateful.

EPILOGUE

*E*VE TOOK RAN'S HAND AND LET HIM HELP HER OUT OF THE BMW. They crossed the green space and he led her along one of the many winding paths through the lush green grass of Mowbray Park.

It was a quiet time of day, the sun shining down through the branches of the trees. There was a pond ahead. Eve could see ducks paddling across the still waters. A lovely white swan held sway over the lesser birds.

"Oh, look!" Eve pointed toward the small gray rabbit hopping toward a brilliant yellow flower bed a few feet away. "Isn't he darling?"

"Maybe it's a she?" Ran teased, smiling. "Maybe there will be lots of little gray bunnies in her future."

Eve looked up at him. The smile on his face was the answer to her silent question.

"Yes," he said. "I would love to make a family with you."

"I would love that, too."

They walked on, winding toward their destination. Eve could see it ahead, a hexagon-shaped, glass-enclosed structure. The Victoria Hall Memorial. The spot was well chosen. In Victorian times, the Victoria Hall would have looked down upon the park.

They paused to read the plaque on the front of the enclosure.

ERECTED TO COMMEMORATE THE CALAMITY WHICH TOOK PLACE IN THE VICTORIA HALL, SUNDERLAND, ON SATURDAY 16TH JUNE 1883 BY WHICH 183 CHILDREN LOST THEIR LIVES.

Inside the monument was the gray stone statue of a seated woman, her head thrown back, a cry of pain on her lips. Draped across the mother's lap lay the body of her small child, killed that day in Victoria Hall.

Eve's throat tightened. She felt Ran's fingertip lift a tear from her cheek.

"They're at peace now," he said. "Can you feel it? You can be proud of what you did to help them."

She glanced around, taking in the serenity of the lush green park. "As Luke said, God helped us help them."

Ran brushed a soft kiss over her lips. They stood in silence for a while, absorbing the quiet peace of their surroundings. Then they both seemed to know it was time to leave.

A new chapter was beginning in their lives. They held hands as they walked back to the car.

Author's Note

This book is a work of fiction. However, much of the story is true. The orphan asylum still exists, though the building, which is now being used as a memory care facility, is in much better condition today than when I began working on this tale.

The Victoria Hall disaster, one of the worst in England's history, resulted in the needless deaths of 183 children. The entertainment involved the occult. The Great Ghost Illusion was the featured act of the day.

The owner of the theater, Frederick Taylor, was well known for his generosity to the poor. Free tickets for the boys in the orphanage, only half a mile away, would have been likely.

On a better note, as a consequence of the tragedy, eight years after it happened, a young engineer named Robert Alexander Briggs, fifteen years old when he survived the disaster, patented a design for a bolt that would keep a door secure from anyone trying to enter from outside while still enabling those inside to escape.

It was the first version of the panic bar we see on emergency exits today. Since the adoption of Robert Briggs's invention, hundreds, perhaps thousands of lives have been saved.

The best possible tribute to the children who died that day.